Praise fo
What You Wi
by Janet Dav

"This thoughtful suspense novel concerns families, secrets, and the human cost of coffee from El Salvador.... Dawson weaves together multiple time lines and character viewpoints...as she conveys the message that 'the price of coffee shouldn't include death.'"

—*Publishers Weekly*

"Janet Dawson's *What You Wish For* is a worthwhile and satisfying read.... In her first stand-alone novel, Dawson gives readers a page-turning read that will satisfy the mystery lover and readers of smart literary fiction alike."

—*Reviewing the Evidence*

"With vivid descriptions of San Francisco and Berkeley from the early 1970s to the current day, and an unflinching look at the grinding poverty, torture, and execution experienced by Salvadoran civilians during that country's civil war, *What You Wish For* is a story that grips you until the very last page."

—*Alameda Sun*

"This is a novel you want to savor as much for the context of the story, as for the story itself.... It provides a powerful contrast between the affluence of San Francisco and the jungles of El Salvador, from which the conflict emerges."

—Killer Nashville Featured Book

"An excellent you-are-there exposé of El Salvador's appalling human rights abuses... *What You Wish For* succeeds in putting a human face on the 'end justifies the means' political philosophy which has savaged the world for far too many decades."

—*Mystery Scene*

Death Rides the Zephyr

MYSTERY FICTION BY JANET DAWSON

Death Rides the Zephyr

a mystery

JANET DAWSON

2013
PERSEVERANCE PRESS / JOHN DANIEL AND COMPANY
PALO ALTO / MCKINLEYVILLE, CALIFORNIA

Copyright © 2013 by Janet Dawson
All rights reserved
Printed in the United States of America

A Perseverance Press Book
Published by John Daniel & Company
A division of Daniel & Daniel, Publishers, Inc.
Post Office Box 2790
McKinleyville, California 95519
www.danielpublishing.com/perseverance

Distributed by SCB Distributors (800) 729-6423

Book design by Eric Larson, Studio E Books, Santa Barbara, www.studio-e-books.com

Cover art © Roger Morris, Two Rock Media. All rights reserved.

10 9 8 7 6 5 4 3 2 1

LIBRARY OF CONGRESS CATALOGING-IN-PUBLICATION DATA
Dawson, Janet.
  Death rides the zephyr : a mystery / by Janet Dawson.
    pages cm
  ISBN 978-1-56474-530-9 (pbk. : alk. paper)
  1. California Zephyr (Express train)—Fiction. 2. Railroad travel—Fiction. I. Title.
PS3554.A949D43 2013
813'.54--dc23
                2012048733

To Mom, as always

Death Rides the Zephyr ——————————

Chapter One ──────────────────

THE *CALIFORNIA ZEPHYR* seemed alive, poised for movement, waiting on the tracks for the conductor's call of "All aboard!"

Jill McLeod reached up and touched the stainless steel diesel locomotive, one of three powerful engines that would pull the train on the first leg of its eastbound run from Oakland to Chicago. She felt the tingle of anticipation, as she always did when she saw the sleek streamliner at the start of a journey.

The snub-nosed front of the first diesel was painted orange. Rectangular plates on either side of the big, round center headlight bore the engine number, 805-A. The emblem below the headlight was square, with a black background showing the Western Pacific Railroad's feather logo and the legend FEATHER RIVER ROUTE. Orange stripes ran down the sides of the locomotive, with WESTERN PACIFIC in black letters below.

Jill turned and greeted the conductor, who'd been conferring with the engineer and his fireman assistant at the ladder leading up to the cab in the first engine. "Good morning, Mr. Wylie."

"Good morning back at you, Miss McLeod," the conductor said as the engineer climbed back into the cab. "A damp morning it is, for sure."

"It certainly is." Earlier, it had drizzled. The moisture in the air curled the ends of Jill's light brown hair, which she wore in the short, curly style known as a poodle cut.

Fog hugged San Francisco Bay and spilled ashore, blurring buildings in the rail yard, and obscuring Berkeley, Oakland, and the hills to the east. The front half of the *Zephyr* stretched out of the oversized train shed at the end of the Oakland Mole, the huge pier and causeway extending from the eastern shore into the bay.

Mr. Wylie was a tall, broad-shouldered man in his mid-forties, clothed in the distinctive uniform of his position. On his billed cap a shiny badge read WESTERN PACIFIC CONDUCTOR, and WP pins decorated each lapel of his dark jacket, worn over a white shirt, tie, and vest. A watch on a chain was tucked into his left pocket. His first name was Arthur, but most people knew him as Red, because of his rusty-colored hair.

Not that she would ever address the conductor by his first name or his nickname. Onboard crew members were supposed to keep things on a "Mister and Miss" basis, even though they traveled together often. While on the road, the conductor was in charge of the train. His was the last word.

"Looks like a full train this run," Mr. Wylie said. "Even if it is just three days till Christmas. Folks are heading home for the holidays."

"I'll have my Christmas with my family when I get back from Chicago," Jill said.

Her holiday celebration would be closer to New Year's Eve. It was Monday, December 22, 1952. The eastbound *California Zephyr*, train number 18, was due to leave at nine o'clock this morning and scheduled to arrive in the Windy City at one-thirty on the afternoon of December 24th, Christmas Eve. After a two-night layover, Jill would board the westbound *Zephyr*, train number 17, scheduled to depart Chicago in mid-afternoon on December 26th. Barring any complications, she'd get back to Oakland two days later, on the afternoon of December 28th.

Jill lived with her family in the nearby island city of Alameda. Her mother had been teary-eyed this morning, because her oldest child would spend Christmas in a Chicago hotel, away from home during the holidays. So Mom made waffles—Jill's favorite— for breakfast. Still in her bathrobe, Jill ate with her parents and siblings in their sunny kitchen, pouring hot maple syrup over buttery squares.

After breakfast, her family gave Jill several early Christmas gifts. Her sister Lucy, who was in her senior year at Mills College, and her brother Drew, a freshman at the University of California in Berkeley, had pooled their resources to buy a book for Jill to read on the train. Mom presented Jill with a red cashmere scarf and matching gloves, the better to stave off that Midwestern cold. Her father gave her a new wallet of soft beige leather, with some green-backs tucked inside. "So you can have a nice Christmas dinner while you're in Chicago," he said. "Go to the Pump Room. Your mother and I ate there once, before the war, and it was a real treat."

Jill put her arms around him and gave him a kiss. "Thanks, Dad. I will."

"We'll see you when you get back," he said. Then he headed out the door, for his rounds at the Alameda Hospital, where he was a general practitioner.

Jill hugged her mother. "I love the scarf and gloves, Mom. They're beautiful." She turned to her younger siblings. "And thanks for the new Agatha Christie. I can't wait to read the book. It's a Miss Marple. She's my favorite."

Lucy grinned. "You know what they say. 'A Christie for Christmas.'"

"I'd better get dressed," Jill said, gathering up her presents. She went upstairs to the room that had been hers since she'd graduated from the University of California, three years earlier. Sophie, Jill's calico cat, curled up on the bed, her orange, black, and white face tucked under her white paws. Jill leaned over and stroked the cat's silky fur. The cat opened her yellow eyes, then took Jill's hand in her forepaws, kicking gently with her hind paws. Jill tickled the cat's stomach, and Sophie purred. Then she got up and stretched before curling into a ball again.

Jill dressed and put on her makeup. Then she picked up her suitcase and an old carpetbag made of faded blue fabric, contain-ing a few extra items for the trip. "I'm leaving now, Sophie," she told the cat. "Guard the house until I get back." Sophie opened one eye and yawned.

Mr. Wylie's voice brought Jill back to the present. "Got your Christmas shopping done?"

"Most of it," she said. "I plan to pick up stocking stuffers in Chicago. How about you?"

He smiled. "Haven't even started yet. Plenty of time. The stores don't close until five on Christmas Eve."

Jill shook her head. "What is it about men? My father's the same. He waits until the last possible minute to do his shopping."

"That's what my wife says. She starts buying presents in the middle of the summer."

The brakeman approached them. He was the crew member who assisted the conductor onboard and applied and released handbrakes. He said hello to Jill before turning to ask Mr. Wylie a question. Jill stepped away. She had plenty to do before the train left.

She walked alongside the three locomotives. The consist—the rail cars that made up the train—began with these engines. The *California Zephyr* was the joint operation of three railroads—the Western Pacific, the Denver & Rio Grande Western, and the Chicago, Burlington & Quincy. The cars that followed the engines, built by the Budd Company in Pennsylvania, were a mix of equipment from all three roads, with the exception of the transcontinental sleeper, which belonged to the Pennsylvania Railroad. The exterior of each car had the legend CALIFORNIA ZEPHYR centered over the windows, and below the windows, the individual car's name. The sparkling, newly washed stainless steel cars, all with "Silver" in their names, gave the train its other title—the Silver Lady.

The baggage car, the Silver Stag, was coupled to the third locomotive. She waved to the baggage man, who stood near his folding desk and equipment locker. Then a long black hearse drove slowly up the platform and parked with its rear doors facing the baggage car's double doors. Two men got out of the vehicle and opened the hearse, revealing four coffins inside. The baggage handler jumped down from the car. The men consulted over the paperwork. Then the baggage man wheeled over the special cart that raised and lowered, especially for loading coffins in the baggage car. The men from the funeral home began unloading the coffins onto the cart, preparing to transfer them to the train.

Jill took a deep breath and held it for a moment, then expelled air in a sigh. A week earlier, the McLeods' neighbors in

Alameda had been overjoyed when their son, a soldier in Korea, had been discharged and sent home, arriving in time for the holidays. These servicemen were going home as well. But they were making their final journey in the train's baggage car, their coffins covered with American flags.

How sad to lose a loved one during the holidays, Jill thought. How sad to lose someone you love at any time of the year.

She walked around the hearse. When she came to the first passenger car, the Silver Pony, she climbed the steps up to the vestibule. This was one of three chair cars in the consist. The other two were the Silver Palace and the Silver Saddle. Each car had seating for over sixty coach passengers. On the upper level of each car was the Vista-Dome, a glass compartment rising out of the roof, with seating for the coach passengers. The Vista-Dome's front, rear, and side walls were windows, with curved glass providing unobstructed views of scenery. At night, only floor lighting illuminated the Dome, allowing clear views of the night sky. The *California Zephyr* touted the train's Vista-Domes in its advertisements and brochures, frequently using the tag line, "Look up, look down, look all around."

The cars with Vista-Domes had what was called a depressed floor under the dome, lower than the rest of the car, with two steps on either side leading down to this level. On the chair cars, the men's and women's washrooms were here, under the Vista-Dome, each with toilets and sinks for the coach passengers. Inspecting the women's washrooms in the public areas of the train was part of Jill's pre-departure routine, so she stepped inside and looked around, finding the washroom clean.

Another part of her routine was putting up her name cards, which identified her as a member of the crew. She took a card from her skirt pocket and slipped it into the holder on the wall. Then she greeted the coach attendant and left the Silver Pony, heading back to the second car, the Silver Palace. This car was slightly different. It contained the conductor's office, a compartment at the right side on the rear of the car, with a bench seat and a desk.

She said hello to the coach attendant for the Silver Palace, then checked the washroom and placed her name card, repeating the actions in the third chair car, the Silver Saddle. Then she entered the Silver Hostel, the buffet-lounge car. At the front of the car she glanced into the washroom, finding it clean, as she expected. She kept walking down the central aisle of the car's coffee shop, which served hot food, snacks, and beverages. The passageway jogged to the right and then left, down the steps, and ran alongside the wall of the lounge. Jill greeted the steward, who was behind the bar, checking glassware and bottles, ready to dispense beverages, both alcoholic and non-alcoholic. Behind him was a small kitchen.

Just beyond the entrance to the lounge were another two steps up, then a curved staircase led up to the Vista-Dome above the lounge. At the foot of the stairs, on Jill's left, a closed door led to the crew dormitory, with space for fifteen crew members, bunks stacked three high, lockers, and a washroom with toilets and showers.

Jill's compartment was at the end of the car, next to that of the dining car steward. The narrow space contained a bench seat that folded down into a bed, a toilet, and a washstand that was pulled down from the wall, then pushed up again when not in use. This served as her quarters for the two-and-a-half-day journey to Chicago. Earlier, she had stowed her suitcase and the blue cloth bag, along with the first-aid kit she'd picked up when she'd arrived at the rail yard.

Jill went through to the dining car, the Silver Plate, and stepped into a hive of activity. Crew members had arrived before dawn, loading supplies from the commissary building into the diner before the train was moved from the yard to the Mole. The pantry was packed with a vast array of food and beverages, enough to feed passengers and crew on the train's eastward journey to Chicago. The train carried crockery, glassware, silver service and kitchen equipment, and linens. Now the *Zephyr*'s chefs were in the diner's stainless steel kitchen, menus planned, ready to prepare those meals.

Jill walked down the passageway that ran alongside the wall of the stainless steel kitchen and pantry, where chefs in white uniforms, aprons, and caps were already preparing for lunch. In the dining section, six waiters in white jackets had covered each of the tables with fresh white cloths and set them with Western Pacific china, heavy silverware, and glasses. Each table held a full water bottle, a silver stand holding the menu, and a bud vase containing a red carnation, and in keeping with the holiday season, a spray of holly. Now they talked among themselves as they waited for departure.

"I seen you over at Slim Jenkins's club last night," one waiter said to another. "Who was that fine-lookin' woman you was with?"

"None of your business," the other man said. "You find your own woman and don't be asking about mine."

The other waiters laughed, and one of them said, "That's telling him, Lester. Morning, Miss McLeod."

She waved at them. "Good morning."

Marcus Gridley, the dining car steward, looked up from his curved counter in the center of the car. The base of the counter was decorated with a mural of carved linoleum, showing an auburn-haired woman in Grecian draperies, seated in a pastoral scene, a bunch of grapes in her hand and more grapes in the basket on her lap.

"Good morning, Miss McLeod," the steward said. "It looks like we have a full house this trip, with people traveling during the holiday season."

"Yes, we do, Mr. Gridley. I hope it will be an uneventful trip."

He smiled. "You and me both."

Jill walked back through the Pullman cars—the Silver Gull, the Silver Palisade, the Silver Pine, and the Silver Rapids—where the sleeping car porters were giving the accommodations one last inspection before the passengers arrived. In each car, she greeted the porters and placed her name cards in the wall holders.

The last car in the train, the Silver Solarium, was an observation-sleeper, with three double bedrooms suitable for two passengers each, as well as a drawing room that could accommodate three people. All four accommodations had enclosed toilet facilities.

Todd Parsons, the porter, wasn't in his tiny compartment at

the front of the car, opposite the electrical locker and a toilet. Jill walked past the bedrooms and took two steps down to the depressed level under the Vista-Dome, where a glass partition looked in on the car's buffet, which provided beverages and a limited menu during the journey. Mr. Parsons was in the small bar, his reflection visible in the mirror etched with a design of birds and branches. The curved counter where he stood was similar to the one in the dining car, with a carved linoleum base. This mural showed plump white birds on a sky blue background.

"Good morning, Mr. Parsons," Jill said.

He looked up. "Morning, Miss McLeod. Ready to go to Chicago?"

"Ready as I'll ever be. How about you?"

"Looking forward to it," he said. "I've got family on the South Side, so I'm spending Christmas with them. Heading back here to Oakland in a few days."

"Me, too," Jill said. "Maybe we'll be on the same train. We'll have 'specials' on this train, all of them back here in the Solarium."

"Yes, ma'am. Got a full house this trip. Seven people, taking all three bedrooms and the drawing room."

The "specials" were "special attention passengers," usually prominent people who had come to the notice of the railroad when they'd booked their accommodations. As such, they were singled out for extra attention from the crew. These passengers might be traveling anywhere on the train; for this trip, the people in question were all traveling on the Silver Solarium. According to the information Jill had received when she'd checked in this morning, three of these passengers would board the train here at the Oakland Mole, after arriving on the ferry from San Francisco. The other four would board in Oakland, at the Western Pacific station at Third and Washington.

"I'll be back to meet the passengers once we get underway," Jill said.

She walked up two steps to the main level, past a small water fountain tucked into a space at her left. Here another set of steps led up to the car's Vista-Dome. These stairs curved slightly, and were edged with Lucite that glowed at night with muted lighting.

In the lounge, comfortable chairs upholstered in sandalwood and brown—five on one side and four on the other—ranged along the sides of the car, which had a rounded end known as a "fish tail." The flowered carpet was tan and beige. Venetian blinds and curtains covered the windows on either side of the car. In the middle of the lounge, within reach of passengers who would sit there, were small, round metal tables with recessed holders for glasses around the perimeter and ashtrays in the middle. At the very back of the car, two settees, each wide enough for two people, faced the car's rear double door. On either side of the door were two small tables built into the sides of the car, just big enough to hold a glass or two. The table on the right held a silver tinsel Christmas tree, about eighteen inches tall, decorated with red and green glass balls and a gold star.

Both this lounge—and the Vista-Dome at the top of the stairs, with seating for twenty-four people—were available for the use of all the sleeping car passengers. Just to the right of the stairs a writing desk held stationery and postcards for the passengers' use, as well as newspapers for them to read. Multiple copies of the *San Francisco Chronicle* and *Examiner* had been delivered to the train before it left the coach yards. The papers were distributed through the cars, including this one.

Jill glanced at the front page. The largest headline was about an explosion at a chemical factory in Japan. There was also a photo and article about the opening of the new Broadway Tunnel in San Francisco the day before. Evidently sightseers had turned out in droves.

She picked up the *Chronicle* and leafed through the first few pages. The death toll in that terrible plane crash had gone up to eighty-six. Two days earlier, on December 20th, an Air Force C-124 cargo and troop transport plane had crashed at Larson Air Force Base in Moses Lake, Washington. Most of the passengers were Air Force personnel from Korea or Northwest bases, catching a ride home for Christmas in a program called Operation Sleigh Ride.

Their poor families, she thought, remembering the coffins being loaded onto the baggage car. She turned the pages of the newspaper, scanning the articles.

On page 8, in the upper right corner, she saw a headline. POLICE BAR ROSENBERG RALLY AT SING SING. She read through the article. A delegation of over seven hundred people seeking clemency for Julius and Ethel Rosenberg had traveled by train to Ossining, New York, site of Sing Sing Prison. But the local police had kept them from marching to the prison. Instead, they'd marched near the train station. The Rosenbergs, charged with passing atomic secrets to the Soviet Union, had been convicted and sentenced to death in the spring of 1951. In October 1952, the United States Supreme Court had ruled against reviewing the case. Now the couple's execution was set for the week of January 11, 1953.

Mr. Parsons came into the lounge. He glanced at the newspaper and pointed at the article. "Those Rosenbergs, d'you think they're really going to the electric chair?"

"Looks like it," Jill said. "It's scheduled for next month. Though I suppose it could be delayed again."

"Don't know what to think about that. Lots of folks think they're not guilty."

"Lots of folks think they are guilty." Jill recalled the discussions her mother and father had had on the subject. Certainly those hundreds of people who had gone to Sing Sing yesterday thought the Rosenbergs were innocent.

She turned the pages, until another headline caught her eye. This one was an editorial. NO ROMANCE IN MODERN WAR. Jill closed the paper and put it back on the writing desk. She didn't think there was ever any romance in war.

Jill had things to do. The passengers would be arriving soon and she wouldn't have a moment to relax until the train was well on its way. She placed one last name card in the wall holder. Then she returned to the Silver Solarium's vestibule and stepped down to the platform inside the huge, echoing Oakland Mole, where the train waited for its passengers. She walked to the rounded end of the observation car, where a small rectangular sign stood out on the car's stainless steel skin. CALIFORNIA ZEPHYR glowed in yellow neon letters against an orange background showing an outline of the Golden Gate Bridge.

A group of Red Caps, the railroad station porters who wore distinctive red headgear, waited for the onslaught of arriving passengers. They gathered around a radio playing what some people called race music, but Jill knew it as rhythm and blues. She recognized the song, Ernie Andrews singing "Pork Chops and Mustard Greens." Her brother, Drew, loved R&B and ever since the record came out last year, he played it constantly.

Then voices drowned out the music, echoing off the Mole's high roof. Passengers from the East Bay cities had the option to board the *Zephyr* here at the ferry terminus, or at the train's first stop, the Western Pacific station located at Third and Washington in Oakland. People had already arrived here by car and bus. Jill saw men in Navy uniforms, not surprising with the Naval Air Station located in Alameda. An officer in dress blues approached, walking arm in arm with a redheaded woman whose knee-length blue coat matched his uniform. Behind them, a little blond girl dawdled, clutching an overnight case and a teddy bear. A young sailor in bell-bottomed trousers hurried past Jill, carrying a duffel bag on his left shoulder. He saw the officer and stopped, snapping a salute. The officer returned the salute and the sailor continued toward one of the Dome chair cars.

Out on San Francisco Bay, a foghorn bellowed its warning. A moment later, Jill heard another horn, signaling the approach of the double-decker ferry from San Francisco.

She quickened her pace and walked to a spot a few yards beyond the end of the Silver Solarium. Here she joined the Pullman conductor, Mr. Alford, who supervised the porters and had overall charge of the sleeping cars. The porters were employed by the Pullman Company rather than the railroads. Now, as the passengers arrived, he would check in those with sleeping accommodations, while Jill greeted people, providing assistance and directions as needed.

The horn sounded again as the ferry docked. Mr. Alford straightened his cap. "Ready, Miss McLeod?"

Jill nodded. "I'm ready, Mr. Alford. Here they come."

Chapter Two ———————————————

THE FLOOD BEGAN. Passengers disembarked at both levels of the ferry, then hurried down the gangplank toward the train. The platform bustled with activity. Red Caps took suitcases, bags, and packages, carrying them to the coach and sleeper cars, or stowing them on carts for transport to the baggage car. Passengers converged on the train, talking, laughing, intent on finding the cars in which they'd be traveling.

A family of five came by, a mother, a father, and three children giggling as they sang that Christmas song that was so popular this year, "I Saw Mommy Kissing Santa Claus." Then their voices faded. Other passengers streamed past Jill, their voices and fragments of conversation replacing the lyrics of the song.

"I'm looking forward to Aunt Millie's mince pie," a woman told her male companion.

"Yeah, it's the best." He laughed as they both hurried past, carrying overnight cases and wrapped packages.

"If we get the contract, we can start work in April," one man said to another. "We'll discuss it on the train and I'll send him a wire when we get to Sacramento."

"...and Johnny Ray," a teenaged girl said to another. "I just love it when he sings 'Cry.' It makes me swoon!"

"Oh, I think he's drippy," her friend said. "I like Eddie Fisher better."

A growing line of passengers queued in front of Mr. Alford, checking in for the sleeping accommodations. The Pullman conductor smiled as he held out his hand. "Good morning, sir. May I check your reservations, please?" The man handed over his tickets. Mr. Alford glanced at them. "Mr. and Mrs. Grayson, I see you're holding two berths in car twelve."

"That's the car called the Silver Pine," Jill said.

"That car is available for occupancy now," Mr. Alford said. "I see you're traveling to Provo, Utah. We are scheduled to arrive there at six thirty-two tomorrow morning. Do have a pleasant trip, Mr. and Mrs. Grayson."

Jill saw an older couple she recognized, walking arm in arm, followed by a Red Cap carrying their suitcases. The man showed his tickets to the conductor.

"Hello, Mr. and Mrs. Gunther," Jill said. The Gunthers had traveled on the *Zephyr* several times before, most recently in August. The woman wore a Christmas corsage, a candy cane with a spray of holly pinned to the collar of her tweed coat. She carried a small beige leather overnight case and a bouquet of red and white carnations.

"Miss McLeod, you remember us," Mrs. Gunther said. "How nice to see you again. Look, Martin, it's Miss McLeod. She was on our train last summer."

"You look lovely, my dear," Mr. Gunther said as he stepped away from the Pullman conductor. He pulled a red carnation from the bouquet and handed it to Jill. "Merry Christmas."

"Thanks, Mr. Gunther." Jill took the flower and sniffed its spicy scent.

"We're going to Salt Lake City to spend Christmas with our daughter and her family," Mrs. Gunther said. "I'm looking forward to the trip. The scenery in the Feather River Canyon should be spectacular, with all the snow. Of course, it's gorgeous all the time."

"Yes, I'm sure it will be beautiful. We're due into Salt Lake at five-forty tomorrow morning. I hope you enjoy your trip."

"Oh, we always do, on the *Zephyr*." Mrs. Gunther took her husband's arm. "Which car are we in, dear?"

"Car sixteen, the Silver Gull, compartment G," Mr. Gunther said.

"First sleeper near the diner," the Red Cap said, stepping forward. "Right this way, sir."

As the Gunthers walked up the platform, another couple stepped forward, followed by a Red Cap carrying two suitcases and an overnight case. The man and woman appeared to be in their mid-thirties. He had a wiry frame and brown hair in a crew cut. His overcoat was unbuttoned, revealing a gray pinstriped suit. The woman's chestnut hair was pulled back into a sleek ponytail that accentuated her long, narrow face. She wore a mossy green suit under her black wool coat.

The man reached into the inner pocket of his overcoat and handed the tickets to Mr. Alford, who glanced at them and said, "Mr. and Mrs. Cole, bound for Chicago."

"That's right," Mr. Cole said. "Heading home."

"We've been on our honeymoon in San Francisco." Mrs. Cole squeezed her husband's arm with her right hand, flourishing her left so Jill could see the wide gold band.

"Congratulations," Jill said. "I hope you enjoyed your stay."

"Oh, I do love San Francisco," Mrs. Cole said. "I always have. It's marvelous, one of my favorite cities."

Mrs. Cole spoke English with a slight accent. Something European, Jill thought. German? Perhaps. She couldn't place it just now.

In addition to the French she'd learned in college, Jill had acquired a smattering of German, Italian, and Spanish. While working on the *California Zephyr*, she'd picked up a few words of even more languages, including Dutch, Swedish, Russian, Polish, Chinese, and Japanese. People from all around the country and all around the world rode the Silver Lady. Jill's ear for languages had proved an asset in this job.

"You're in compartment B aboard the Silver Gull," Mr. Alford told the Coles. "That's car sixteen. The Red Cap will show you the way. We should arrive in Chicago at one-thirty on the afternoon of December twenty-fourth."

"Just follow me, sir," the Red Cap said, moving past the Coles as he headed for the sleeper section. Mrs. Cole squeezed her husband's arm again, her laugh tinkling as she tilted her head toward his.

Jill turned and smiled at the next passenger. This was one of her "special attention" passengers, traveling aboard the Silver Solarium. Jill recognized Lydia Stafford from the photo on the jacket of her latest novel. Jill had purchased the book and wrapped it up for her mother, the package now waiting at home under the McLeods' Christmas tree. Had she known the author was going to be on the train, she'd have brought the book with her, to get an autograph.

"Miss Stafford, it's a pleasure to have you aboard," Jill said. "I enjoy your books."

"Thanks." Miss Stafford returned Jill's smile and handed her ticket to the conductor. She was in her thirties, with brown hair swept back from a high forehead in a short ear-length bob, showing off her pearl earrings. Her wool suit was a herringbone tweed. Behind her the Red Cap carried a small overnight case and a Smith-Corona portable typewriter.

The conductor checked the ticket. "That's bedroom C on the Silver Solarium, the Dome observation car, which is right here behind us. Have a pleasant trip, Miss Stafford."

Next in line was a middle-aged man in a gray suit and tie, accompanied by a woman who wore a blue wool coat over her stylish blue dress, showing off sapphire-and-gold jewelry. The Red Cap a few steps behind them pushed a baggage cart carrying two suitcases and two overnight cases.

The man presented two tickets to the conductor. "We're going to New York City."

Now that accent was pure Brooklyn, Jill thought.

The conductor examined the tickets. "Welcome aboard, Mr. and Mrs. Perlman. You'll be traveling on the Silver Rapids, car eleven. That's our transcontinental sleeper. Once we get to Chicago it will be transferred to the Pennsylvania Railroad for the trip to New York City."

"Yes, I know. We've ridden the through sleeper before." Mr. Perlman took the tickets from the conductor and beckoned to his wife. "Come on, Blanche. Let's get settled in and…" His voice faded as he and his wife walked toward their car, followed by the Red Cap with their baggage.

More passengers lined up with tickets in hand, a family of

four, traveling to Winnemucca, Nevada. Jill directed them to the first coach car, the Silver Pony. Then, in rapid succession, came passengers headed for points all along the *California Zephyr's* route—from California all the way to Illinois, and some like the Perlmans, heading for other destinations in the eastern United States. They were young and old and every age in between, some traveling on their own, some accompanied by families.

A young woman in a pleated skirt and cardigan fumbled with her small suitcase and held out her ticket to the conductor. "I am going to Chicago," she said in an accented voice.

Jill placed the accent. "*Vous êtes française?*"

The woman's face brightened and she spoke to Jill in French. Her name was Solange LeGros, she said. She was an exchange student at the University of California in Berkeley, and she thought this trip would be a wonderful way to see the United States.

Jill glanced at the ticket. "*Bienvenue,* Mademoiselle LeGros. You'll be traveling in the third chair car, the Silver Saddle. It's car number twenty. I, too, went to the University of California. If you have any questions about Berkeley, I'd be happy to talk with you. And yes, this is a great way to see our country. I hope you enjoy the trip. You'll see some beautiful scenery."

As the young woman moved away, Jill saw a middle-aged man coming down the ramp from the ferry. He wore a tan overcoat and carried a small leather valise. He stopped at the foot of the ramp, set the valise next to his feet, and smoothed his sandy hair, receding from his forehead. Then he removed the wedding band from his left hand and slipped it into his pocket.

Jill hid a rueful smile. She'd seen that move before, the married man who had decided to be single for the duration of the trip.

Now he picked up the valise and walked up to Jill instead of the Pullman conductor. With his other hand, he pulled his ticket from the inner pocket of his overcoat. "Hi, honey. I'm Brad Washburn. What's your name?"

"I'm Miss McLeod. May I help you, Mr. Washburn?"

He chuckled and leaned closer, waving his ticket at her. "Oh, listen, honey, I'm sure you could help me a lot. Got a bedroom on one of the Pullmans. Hope to get some rest and relaxation on the way to Omaha."

She glanced at his ticket. "You're in bedroom J on the Silver Gull, Mr. Washburn. That's car sixteen, just before the dining car."

"Why don't you escort me to my bedroom, honey?" He moved closer still. She could smell the Old Spice cologne that he'd splashed on that morning.

Jill took a step back and gestured toward the Pullman conductor. "I must stay here to assist other passengers, sir. Please show your ticket to the conductor so he can check you in. Then the porter for that car will help you get settled."

"I'm sure I'll see you later on the train, honey."

"I'm sure you will," Jill said. Though she wished she could avoid it.

Mr. Washburn flourished his ticket at Mr. Alford. Then he tucked the ticket into his overcoat and shifted his leather valise from one hand to the other. The valise rattled. She glanced down at the half-open zipper and saw several bottles inside the valise. Definitely not Old Spice. More like Old Crow. Mr. Washburn was looking for more than rest and relaxation on his journey to Omaha. He'd be partying in his bedroom and looking for female companionship.

Jill glanced at the passengers approaching the conductor and saw the other two "special attention" passengers who had traveled on the ferry from San Francisco. Angelo Constanza was a noted tenor who had performed with the San Francisco Opera this past season and stayed in the city to give a series of concerts. Now he and his wife, Sophia, were traveling to Chicago, in the drawing room on the Silver Solarium. At nearly eighty dollars for two people all the way to the Windy City, this was the most luxurious accommodation afforded by the *California Zephyr*.

Jill greeted the couple in their native Italian, then switched to English as Mr. Constanza showed their tickets to the conductor. Then the Constanzas followed the Red Cap who wheeled their luggage toward the observation car entrance.

"I'm Mrs. Clive. I have a bedroom on this train." The woman had an imperious voice. She presented her ticket with a haughty flourish, tilting her pointed chin upward. She appeared to be in her forties, dressed in an expensive beige suit. She had a fox stole draped over her cashmere coat and a tiny hat perched on her tightly permed brown hair.

The Pullman conductor examined her ticket. "Yes, ma'am. I see you're traveling to McCook, Nebraska. You're in bedroom D on the Silver Palisade, car fifteen." He handed the ticket to her.

Mrs. Clive took the ticket and directed her waspish voice to the Red Cap who was carrying two leather suitcases and an overnight case. "Be careful with those cases." Then she looked past Jill and her eyes widened. "Is that Angelo Constanza, the tenor? He's traveling on this train? How lovely. I'll have to renew our acquaintance. I met him at a party in Pacific Heights. And saw him perform, of course. He was marvelous in *Pagliacci* and *Aida*. And his Alfredo in *La Traviata*. Oh, simply divine." The woman gave Jill a condescending smile. "I don't suppose you've ever heard him sing."

Jill smiled. "As a matter of fact, I have. And you're right, he is marvelous."

Mrs. Clive's smile cooled. She opened the handbag hanging from her left wrist and took out a cigarette case that looked like an envelope, with a stamp engraved in the upper right corner. With one gloved finger she opened the flap on the other side and shook out a cigarette. The tall man behind her quickly held out his own cigarette lighter, a battered Zippo. "Oh, thank you," she told him as the flame flared. She lit her cigarette and inhaled smoke, tucking the case in her purse. "Now, the Silver Palisade. Which car is that?"

"Just follow me, ma'am," the Red Cap said. Mrs. Clive moved off, her heels tapping on the platform.

Jill glanced up at the tall, dark-haired man, who carried a small leather suitcase in his left hand. His right hand still held the cigarette lighter. Now Jill saw that it had an inscription on the side, but she couldn't quite read it. He smiled at Jill, shut the lighter, and tucked it into his pocket.

"Heading for Denver, I see," the conductor said. "Well, Mr. Paynter, you're in bedroom A on car sixteen, the Silver Gull. We're due to arrive in Denver tomorrow evening at seven."

The man thanked the conductor and moved away, whistling as he swung his suitcase. Jill turned to answer a question posed by another passenger. Then she gave a young couple directions to the first chair car. The flood of passengers from the ferry slowed to a trickle as people moved toward their cars and boarded the train.

"Are you in the army? My mom was in the army. My dad, too."

Jill smiled down at the little boy. He was about six, with dark hair and brown eyes.

"I'm a Zephyrette," she said. Indeed, her tailored teal-blue suit could be mistaken for a military uniform. The jacket had a monogram on the left breast pocket, reading ZEPHYRETTE, and so did her garrison cap. The white blouse under the jacket also had a CZ monogram and she wore a *Zephyr* pin as well.

"What's a Zephyrette?" the boy asked, stumbling a bit over the unfamiliar word.

"I'm a hostess for the train," Jill told him. "I do all sorts of things, like make announcements on the public address system. If you hurt your finger I'll give you a bandage. And if your mom and dad want to get away by themselves for a while, I'll entertain you."

"I'll take you up on that," the boy's mother said with a laugh. She, too, had dark hair and brown eyes. Under her short tweed jacket she wore a simple, full-skirted dress made of topaz jersey. She had another little boy in tow, this one about four. She held his hand. In the other hand, she carried a large purse and a blue overnight case. "Sometimes keeping up with these two just wears me out. We're the Bensons, headed for Colorado, to spend Christmas with family. And we're all very excited about our first trip on the *Zephyr*."

"Welcome aboard, Mrs. Benson," Jill said. "You're in for a treat. You'll see some beautiful scenery along the way, in the Sierra and the Rockies. Since it's so near Christmas, I've planned a party for the children onboard. I'm sure your boys would like that."

"Yes, they would," the woman said.

"We want to look at the engines," the older boy said. "Can we do that, Mom? Please?" His younger brother echoed the request.

"Wait till your dad is finished with the luggage," his mother said. She glanced back at her husband, a slender blond man in a blue suit and tie who was handing the family's suitcases to a Red Cap. Then he stepped up to the Pullman conductor, tickets in hand.

"Those are diesel locomotives," Jill told the boys, "three of them, from the Western Pacific Railroad. When we get to Salt Lake City, we change to five engines, from the Denver and Rio Grande Western. We need the extra power to pull the train over the Rocky Mountains."

"Billy and Chip are mad for trains," Mrs. Benson said, as her husband joined them.

"I'm Miss McLeod, the Zephyrette. If there's anything I can do to help during the journey, please let me know. I'll come around later to make dinner reservations. And I would be happy to keep an eye on your boys if you and Mr. Benson would like some time alone."

"Sounds like a good deal," Mr. Benson said with a pleasant smile. He consulted the tickets. "We've got two bedrooms on the...Silver Palisade."

"That's car fifteen," Jill said. "I'll show you where it is."

Jill walked with them to the Silver Palisade and beckoned to Frank Nathan, a tall, slender Pullman porter in a tailored uniform and cap. He stood near the metal step box at the car's vestibule, calling out the number of his car.

"Good morning," Jill said. "The Bensons are traveling on this car."

"You go on, Norma," Mr. Benson said, handing the tickets to his wife. "I'll take the boys up to look at those locomotives."

Frank Nathan touched his cap and glanced at the tickets. "Very good, sir. Mrs. Benson, you and your family are in bedrooms E and F. May I take that overnight case?" He reached out his hand and Mrs. Benson gave him the case. He set it in the vestibule, then held out his hand again. "Now, watch your step, please." She climbed the steps up to the vestibule and he followed. Mr.

Benson took his sons by their hands and headed for the front of the train.

A moment later Mr. Nathan returned to the vestibule and waved in Jill's direction before he stepped down to assist other passengers.

"That's my son Frank."

So that's who the porter was waving at. Like her son, the older woman was tall. Her face, with its high cheekbones and full lips, was the same dark coffee brown. Her short black hair, threaded with silver, was combed back from her round face. A sprig of holly decorated the lapel of her gray wool coat, worn over her plain gray dress.

To the woman's left was a little girl, about nine, blond with blue eyes, a dusting of freckles on her thin face. She wore a green sweater buttoned over a white blouse and a green-and-blue-plaid skirt. In one hand she carried a small pink overnight case. The other hand cradled a button-eyed teddy bear made of corduroy, the same golden-brown color as the maple syrup Jill had poured on her waffles that morning.

"I'm Stella Nathan," the woman said.

"I'm Jill McLeod. I'm the Zephyrette on this run."

Mrs. Nathan nodded. "I know. Your father is Doctor Amos McLeod. I used to keep house for the Ericsons, across the street from your family. Frank told me you'd be on this train. I need to ask you a favor, Miss McLeod."

"What sort of a favor?"

Mrs. Nathan put her left hand on the little girl's shoulder and drew her closer. "This is Emily Charlton. I was housekeeper for her father. They lived in officers' quarters at the Naval Air Station in Alameda. Emily will be on the train, all the way to Denver. I'd really appreciate your keeping an eye on her."

The little girl looked familiar. Then Jill realized this was the child she'd seen earlier, with the Navy officer and the redheaded woman. Now she saw them again, talking with another couple. They turned and walked toward Mrs. Nathan and the little girl, who had remained silent through this exchange, staying close to Mrs. Nathan, a look of apprehension on her face.

"Those aren't her parents?" Jill indicated the Navy officer and his wife. No, as the young couple approached, she saw that the child didn't resemble either of them. The woman's hair was a vibrant carroty red, and the man was dark.

Mrs. Nathan shook her head. "The Fielders? No, they're the next-door neighbors. Emily's been staying with them. You see, her daddy passed recently. Her mama passed some time ago. She's going to Denver to live with her grandma."

"Is she traveling alone?" In her head, Jill reviewed the *California Zephyr's* policies on children traveling alone. She'd turn the girl over to Traveler's Aid in Denver.

"She's supposed to have someone with her." Mrs. Nathan frowned. "A Mrs. Grace Tidsdale. But she's not here yet."

"Don't worry, Stella. I'm sure Mrs. Tidsdale will be here soon." The Fielders now joined them. Lieutenant Commander Fielder had an aviator's insignia on his uniform. Beneath her roomy blue coat, Mrs. Fielder wore a maternity blouse over her protruding abdomen. She turned to Jill and smiled. "Hi, I'm Maxine Fielder. This is my husband, Chet."

"Jill McLeod. I'm the Zephyrette on this run."

"She's Dr. McLeod's daughter," Mrs. Nathan said. "She'll keep an eye on Emily."

"Thanks, we'd all appreciate that," Commander Fielder said. "Emily's bags are checked through to Denver."

The Navy officer held out the ticket to Emily, along with a small zippered purse with a strap. It was made of bright red silk. Jill had seen dozens like it in Chinatown.

"This is your train ticket, Emily," the commander said. "Keep it safe. And here's a little purse with some money for you to have on the train, to buy your meals and other things if you like."

"Thank you." Emily's whisper was so low that Jill barely heard it. The little girl took the ticket and tucked it into her skirt pocket. She hung the purse on her shoulder.

"You're going to stay in a bedroom in that car right over there, where Frank is," Mrs. Nathan added. "It's called the Silver Palisade. Frank will look after you, and so will Miss McLeod. I do wish Mrs. Tidsdale would get here. This train is about to leave."

"We have some time," Jill assured her. Not much, she thought, consulting her wristwatch.

Emily tugged Mrs. Nathan's hand. The woman pulled the child away from the group, then she knelt, talking with the child in a low voice.

"Mrs. Nathan tells me Emily's father died recently," Jill said.

"He was killed in Korea, just after Thanksgiving," Chet Fielder said.

A shadow passed over Jill's face. "I'm sorry to hear that."

"Emily has been living with us since her father died. I wish that could go on indefinitely but Chet's getting ready to deploy to Korea himself." Mrs. Fielder stopped and looked worried. With an effort she returned to her previous cheery expression. "We're giving up our quarters on base. I'm moving down to San Diego to stay with my mom until Chet comes home." She patted her belly. "The baby's due in two months."

"Is Mrs. Tidsdale a relative of Emily's?" Jill asked.

Maxine Fielder shook her head. "She's no relation at all. Emily's grandmother, Mrs. Charlton, doesn't want Emily to travel alone, and I can't blame her, under the circumstances. Her plan was to come out here and take Emily back to Denver. But Mrs. Charlton fell and broke her ankle. Her son, Emily's uncle Robert, arranged for someone to escort Emily. I gather Mrs. Tidsdale is a friend of his who lives in San Francisco."

Mrs. Fielder glanced at her watch and frowned. "I have no idea what Mrs. Tidsdale looks like. I've never actually met her, or even talked with her. All I know is, she is supposed to meet us here, at the Oakland Mole. I thought she'd be on the ferry. I hope she gets here soon. Stella and I want to talk with her about Emily, before the train leaves."

"Emily's nervous about the trip, traveling with a stranger," Mrs. Nathan said as she rejoined the group, holding the little girl's hand. "She's still upset about her daddy."

"I'll do my best," Jill said, "to keep an eye on her and cheer her up. Emily will be in Denver in time to open presents Christmas morning."

A man and a woman approached Jill with questions. She

stepped away and talked with the passengers. When they moved away toward their car, she glanced at her watch again. The train was due to leave soon.

As if to underscore that fact, Mr. Wylie's voice boomed out as the conductor walked past, calling, "Now boarding, the *California Zephyr*. Destination Chicago, with stops in Stockton, Sacramento, Marysville, Oroville, Portola, Winnemucca..."

Jill walked toward the Silver Palisade. The Fielders and Mrs. Nathan, holding Emily Charlton's hand, still waited near the entrance to the sleeping car. The little girl looked forlorn as she clutched her well-worn corduroy teddy bear. There was still no sign of Mrs. Tidsdale.

"Emily should go ahead and board." Jill looked up at Mr. Nathan, waiting in the vestibule. "She's in bedroom A."

The porter held out his hand. "I'll put that case in your bedroom while you say your good-byes."

Emily handed him the pink overnight case and he stepped into the passageway. Maxine Fielder hugged the little girl and her husband patted Emily's head. Then Emily flung her arms around Stella Nathan. The housekeeper returned the embrace, then looked up at Frank, who'd returned to the vestibule.

"Go on with Frank," Mrs. Nathan told the little girl. "He and Miss McLeod will take care of you."

Emily sighed and gripped her teddy bear. Then she climbed the steps to the vestibule. The conductor was coming back this way, calling, "All aboard."

Jill scanned the platform. No sign of any last-minute arrivals. What had happened to Mrs. Tidsdale? Was she elderly, forgetful? Had she mistaken the departure time? Whatever the reason, she was going to miss the train.

Then she saw a Red Cap hurrying along the platform, carrying a suitcase and an overnight bag. The woman walking behind him had a tiny red hat perched on her brassy blond hair. She wore a bright red dress. A mink jacket swirled around her swaying hips. She was wreathed in smoke from the cigarette she carried in one bejeweled hand. Her fingernails were the same bright red as her lipstick.

Frank Nathan jumped down from the Silver Palisade vestibule to take the woman's luggage from the Red Cap. The woman stopped and put one hand on her hip, weaving back and forth on her high-heeled pumps. She hiccupped. Jill caught the unmistakable reek of whisky.

The blonde winked one mascaraed blue eye. "Never fear, Tidsy's here."

Chapter Three

MRS. GRACE TIDSDALE tossed her cigarette to the platform and ground it out with the toe of her red leather pump. Then she pulled a red leather change purse from her matching handbag and tipped the Red Cap. She clambered up the steps to the Silver Palisade vestibule, oblivious to Stella Nathan's withering glare and the shock on Maxine Fielder's face. Once aboard, she wove from side to side, as though the train was already moving.

"You mus' be Em'ly." She slurred her words as she reached out one hand to touch the little girl's hair. Emily shrank back, eyes widening in alarm as she clutched her teddy bear. "I'm Mrs. Tidsdale. Call me Tidsy. I'm going to ride the train with you. Won't that be fun? Choo choo!" She snorted with laughter as she ran a red-tipped hand through her blond curls. Then she turned to Frank Nathan and smiled. "Now, Porter, if you'll escort Emily and me to our bedroom, we'll get settled in."

"Yes, ma'am," he said. With quick, practiced movements he leaned down and grabbed the step box, standing it on its side in the vestibule. When he closed the door, the steps raised until the vestibule floor was flat, extending from door to door. He locked the door. Then he picked up Mrs. Tidsdale's luggage. "This way, ma'am. You and Emily are in bedroom A." He moved down the passageway. Mrs. Tidsdale teetered behind him. Jill and Emily followed.

The Silver Palisade was, in railroad parlance, a ten-six sleeper. Just past the porter's accommodations were ten roomettes designated by numbers, five on either side of the central passageway, each suitable for one person. A roomette to Denver was $21.50;

to Chicago, $29.40. In the middle of the car a door on the left hid the soiled linen locker. Here the corridor jogged to the right, then left again, leading to six double bedrooms designated by letters, doors on the left facing the windows on the right side of the car. The term "double bedroom" meant the compartment could accommodate two people, one in a bench seat that transformed into a lower berth, another in an upper berth that the porter unlocked with a key and then lowered. In the case of a family traveling together, such as the Bensons in bedrooms E and F, a door between two double bedrooms could be opened to allow passage between the two bedrooms. Or the entire wall could be folded aside, to make a larger space. The Bensons were paying $33.95 each for those bedrooms.

Frank Nathan stopped just outside bedroom A and gestured to Mrs. Tidsdale, who wobbled a bit as she entered. The porter deposited her luggage inside. "Here's where you control the heat and ventilation," he said, pointing. "And here's the call button. You just press that if you need me. Now, that bench seat makes into the lower berth. When you and Emily are ready for bed, I'll lower the upper berth from the ceiling."

He opened a door. "Here's the lavatory. That sink folds down from the wall, like this." He reached out and demonstrated, pulling the sink down, then raising it again. "When you're done with it, you just push that sink up against the wall, and the water drains out in the pipes between the walls." He shut the door to the lavatory and stepped into the doorway, pointing. "Just ahead of us are the dining car and the buffet-lounge car. There's a Vista-Dome above the lounge. And there's another Vista-Dome back in the observation car at the end of the train."

"Where can I get a drink?" Mrs. Tidsdale asked.

"You can purchase beverages in the lounge car or the observation car. Now, the dining car will be open for lunch between noon and two o'clock. You don't need reservations for lunch, or breakfast either. You do need reservations for dinner. Miss McLeod here, our Zephyrette, she'll come around and make reservations. Dinner is generally between five and eight but we do have early dinners, for folks traveling with children." He looked past her and smiled at Emily. "As for breakfast, first call is six in the morning, and last call is nine."

"Thank you, Porter." Mrs. Tidsdale pulled out her change purse and tipped him. "We'll call you if we need you."

Frank Nathan stepped out of the compartment. Jill entered and settled Emily and her teddy bear onto the bench seat near the window. Stella Nathan and the Fielders were visible outside on the platform, waving at the little girl.

Mrs. Tidsdale hiccupped again. "Tidsy needs to sit down." She plopped onto the bedroom's small free-standing chair, mink coat rumpled around her, as though boarding the train had sapped her energy. She had a large square-cut ruby ring on her left hand, a big diamond on her right. Her red dress was well cut and expensive, made of silk crepe. She was in her late forties, Jill guessed.

The whistle blew twice, the signal that the train was moving forward. The eastbound *California Zephyr* pulled away from the Oakland Mole. Emily scrambled to her feet and waved at Mrs. Nathan and the Fielders. When they were no longer visible, the little girl turned, tears streaking her face.

"I'm sure you'll enjoy your trip, Emily," Jill said. Emily didn't look convinced. Jill turned to Mrs. Tidsdale. "I'm Miss McLeod, the Zephyrette for this run. Please let me know if there's anything I can do to help you with Emily."

Mrs. Tidsdale looked up. "What? Oh, yeah, sure. Thanks." She glanced down at Emily's teddy bear, tracing its yarn nose and mouth with one blood red fingernail. Then she smiled at Emily. "Do you play cards, sweetie?" The little girl shook her head. "I'll teach you how to play poker. It's really easy."

Jill retraced her steps. Frank Nathan was at the rear of the car, in the doorway to the porter's compartment. He shook his head and frowned, speaking in a low voice. "Nine o'clock in the morning, and that woman's drunk. Mama's fit to be tied."

"So are the Fielders," Jill said. What a mess. But it was too late to do anything about Emily's unsuitable escort. "We'll just have to keep an eye on Emily. *And* Mrs. Tidsdale."

The *California Zephyr* threaded its way through the Oakland rail yard, passing warehouses and piers near the waterfront. The engineer blew the horn—two long whistles, followed by one short and another long. There was a whole language of horn signals, and this one meant the train was approaching a public grade crossing, any street or road where vehicles or people could cross the tracks.

The trip from the pier to the next stop took about eleven minutes. Soon the *Zephyr* slowed, heading down Third Street in Oakland. The horn blew one long blast as it approached the Western Pacific station at Third and Washington. When the train stopped, it blocked auto traffic on Broadway, the main thoroughfare that led through downtown Oakland. But they would be here a short time. Frank Nathan opened the vestibule doors. When the steps unfolded, Jill followed him off the train and greeted boarding passengers.

"Here, George, take this suitcase," one man said, shoving a valise at Frank Nathan. The porter took the bag, but his mouth tightened. Jill knew why. Porters took offense at being called "George," instead of their proper names. They considered it demeaning and derogatory. The name dated back to the early days of the sleeping cars, and came from the first name of the founder, George Pullman. Sometimes the porters were called "Sam" or "Sambo"—and worse. That's why Jill was careful to address all her fellow crew members by their last names, with "Mister" in front.

A middle-aged man was the last to climb the steps into the Silver Palisade's vestibule. He was tall, thin, and bespectacled, with black hair going gray, and he wore a tan overcoat and carried a battered leather bag. He showed his ticket to Frank Nathan, who held out his hand for the man's suitcase.

"Thank you," the man said, his voice flavored with an accent. "I'll carry my own bag."

"As you wish, sir," Frank Nathan said. "You're in roomette two."

Jill climbed up to the vestibule as the conductor approached, calling, "All aboard." The conductor boarded the train. Frank Nathan closed and locked the doors. Then the *Zephyr's* whistle blew as the train pulled out of the station. Mr. Wylie walked forward, toward the front of the train, while Jill headed the opposite direction.

The engineer blew the train's warning signal almost continuously as it crossed the streets of the waterfront district, with its fruit warehouses and meat-packing plants. The *Zephyr* picked up speed as it headed through the Fruitvale district and East Oakland, where the canneries and factories operated, then through the small community of San Leandro.

Jill made her way through the Silver Pine, a sixteen-section sleeper, with semi-private seats that made into berths. These were reasonably priced—$15.40 for a lower berth to Denver; $11.75 for an upper. An older man hailed her, and she paused to answer his question. "Yes, sir, you do need reservations for dinner in the dining car. I'll be coming through the cars later to take those. Breakfast and lunch are first-come, first-served."

"Is there a Vista-Dome for the Pullman passengers?" a young woman asked, looking up from the book she held.

"Yes, ma'am. The Dome above the lounge car is reserved for passengers on the sleeper cars. That's the first car forward from the diner. You can also use the Vista-Dome in the observation car, the last car in the train."

Jill excused herself and walked through the next car, the Silver Rapids. The transcontinental sleeper was a ten-six sleeper, like the Silver Palisade, with ten roomettes and six double bedrooms. Though identical in design to other *Zephyr* cars, this one actually belonged to the Pennsylvania Railroad, and would be attached to a Pennsy train in Chicago for its run to New York City.

Jill stopped to say hello to Mr. and Mrs. Perlman, who were coming out of their bedroom, heading back to the observation car and its Vista-Dome. Many of the passengers, both coach and sleeper, went immediately to the Domes to claim one of the upper-level seats, all the better to see the scenery from the wraparound window. All told, the five Dome cars on the train—three coach plus the buffet-lounge car and the observation car—provided a total of 120 seats for *Zephyr* passengers.

Jill followed the Perlmans back to the Silver Solarium. The bedroom doors were closed, but from bedroom C, she heard the sound of keys striking a platen. Evidently Miss Stafford planned to use her travel time to write.

The Constanzas, who were traveling in the drawing room, were in the lounge at the end of the Silver Solarium. They were both reading paperback detective novels, an Agatha Christie for Mrs. Constanza and a Raymond Chandler for the opera singer.

"Good morning," Jill said. "It's a pleasure to have you aboard the *California Zephyr*. I heard you sing once, Mr. Constanza, in Denver. It was the summer of nineteen forty-six. You performed in *Naughty Marietta*, at the Denver Post Opera in Cheesman Park."

Mr. Constanza smiled. "Such a lovely tradition, to have music in the park, free to all the people who bring picnics and sit on the grass. I have performed in the Post Opera several times. In 'forty-eight it was *Rose-Marie*, and this past summer, *The Student Prince*. I do enjoy the operettas. A change of pace from grand opera."

Jill smiled, remembering those summer evenings in Denver. "We lived with my grandmother during the war, while my father was in the Navy. She lives in the Cheesman Park neighborhood so we'd walk to the park and claim a space on the lawn. We saw some wonderful performances, including yours. Please let me know if there's anything I can do to make your journey more enjoyable."

She chatted with the Constanzas a while longer, then went upstairs to the Vista-Dome to meet the other four "special attention" passengers who had boarded at Third Street in Oakland. Mr. Benjamin Finch owned several of the big canneries that operated in Oakland's Fruitvale district, and his wife, Margaret, was prominent in social circles. Jill had certainly seen their picture in the pages of the *Oakland Tribune* and the *San Francisco Chronicle*. As Jill introduced herself, Mr. Finch offered his hand, and Mrs. Finch looked up from the book she was reading. It was that novel *Giant* by Edna Ferber, the one that Jill's mother had liked so much.

Margaret Finch was an attractive woman with short brown hair and bangs, her hairstyle similar to that of the next First Lady, Mamie Doud Eisenhower. "It's a treat to be traveling with such a renowned opera singer," she said. "I went over to the War Memorial Opera House earlier this fall and saw Mr. Constanza in *La Traviata*. I'm fond of opera, but Ben isn't."

He didn't look like the opera type, Jill thought. The cannery owner was a big man with powerful shoulders, who looked as though he'd worked on the line in one of his canneries. Now he laughed. "I'll take Benny Goodman any day."

The Finches had two daughters. Nan, who was about twelve, sat in one of the forward chairs. She looked as though she was ready to read her way through the journey. In the chair next to her was a stack of blue-backed books with familiar covers—the Nancy Drew books by Carolyn Keene.

Cathy, who appeared to be nine or ten, stood at the front of the Vista-Dome, her arms spread wide. "It's like flying," she said as the train left the small town of Hayward, heading south. On the left, the East Bay hills rose, their slopes green with winter rain. To the right was San Francisco Bay, the sun glinting off the water through a break in the clouds.

"The Constanzas are in the drawing room," Mrs. Finch said. "I haven't met whoever is traveling in bedroom C, but I hear a typewriter, tapping away. Do tell me, Miss McLeod. Is the mystery passenger a reporter, a writer?"

"A writer," Jill said. "Miss Lydia Stafford, the novelist."

"Oh, my goodness," Mrs. Finch said. "The one who wrote that book about the California Gold Rush?"

Jill nodded. "The very same."

"I loved that novel. What a treat. I can't wait to talk with her. Of course, with all that typing, she must be working on another book."

Jill talked with Mr. and Mrs. Finch for a few minutes, then she excused herself and went down the stairs to the main level of the observation car. The train picked up speed as she walked forward to the next car, humming "Ah! Sweet Mystery of Life," from *Naughty Marietta.*

She paused to introduce herself to several other passengers traveling on the transcontinental sleeper, people bound for cities all over the eastern part of the country—Cleveland, Buffalo, Philadelphia, New York City, even Boston. Then she walked forward to the Silver Pine. A boy of about ten ran down the aisle toward her. "Slow down, George," the boy's father said. "Don't bump into this nice lady."

George skidded to a halt and grinned up at Jill. He stuck out his hand. "I'm George Neeley. Who are you? Why are you wearing that uniform? Do you work on the train?"

Jill smiled and shook the boy's hand. "Welcome aboard, George. Yes, I do work on the train. I'm a Zephyrette, and my name's Miss McLeod."

"You get to ride the train all the time? Wow, that's great. I'd like a job on a train. I want to drive a locomotive."

"That's quite a big job," Jill said. "But if you want to drive a locomotive, I'm sure some day you will."

"You going all the way to Chicago?" George asked.

"Yes, I am. How about you?"

"We're going to Nebraska," he said. "My grandma lives in Hastings."

She made her way to the Silver Palisade, stopping to check on Emily and Mrs. Tidsdale. Emily had her nose to the window, looking out, while Mrs. Tidsdale seemed lost in thought as she puffed on a cigarette.

Jill continued forward to the Silver Gull, which was a six-five sleeper, with six double bedrooms alternating with five larger compartments. The porter in charge of this Pullman was an older man named Si Lovell. She said hello and asked him where the Gunthers were. "They're in compartment G, Miss McLeod," he told her.

"Thanks, Mr. Lovell."

Compartment G was in the middle of the car. She stopped to say hello to the Gunthers, who were settled in, Mrs. Gunther on the bench seat that would turn into a lower berth at night, and Mr. Gunther in the free-standing chair. After chatting with them, she turned and walked forward again. Several of the other compartments and bedrooms were empty, awaiting passengers who had yet to board.

At the front of the sleeper car, on the left, was the porter's seat, where Mr. Lovell rode. Opposite this was a toilet for his use, as the compartments and bedrooms had their own toilets, and several lockers, for clean and soiled linen.

The next car was the diner. Jill walked past the tables, some set for two and others for four passengers. There were radios in the buffet-lounge car and observation car, operated by the attendants in those cars. But here, in the middle of the dining car, near the linen locker and the steward's counter, was the master control board for the train's radio and public address system. Recorded music had played while passengers boarded.

Now Jill turned off the music, keyed the mike, and began her welcome-aboard message, the first of many announcements that she would make during the trip.

"Good morning, ladies and gentlemen. This is Jill McLeod, your Zephyrette. On behalf of the Western Pacific, Rio Grande, and Burlington Railroads, I want to welcome you aboard the *California Zephyr.*

"In case you are not acquainted with some of the unusual features of this train, I should like to tell you something about them. This public address system will be used during the day and evening hours in announcing station stops, meal periods, and to call your attention to some of the points of special interest. To insure the reception of these announcements in roomettes and bedrooms, the occupants of those rooms should keep their radio panel at station number four.

"The buffet car, which is located behind the coaches, offers beverage refreshments, sandwiches, coffee, and snack items, and is open now and until midnight for refreshment service and until ten P.M. for food service to all passengers.

"Refreshment service is available in the observation car for sleeping-car passengers. The diner is located between the coaches and the sleepers. Dinner is served on a reservation basis in order that tedious standing in line may be avoided. You will be given an opportunity this afternoon to secure seat assignments for dinner this evening. No reservations are necessary for breakfast or lunch in the dining car, nor for meal service in the buffet car.

"The Vista-Domes of the three chair coaches are for the enjoyment of the coach passengers and the seats are not reserved. The Vista-Domes of the buffet car and of the observation lounge car are for the enjoyment of the sleeping-car passengers, and here again, the seats are not reserved.

"The Vista-Dome affords a marvelous opportunity for camera fans, the best results being secured by using twice the normal exposure time.

"When passing through the train, and when leaving the Vista-Dome seats, please watch for the steps. We have endeavored to make them conspicuous. Two steps will be found at each end of the corridor, directly under the Dome. In the folder rack of your car, you will find not only timetables, but a leaflet entitled 'Vista-Dome Views.' This folder should add materially to your enjoyment of the trip as it describes chief points of interest along the way. The inside back cover explains the various features of the train.

"If you have any questions concerning the adjustments of the roomette and coach seats, the foot and leg rests, or the Venetian blinds, please ask your porter. You may hand me mail to be posted at any time.

"As I pass through the train, I hope you will stop me if you think I can be of service. We are anxious to do all we can to add to the comfort and enjoyment of your trip. Thank you for your attention."

Jill replaced the mike. Recorded music would be played at various times during the journey, along with some news programs, and it was Jill's job to monitor the broadcasts and adjust the volume so that it wasn't too loud, allowing passengers to carry on conversations in a normal tone of voice.

Jill walked forward through the train and met Mr. Wylie, the conductor, in the first Dome coach car, the Silver Pony. Together they walked back through the train, car by car. Passengers expected to see men onboard the train, but many people weren't used to seeing the train's sole woman crew member.

There were attendants in each of the chair cars, but unlike the Pullman porters in the sleepers, the chair car porters were employees of the Western Pacific Railroad, part of the train crew that would change at various stops along the journey.

The *Zephyr* slowed, blowing its grade-crossing warning. They were approaching the small town of Niles. This was a flag station. That meant the train would stop only if there were passengers waiting to board. As it happened, there were three, a family traveling in the third coach car, the Silver Saddle. The whistle blew and the Silver Lady began its journey through Niles Canyon, winding through tree-covered slopes, with Alameda Creek below. The man who'd boarded the Silver Palisade at Third and Washington had already settled into his roomette, the pocket door open, with books and file folders piled onto the seat beside him, and spilling from the briefcase on the floor in front of him.

Jill paused in the doorway. "Good morning, I'm Miss McLeod, the Zephyrette on this run. If there is anything you need, please let me know."

The man quickly tucked the paper he'd been reading into a manila folder, as though he didn't want her to see what it was. He set the folder on the stack of books and looked up, pushing his horn-rimmed glasses up his long nose. He smiled, lines crinkling the skin around his hazel eyes and his wide mouth.

"Thank you, Miss McLeod. I will call on you if necessary."

Again she noticed his accent. European, Jill thought. Like that Mrs. Cole who'd boarded the train at the Oakland Mole. But this man sounded familiar, and now, as Jill stared at him, he looked familiar as well. She had seen him before.

"We've met," she said. "At the university in Berkeley. You're a professor in the physics department, Dr. Laszlo Kovacs."

He nodded. "That's right. Were you in one of my classes?"

She shook her head. "No. I was a history major. I heard you speak at a colloquium, though. It was at the Faculty Club, in March of nineteen forty-nine. There was a reception afterwards. I was with a friend and he introduced us. He was a physics major. He took several of your classes and considered you his advisor."

"And who is this young man?" The professor asked. "I'm sure I'd remember him."

"Steve Haggerty." There, she'd said his name. "We both graduated that spring."

The professor nodded. "Steve Haggerty. I do remember him. A very intelligent young man, with a good head for theoretical physics. He was interested in engineering as well. Yes, and now I recall that evening at the Faculty Club." He stopped and frowned, then he spoke again. "He introduced you as his fiancée. You were engaged to be married."

Dr. Kovacs looked down at Jill's unadorned left hand. She resisted the impulse to hide her hand. She'd taken the ring off and put it away.

"It's none of my business, of course," Dr. Kovacs began.

"Steve is dead." Jill put on her brave smile, the one she used whenever Steve was mentioned. "He was killed in Korea."

Dr. Kovacs hesitated, as though he didn't know what to say. "I am so sorry."

"I'm fine," Jill said. "It's been two years now."

It had been two years and twenty-one days, to be exact. She should stop counting. She had to move on. Not that she'd ever forget Steve or all the plans they'd made, plans that wouldn't happen now.

Jill changed the subject. "Where are you heading, Professor Kovacs?"

"Denver," he said, picking up a file folder.

"Do you have family there?"

He shook his head. "No family. I have friends who teach at the University of Colorado in Boulder. They've invited me to spend the holidays with them. After New Year's Day, I am going on to the University of Chicago, for a conference."

"I'm sure I'll be seeing more of you on the trip," Jill said. "Excuse me."

She walked forward and stopped in the middle of the Silver Palisade, looking out the window. The train was coming out of Niles Canyon. The engineer blew the whistle as the train approached the station in the little town of Sunol, another flag stop, but here there were no passengers. Once out in the countryside, the *Zephyr* picked up speed and headed northeast toward Pleasanton and Livermore.

Ah! Sweet mystery of life. Now she couldn't get the tune from *Naughty Marietta* out of her head.

Jill recalled what Steve had told her about Dr. Laszlo Kovacs. He was from Hungary, a Jew who'd escaped Europe before the war. His family had died in the Holocaust. She wished she could take back the question about his family. She'd have to make it up to the professor, and be extra nice to him.

Suddenly thoughts of Steve overwhelmed her, making her feel sadness for things that would never be. Those feelings were usually kept at bay. But it was December, the anniversary of her fiancé's death. That, and the fact that Dr. Kovacs had talked about Steve, brought those memories. Was that the prickling of tears in her eyes? She hurried through the sleeper cars to the Silver Hostel, to her compartment at the rear of the car. She went inside, locked the door, and sat down. The memories she'd kept at bay washed over her.

Chapter Four

JILL HAD NEVER heard of Chosin Reservoir until Steve died there. She had taken classes in Asian history while at Cal, and she read the newspapers religiously, priding herself on being well read and well informed. So she knew the history. Korea had been occupied by the Japanese in 1905 and annexed in 1910. The peninsula was liberated by the Allies in 1945, with Soviet troops pushing the Japanese from the north and United States forces landing in the south. Korea was a country divided by ideology and in 1948 it was divided in fact, at the 38th parallel. Elections in the south brought anti-Communist Syngman Rhee to power. The north was ruled by a Communist called Kim Il Sung.

The Russians withdrew from Korea in 1948. United States troops remained in the south until early in 1949, the last of them leaving in June, not long after Jill and Steve graduated from the university.

She met Steve Haggerty in the spring of 1948, as she finished her junior year at Cal. It was a blind date set up by her friend Marcia, who was dating Steve's roommate, Dean. The four of them went to a concert at the Greek Theatre on campus. Steve had the bluest eyes she'd ever seen, and an easy smile to go with them. She liked him from the start, and he seemed to like her. After the concert was over, he suggested a movie the following weekend. She said yes, trying not to appear too eager. One date led to another, and soon they were seeing each other every weekend, and sometimes during the week, sharing their lunches on the benches below the Campanile, just a few steps from LeConte Hall, which housed the physics department.

That Thanksgiving, Steve took Jill up to Sacramento to meet his family. Steve's father and uncle both worked for the Western Pacific Railroad. Mick Haggerty was a mechanic based in the Sacramento rail yard, where he repaired the big diesel locomotives that pulled the trains. His younger brother Pat was a conductor and he lived up in Oroville. Jill liked both men as soon as she met them. And she adored Steve's mother, Betty, a good-humored woman who immediately took to Jill. Steve was the oldest of five children, with two brothers and two sisters. And there were lots of aunts, uncles, and cousins there for the Thanksgiving dinner, crowding around the table and filling the two-story house where the Haggertys lived, in midtown Sacramento, not far from the Western Pacific Depot.

By that time Jill was in love with Steve. Through that last semester in school, spring of 1949, they talked about marriage, on long walks through the wooded hills and grassy lawns of the campus, and sitting on the banks of Strawberry Creek. The formal proposal came in April, when Steve gave her an engagement ring set with a small square-cut diamond. They set the date, in August 1950, and continued making plans, for the ceremony, the honeymoon, and their lives together. They would wait a few years before having children. Jill planned to get her teaching credential and look for a job teaching history to junior high or high school students. Steve, with his degree in physics and his interest in engineering, talked of building bridges and roads. But first he had a commitment to fulfill, as an officer in the Marine Corps.

Steve had gone through college in the Navy Reserve Officers' Training Corps, four years of education in exchange for a commitment to serve in the Navy or Marine Corps. He'd chosen the Marines, since his father had been in the First Marine Division, "The Old Breed," in the Pacific during World War II. After graduation, Steve had received his commission as a second lieutenant. In June 1949 he reported for duty at Camp Pendleton in Southern California, while Jill waited for him.

Not that she was idle. The receptionist in her father's medical office had quit to get married, so Jill took the job, temporarily, of course. She lived at home and saved her money, picking out china and silver patterns, looking at furniture, mentally furnishing the home she and Steve would share once they were husband and wife. Several times she took the train down the coast to visit Steve in Oceanside, the site of Camp Pendleton. He borrowed a car from a friend and they spent time exploring San Diego.

On June 25, 1950, North Korean troops poured into South Korea. Jill was ready to go ahead with the wedding, move up the date if necessary, to forgo the church ceremony and stand in front of a justice of the peace. But Steve was cautious. He wanted to wait. He knew his unit was going to Korea. So they postponed the wedding. In September, Steve's regiment was in Korea, assaulting the beaches at Inchon. By October the Chinese army had joined the fray.

Chosin Reservoir was a man-made lake in the northeast of the Korean peninsula. In the battle that began in late November and lasted until mid-December, the First Marine Division had been outnumbered by the Chinese army, assaulted not only by enemy troops but the worst weather in fifty years, with snow, wind, and temperatures dropping to forty below zero. The American troops fighting there called it "Frozen Chosin."

Steve died on Friday, December 1, 1950, in a place called, ironically, Hell Fire Valley. Jill found out about it several days later, on Tuesday, December 5th.

They'd just finished dinner that evening. Her brother, Drew, had set the table, so it fell to Jill and Lucy to help Mom clean up the kitchen and wash dishes. Then the whole family sat down at the dining room table, playing cards. When the doorbell rang. Jill got up from the table and went to the foyer to answer it.

She was surprised to see Steve's Uncle Pat on the porch. What was he doing here?

Jill invited him in and introduced him to her family. Pat refused Lora McLeod's offer of coffee and he looked at Jill with a somber face. Jill didn't connect the dots, but her father did. Amos McLeod crossed the living room and put his arms around his elder daughter.

Pat Haggerty cleared his throat, took a deep breath, and said, "I was on a run from Oroville to Oakland. When I stopped in Sacramento, Mick was at the station. He asked me to come over and see you. He and Betty...they got a telegram this morning."

"Frozen Chosin" reached out and placed icy fingers on Jill's skin. She sat down abruptly in the wing chair, her face wet with the tears that were streaming from her eyes.

Next thing she knew, Pat was gone. She was in her bed upstairs, her sister hovering with a hot water bottle, her brother in the doorway. Her parents sat on either side of her, speaking words that were supposed to comfort her. Her cat, Sophie, instinctively knowing something was wrong, burrowed into Jill's left side, kneading with her paws.

Jill stared up at the ceiling as her parents' voices washed over her. She thought about the last time she and Steve were together, that August weekend in San Diego, right after his division had been mobilized at Camp Pendleton. They had walked arm in arm on a beach, and later, as the sunny afternoon gave way to evening, they clung together, passion stoked by the impending separation. But they hadn't made love. Fear of pregnancy and the uncertain future had stopped her, stopped both of them.

I wish I had, she thought now. I wish I was pregnant. At least I'd have something of him. Something besides photographs. And...

The engagement ring was on the third finger of her left hand. She raised it from Sophie's soft fur and looked at the golden band with its little diamond promise. Then she dropped her hand and stroked the cat, finding comfort in the calico's warm body and steady purr.

Jill wore the engagement ring when she and her parents took the train up to Sacramento for the memorial service for Steve. On the way back, staring out at the rich farmland of California's Central Valley, she wondered what she would do with the rest of her life. When she got home she took off the engagement ring, wrapped it in a lace handkerchief, and tucked it into her jewelry box.

"Now what?" Jill asked herself, looking in the mirror. On the bed, Sophie meowed as if to say she didn't have the answer.

Teaching? That was what Jill had planned to do, but it didn't appeal to her now. Nor did spending the next few years working in her father's office near the hospital.

She met Uncle Pat one afternoon three months later, in a

hole-in-the-wall café near the Western Pacific depot at Third and Washington. It was March of 1951. Whoever had been at the table before them had discarded that morning's *San Francisco Chronicle*. While Pat went to the counter to fetch coffee for both of them, Jill glanced through the newspaper. The headlines were full of the Rosenberg espionage trial that was taking place in New York City. David Greenglass, Ethel Rosenberg's brother, was on the stand, and it looked like his testimony was implicating his sister and brother-in-law.

March already. She folded the newspaper and deposited it on another table. March had memories associated with it, just as December did, and always would. Jill's birthday was at the end of the month. Last year Steve had sent her a bouquet of lush red roses, and a little gold locket on a chain, something else she'd tucked away, out of sight.

She pushed the memory aside and smiled up at Uncle Pat as he set two crockery mugs of coffee on the table. He was in town, laying over at the end of a run, due to head back to Oroville the following day. He'd called and asked her to meet him for coffee.

"I feel restless," she told him. "I want to do something different, something besides working in Dad's office. Travel maybe, but I can't afford it. I need a different job."

Pat stirred sugar into his coffee and took a sip. "I got just the ticket. Why don't you become a Zephyrette? You'd be good at it."

"A Zephyrette?" Jill tried on the idea. She knew about Zephyrettes, of course. She'd ridden the *California Zephyr* several times to Denver, where her grandmother and the rest of her mother's family lived. She smiled. "That would be fun. And you're right, I'd be good at it. That's a great idea, Pat. How do I get to be a Zephyrette?"

Pat grinned. "Good to see you smile, kid. It's been a while. Well, how to go about it? I'm not sure, but..." He looked up and waved at a willowy brunette in slacks who'd just entered the café. "Here's someone who can answer that question. Hey, Fran. Grab some coffee and join us."

"Hey, yourself, Pat." The brunette got a mug and walked over to their table.

Pat made the introductions. "Fran Ellis, meet Jill McLeod. I'm doing some recruiting for you, Fran. Jill's interested in becoming a Zephyrette. What's the first step?"

"You're in luck," Fran said. "Mama McPeek's in town."

"And who is Mama McPeek?" Jill asked.

Fran laughed. "Her name is Velma McPeek. She's our den mother, so to speak. The way I hear it, she sort of invented the Zephyrettes. She's based in Chicago, but she rides the rails quite often. Checking up on us girls to make sure we make all the proper announcements at the proper times. I happen to know we are short a Zephyrette because one of the other girls based here just quit. There are only ten or eleven of us, with six on the road at any one time, three in each direction. And a couple laying over in Chicago and San Francisco."

"How often do you travel?" Jill asked.

"About three round trips a month. How old are you, Jill? The girls are supposed to be between twenty-four and twenty-eight."

"I'll be twenty-four later this month," Jill said.

Fran looked her over. "I can't tell how tall you are since you're sitting down. You've got to be between five four and five eight. I'm a whisper over five eight but I made the cut."

Jill smiled. "Five four and a half."

"Close enough. Good character and a pleasing personality?" Fran asked.

"I can vouch for both," Pat said, saluting Jill with his coffee cup.

"I thought as much," Fran said. "College degree or nurse's training? Do you speak any languages?"

"Bachelor's in history from UC Berkeley," Jill said. "My father's a doctor and I've been working as a receptionist in his office. I know my way around a first-aid kit. Got a merit badge in first aid when I was in the Girl Scouts. I took French in high school and college. I can ask for directions in Spanish, Italian, and German. And I can say 'Happy New Year' in Chinese."

Fran laughed. "*Gung hay fat choy*. Living in the Bay Area, so can I. That's great. Sounds like you're covered in the language department. Let's see, you've got to be single. But I guess you are. You're not wearing a ring."

Jill's smile dimmed a bit and she rubbed her ring finger, thinking of the engagement ring hidden in her jewelry box. "Yes, I'm single."

"As far as I'm concerned, you've got the job," Fran said. "Of course, you've got to talk with Mrs. McPeek. Give me your phone number and I'll see what I can do."

Three days later Jill took the ferry to San Francisco, where she had an interview with Mrs. Velma McPeek at the Western Pacific Railroad headquarters on Market Street. A week after that, Jill boarded the *California Zephyr* for an eastbound run to Chicago, as an employee rather than a passenger. This was her on-the-job training, accompanying Fran Ellis, who was the Zephyrette on the run. She shadowed Fran and soaked up as much information as she could on the eastbound and westbound journeys. Then, six days after her return to Oakland, Jill was riding the rails on her own.

By the time Jill celebrated her twenty-fourth birthday at home with her family, Julius and Ethel Rosenberg had been found guilty of espionage and sentenced to death.

Three railroads—the Western Pacific, the Denver & Rio Grande Western, and the Chicago, Burlington & Quincy—operated the *California Zephyr*. The conductors, brakemen and stewards were employees of the various railroads. And the Pullman porters worked for the Pullman Company. But the Zephyrettes were considered Western Pacific employees and paid by that road.

As Fran had said earlier, there weren't that many Zephyrettes. Jill was one of eleven. There were six young women based in the San Francisco area and five in Chicago, plus the occasional trainee. Many of the Zephyrettes stayed only two or three years, but Fran had been working for the *CZ* since the start, in March of 1949. Once Jill was on her own, she made three round trips a month. When she wasn't on the road, she helped out in her father's office.

Weeks blurred into months and a year passed, now almost two. Hard to believe, but in three more months, March 1953, Jill would celebrate her twenty-sixth birthday, and her second anniversary as a Zephyrette.

Chapter Five

ANNIVERSARIES. DECEMBER WAS the second anniversary of Steve's death. It didn't do to dwell on the past. She was over it by now. Or was she?

Little things triggered the memories. Anniversaries, like December, or March, or the day in April when Steve proposed. Like Nat King Cole singing "Mona Lisa." That velvety voice wrapped around the lovely melody reminded her of slow dancing, Steve's arms wrapped around her, pillowing her cheek on his broad, comfortable shoulder.

Stop it, she told herself. Stop thinking about Steve. But that was hard to do, when little things reminded her. Like December—and Professor Kovacs.

Jill glanced at her watch. She'd been sitting here too long. She stood and lowered the small stainless steel sink from the wall of her compartment. She washed her face. Then she freshened her makeup, inspecting her face in the mirror.

Someone knocked on her door. "Miss McLeod? You in there?"

She opened the door and saw the car attendant for the Silver Palace, the second Dome chair car. "What is it?"

"A little girl on my car took a tumble coming down the stairs from the Vista-Dome. You know how the kids are. They will run up and down the aisles and play on those stairs. Anyway, the little girl scraped some skin off her knee and it's bleeding a bit."

"I'll be right there."

Jill grabbed the first-aid kit and left her compartment. When she glanced out the windows, she saw the train had left Livermore and was heading up the switchbacks that would take it over

Altamont Pass. She walked forward to the Silver Palace, where the girl was sitting with her mother in their seats in the middle of the car. The scrape on the child's right knee had stopped bleeding. Jill cleaned the wound, asking the child's name and age just to distract her.

"My name's Tina," the girl said, "and I'm nine."

"That's a good age," Jill said. "There's another girl on the train who's nine. Her name is Emily. She's traveling in one of the sleeper cars. Now this might sting a little bit, but only for a few seconds."

Tina winced as Jill put some Merthiolate, a topical antibiotic, on the scrape and covered the spot with a large bandage. "Now be more careful going up and down the stairs," Jill said.

The little girl nodded. "I will."

After Jill said good-bye to Tina and her mother, she moved to the vestibule of the car and reached into her skirt pocket. She pulled out a pencil and a small notebook, wrote down the time and a brief description of what happened. She kept notes during the run, so she could refer to them when she filled out the detailed trip report she was required to submit at the end of the run. The trip report contained information about the journey and her activities each day she was on the road, noting any complaints, accidents, medicine administered, the names of the special attention passengers or any other notable people aboard. In short, anything and everything, a picture of the train and the people on it.

She walked forward to the first Dome coach car, the Silver Pony, where she was hailed by a woman who was experiencing motion sickness. Jill always kept a remedy called soda mints in her pocket, so she gave the woman a few. Then Jill climbed the stairs to the Vista-Dome. It was a clear day, with just a few high clouds. As the train descended the east side of Altamont Pass, she looked out at the broad sweep of California's Central Valley. Once the train was out of the hills, it picked up speed, heading through the little towns where farmers tilled the rich soil along the San Joaquin River. The whistle blew its warning near crossings, and children on the streets and in backyards waved at the Silver Lady.

The *Zephyr*'s next scheduled stop was just before noon in

Stockton, the city at the eastern end of the vast watery delta, where the San Joaquin met the Sacramento and the two rivers mingled and flowed toward San Francisco Bay. The train slowed, moving through the town, and blew its whistle before stopping at the station. Jill checked her watch. Right on schedule. The stop was only a minute long, time enough to board a few more passengers. Sacramento, the state capital, was the next stop, about an hour away.

After the train left Stockton, Jill walked to the diner to make her second announcement. "Your attention please. No doubt you will be interested in watching the approach of the westbound *California Zephyr*. We'll be meeting it soon."

That usually happened near the small town of Kingdon, just north of Stockton. Jill walked forward to the first chair car and took the steps up to the Vista-Dome. Every seat was taken, with passengers talking about the two trains meeting. In the distance she saw number 17, the westbound train, approaching number 18, the eastbound train. Whistles blew on both trains as the gap between them narrowed. Then the trains passed each other in a blur of silver cars.

Jill descended from the Vista-Dome and headed back through the chair cars to the Silver Hostel. In the coffee shop section, four people at one table were talking and eating sandwiches. At another table, a young woman in a full gray wool skirt and a red cardigan sweater dealt herself a hand of Solitaire as the steward brought her a cup of tea. She took a sip and grimaced.

"You Yanks don't know how to make a proper cuppa," she said, looking up.

Jill smiled. "Believe me, it's not the first time I've heard one of your countrymen—or women—say that."

"I don't doubt it. Though this will have to do. I'm Evelyn Wolford, by the way. And you're the Zephyrette."

"Miss McLeod," Jill said. "What part of England are you from?"

"London, born and bred," Miss Wolford said.

"I read about that terrible fog in London, earlier this month," Jill said. The killer fog, as the newspapers called it, had begun

December 5th, when cold weather and a lack of wind trapped a layer of pollutants over the British capital. It lasted four days, and in the weeks since, a number of people had died of respiratory problems, according to the articles Jill had seen in the newspaper.

The young Englishwoman shook her head. "Dreadful business, that. We Londoners are used to our 'pea-soupers,' but this was different. It had been so cold that people were burning lots of soft coal to keep warm. My sister said she couldn't even see to walk along the sidewalk, had to shuffle along as though blind. And it seeped indoors. Lots of fatalities from breathing the stuff. I expect the toll will go up."

"Have you been visiting the United States for long?" Jill asked.

"Spending a year at Cal doing graduate studies in sociology."

"My alma mater," Jill said. "My degree is in history. There's another young woman aboard who's studying at Cal. Miss LeGros, traveling in one of the chair cars."

"I'll look for her. We can have a natter and compare notes on Berkeley. I'm off to New York City to spend the holidays with friends. Got a berth in that car, what's it called? Ah, the Silver Rapids."

Jill nodded. "The transcontinental sleeper. When we get to Chicago, that car gets hooked up to a train from the Pennsylvania Railroad for the trip to New York."

"Sounds grand. Wonderful opportunity to see your country."

"Someday I'd like to see yours. I feel as though I know it."

"With a name like McLeod, I imagine your ancestors came over from Scotland," Miss Wolford said.

"A long time ago," Jill said. "What I meant, though, is that I've read so many books set in England that I feel I know it. I love Agatha Christie."

"Ah, yes, Agatha. I've read most of hers. I'm actually quite fond of the Lord Peter Wimsey books by Dorothy L. Sayers."

"I've read those, too," Jill said. "It's been nice talking with you, Miss Wolford."

After leaving the coffee shop, Jill headed back to the lounge section. She peered in and saw a man and a woman seated in the corner. He was talking loudly, pounding his hand on the table for emphasis, and attracting stares from other passengers. "I'm telling you, all those Jews are Commies. They're infiltrating the government, that's what Senator McCarthy says."

His wife looked up from her embroidery. "Oh, keep your voice down. Nobody wants to hear what you think. Besides, I'd just as soon you didn't talk about politics."

Jill passed the dormitory section at the rear of the car and made a quick stop in her compartment. Then she continued to the dining car. It was past noon now, and lunch service was in full swing. As she entered the Silver Plate she glimpsed the kitchen, where the chefs were in constant motion, preparing meals so that the waiters could deliver them to the passengers seated in the table section. A so-called "air curtain" kept cooking odors from permeating the dining section.

Jill walked down the corridor that ran alongside to the kitchen, excusing herself as she stepped past three coach passengers who were waiting in line to be seated. Although she would later make reservations for dinner, there was no reserved seating. Instead passengers were directed to tables by the dining car steward. It was a great way for people to meet their fellow passengers, the people with whom they'd share the train for the duration of their journey.

In the center of the car, Jill stepped behind the counter to let a man and a woman pass, heading up the corridor to the forward coaches. The steward was at the rear of the car, seating passengers who'd come forward from the sleeper section.

The dining car seated forty-eight passengers when filled to capacity. There were thirty-two seats in the main section, and at either end, semi-private nooks that could accommodate another sixteen additional people. Floral reliefs decorated the walls and ceilings. The carpet, a pale green, set off the red leather chairs. The windows had Venetian blinds as well as drapes in contrasting red, green, and cream.

The steward returned to his counter. "Are you here for lunch, Miss McLeod?"

"No, thank you, Mr. Gridley. I'll wait a while."

He nodded and turned to the coach passengers waiting to be

seated, beckoning them to a nearby table. After they were seated, Jill walked down the central aisle between the tables. As she neared the rear of the car, she saw the Gunthers facing her, at a table on the right. Opposite Mrs. Gunther, Emily Charlton pulled crusts off the bread on her chicken sandwich. Next to the child, Mrs. Tidsdale waved her spoon as she chatted with the Gunthers, pausing now and then to dip thick green pea soup from the bowl in front of her. The waiter appeared, with a chicken salad for Mrs. Gunther and a hot roast beef sandwich for Mr. Gunther.

Jill stopped to say hello to the four at the table, then continued to the rear entrance of the dining car. At another table for four, Miss Stafford, the writer, was talking with the Perlmans, the couple traveling on the transcontinental sleeper.

"I'm spending Christmas with my brother in Chicago," Miss Stafford said. "After that, I'm going to New York to visit friends. I really want to see this new play, *The Seven-Year Itch*. I've heard it's good."

"Oh, yes, it is," Mrs. Perlman said. "We were there opening night in November. I loved it. Wonderful, so funny."

Her husband looked up from his menu. "It was okay. Blanche liked it more than I did."

"That was you laughing in the seat next to me," Mrs. Perlman said, poking her husband with her elbow. "You enjoyed it more than that Mary Chase play we saw earlier in the year."

"You've convinced me," Miss Stafford said. "I'll definitely put *The Seven-Year Itch* on my list of things to see. What other shows would you recommend?"

"*Dial M for Murder*. You definitely want to see that one." Mrs. Perlman picked up her menu. "Now, let's see. I think I'll have the chicken."

"That Shrimp Newburg looks good. In fact, that's what I'll have." Miss Stafford marked her meal check and gave it to the waiter.

In the space next to a storage locker, Dr. Laszlo Kovacs waited for the steward to seat him. He smiled at Jill.

"Good afternoon, Professor Kovacs," Jill said. "I hope you're enjoying the trip."

Before the professor could answer, two other people entered the dining car, a man in gray pinstripes and a woman in a green suit. They were the Coles, the newlyweds who were traveling in the Silver Gull. The professor glanced back at the new arrivals and his polite smile turned into a frown. Emotions flickered over his face.

Mrs. Cole's full red lips turned upward in her narrow face, but the smile didn't quite reach her hazel eyes. "Hello, Laszlo."

Dr. Kovacs nodded, a tight formal move. "Rivka. What a surprise to see you."

Mrs. Cole laughed, smoothing back her chestnut ponytail. "Oh, it's Rita now. Much more American. Where are you working these days?"

"At the University of California in Berkeley," Dr. Kovacs said.

"Who's this, honey?" Mr. Cole put his arm around his wife's waist.

"This is my ex-husband, darling," Mrs. Cole said. "Laszlo Kovacs. I've told you about him. Laszlo, this is my husband, Clifford Cole. We just got married."

"Oh, yeah." Mr. Cole smiled and stuck out his hand. "Pleased to meet you."

The professor hesitated, then returned the handshake. "Congratulations on your marriage. I hope you'll be very happy."

"Oh, I am very happy indeed." Mrs. Cole smoothed her collar, showing off her wedding ring. "We spent our honeymoon in San Francisco and we're on our way back to Chicago. Where are you going, Laszlo?"

"Denver, then Chicago."

"Bet you're going to the Institute in Chicago," she said.

Dr. Kovacs didn't respond to this. Instead he said, "I'm spending the holidays with the Walkers. He's teaching at the University of Colorado in Boulder."

Mrs. Cole rolled her eyes, and her voice was tart. "Lloyd and Ella, and those endless games of canasta." Mr. Cole looked curious, so she added. "The Walkers were our neighbors in New Mexico."

Her husband gave an incurious shrug. "Oh, yeah? Never been to New Mexico. I hear it's real pretty."

The dining car steward stepped up and beckoned Dr. Kovacs.

The professor followed him down the aisle. As he passed the table where Emily and Mrs. Tidsdale were sitting, Dr. Kovacs looked down, just as Mrs. Tidsdale looked up and smiled. Their eyes met and Dr. Kovacs frowned again. Then he moved away, taking a seat indicated by the steward, at a table already occupied by a man, a woman, and a teenaged girl.

Curious, Jill thought. It was as though the professor and Mrs. Tidsdale knew each other, or thought they did. But if that was the case, why hadn't they spoken?

The steward returned and placed the Coles at a table opposite two elderly women. Mrs. Clive was sitting at a nearby table, upbraiding a waiter as she pointed at her soup. "This is cold. Take it back to the kitchen and bring me another bowl."

"Yes, ma'am," the waiter said, whisking the offending bowl from the table.

"Not the standard of service I'm accustomed to," Mrs. Clive said. She waved at Jill. "How long before we get to Sacramento?"

Jill looked at her watch. "We're due in at twelve-fifty." And I have things to do before we get there. She left the dining car and walked back through the sleeping cars to the Silver Solarium. "We're coming into Sacramento soon," she told the passengers in the lounge at the rear. "We'll have a longer stop, so I can mail letters and postcards if you want, or send telegrams from the Western Union office at the station."

"I would like to send a wire," Mr. Finch said. "Just a moment, I'll write it out for you." He stepped to the writing desk, which was supplied with *California Zephyr* stationery, envelopes, and postcards, and picked up a pen. As he scribbled, both his daughters came down the stairs from the Vista-Dome.

"Can we go up to the lounge?" the older girl, Nan, asked.

Mrs. Finch smiled. "That would be fine. I'm sure I can count on both of you to behave, and not get in the way of the train crew. Miss McLeod is going to send a wire for your father when we get to Sacramento. She can mail postcards, too, if you want to write out a few."

Cathy, the younger girl, said, "I want to send postcards. One to Grandma, and one to my friend Margaret. But I don't have any stamps."

"I do." Jill reached in her pocket for the stamps she carried, two cents for postcards and three for letters. "Just let me know how many stamps you'll need."

Nan and Cathy both took postcards from the writing desk and wrote notes on three cards each. Jill counted out the stamps and the girls affixed them to the postcards. Mr. Finch handed her his wire and took out his wallet, removing several bills. "That should take care of the wire and the stamps," he said.

"Thank you. I'll bring your change once we're out of Sacramento." Jill left the Silver Solarium and walked through the sleeper cars, collecting postcards and letters to be mailed. When she reached the Silver Palisade, she stopped at bedroom A. Emily and Mrs. Tidsdale had returned from the diner. "Do you want to send a postcard?" Jill asked the little girl.

Emily hugged her teddy bear. "Who would I write to?"

"What about Stella?" Jill asked. "You could tell her all about your train trip."

"That's right," Mrs. Tidsdale said, lighting a cigarette as she leaned back in the seat. "Go ahead and write out a card, sweetie, and Miss McLeod will mail it when we get to Sacramento."

"Stella lives on Taylor Street," Emily said, "but I don't know the number of the house."

"I do." Frank Nathan appeared, holding a postcard and a pen. "I can write out Mama's address, and you can write the rest."

Emily nodded and took the card. While she was writing out her message, Jill knocked on the doors of the other bedrooms. There was no answer in B or D, and bedroom C was empty. The door to bedroom E was open. Inside, Jill saw Mr. and Mrs. Benson together on the bench seat, a copy of that morning's *San Francisco Chronicle* open to an inside page. He was pointing at the article Jill had seen earlier, about the Rosenberg supporters marching near Sing Sing.

"Well, I think they're guilty," Mr. Benson said. "Always have, from the start."

Mrs. Benson sighed. "Julius, yes. I believe that. But Ethel? I'm not so sure."

"Yeah, but her brother, what he said at the trial about her typing up the notes."

"I know," Mrs. Benson said. "But I'm not sure he told the truth. A man will say anything to save his own skin. I just think the electric chair seems harsh. We're not at war now."

"Passing secrets to the Reds is treason," Mr. Benson said. "And we were at war when it happened, even though the Russians were our allies."

"I just think about their kids. Two little boys, just like us. Their youngest is about the same age as Billy."

"Who's the same age as me?" Billy came into view, followed by his younger brother, Chip. The porter had opened the wall between the two bedrooms, making the two bedrooms into one large room for the family.

"A little boy who lives back east," his mother said. She looked up and saw Jill. "Oh, hi, Miss McLeod."

"I'm collecting postcards to mail in Sacramento," Jill said. "I have stamps if you need them."

"I brought stamps with me." Mrs. Benson reached for her handbag and took out a handful of postcards, all stamped and ready to mail. Jill took the cards and glanced at them. They were all destined for addresses in Colorado and New Mexico. "The boys wrote to all their cousins, and their grandmother."

"I wrote my *Abuela*," Billy said. "That's Spanish for grandma."

"I know." Jill smiled at Mrs. Benson. "You're from New Mexico, then."

"That's right. My parents live in Española. Papa was an engineer on the Chili Line, until they shut it down in 'forty-one. It ran from Antonito, Colorado, down to Santa Fe, New Mexico. The official name was the Santa Fe Branch, but everyone called it the Chili Line, because it carried a lot of chile peppers."

"I've heard of that line," Jill said.

"It's narrow gauge," Billy said. "Grandpa told me. That's because of the mountains."

Jill smiled. "Narrow gauge is the space between the insides of the rails. Sometimes the distance is as small as two feet, and other times it's about three and a half feet."

"My grandpa says in Colorado it's three feet," Billy said. "It takes up less space when they put the rails in the mountains."

"Do you know what standard gauge is?" Jill asked.

Billy screwed up his face. "Four feet and...eight inches. And a half inch."

"That's right. You really know a lot about railroading."

"I told you they were mad for trains," Mrs. Benson said.

The younger boy, Chip, tugged on Jill's sleeve. "Grandpa's an engineer. He took us on a ride in the engine. I got to toot the horn."

"It sounds like you're quite the railroading family," Jill said.

"We sure are," Mrs. Benson said. "My Aunt Becky was a Harvey Girl at the station in Albuquerque. Dad's retired now, from the Denver and Rio Grande Western. My brother Rico is a brakeman. He's based in Alamosa, Colorado."

"Toot, toot," Chip said. Then he dashed around the room and out the door of bedroom F, yelling, "Toot, toot, toot."

Billy stepped past Jill into the corridor, adding his voice to that of his brother. Ed Benson got up and followed the boys outside. "Settle down, you two."

Just then Mrs. Clive rounded the corner, returning from the dining car. She stopped, glaring at the little boys running along the passageway. She looked as though she'd bit into a lemon, then went into bedroom D and shut the door.

"Let's keep the noise down, boys," Mr. Benson said. He smiled at Jill. "Don't want to disturb the neighbors. Probably too late for that, though."

"Let's go up to the Dome," Billy said.

"Good idea," Mrs. Benson said. "We'd better let you go, Miss McLeod. I'm sure you have a lot to do before we pull into Sacramento."

"Yes, I do." Jill glanced at her watch. Frank Nathan and Emily appeared in the passageway, Emily holding the postcard she'd written for Stella. She handed it to Jill, who tucked all the postcards she'd gathered into her jacket pocket.

She headed for the next car, the Silver Gull, and said hello to the Gunthers, who were just returning to their compartment. She waited while Mrs. Gunther wrote out a postcard to send to her sister in Oregon.

By the time she reached the Silver Pony, Jill's pockets bulged with cards and letters, and she had more telegrams to send. Sacramento loomed in the distance. The *Zephyr* slowed as it moved through the outskirts of the city, blowing its horn at each crossing. Jill glimpsed the domed capitol building. Then the train pulled into the Western Pacific Depot at Nineteenth and J Streets. As soon as the train stopped, Jill stepped down to the platform and hurried toward the one-story Mission Revival–style building. She dropped envelopes and postcards into a nearby mailbox.

Teresa Brewer's perky voice sang out from a radio in the Western Union office, urging everyone within range to put another nickel in the nickelodeon. The man behind the counter was unwrapping a piece of Juicy Fruit gum when Jill walked in. He stuck the gum in his mouth, reached for the pencil tucked behind his ear, and scanned the wires she handed to him, tallying up the cost. On the radio, the music changed. Rosemary Clooney sang her hit, "Tenderly." Jill paid the man behind the telegraph office counter and left the building, walking toward the train.

At the vestibule of the Silver Palisade, Frank Nathan was stowing a suitcase and a worn carpetbag in the vestibule. A woman waited near the step box. She wore a dove gray dress with a blue shawl around her shoulders. Silver threads mingled with dark in her hair, worn in a loose bun at the nape of her neck. She held a white cane in her right hand.

"I've got your case in the vestibule, ma'am," the porter said. "You're in bedroom C. Now, if you'll take my arm, I'll help you up the steps."

With her left hand, the woman grasped Mr. Nathan's arm. The tip of her cane flicked over the step box. The shawl slipped from her shoulders and fell to the platform. Jill stooped to pick it up. "I'm right behind you, ma'am," she said. "I have your shawl. I'll give it to you when we get aboard."

"Thank you." With Mr. Nathan's assistance, the woman carefully climbed the steps into the vestibule. She turned, her head erect and her sightless eyes a clear light blue. "Are you traveling on this car?" she asked as Jill draped the shawl around her shoulders.

"I'm Miss McLeod, the Zephyrette. If there's anything I can do to help you during the trip, please let me know."

"I appreciate your assistance, both you and this young man.

I'm Mrs. Tatum, by the way, Alberta Tatum. Bound for Grand Junction, Colorado." She nodded her head. "And what is your name, Porter?"

"Frank Nathan, ma'am. I'll be with you all the way to Colorado. Now, if you'll come with me, your bedroom is this way." He escorted Mrs. Tatum to bedroom C, then went back to the vestibule for her luggage. He set the suitcase and carpetbag inside, telling her where they were. She took a change purse from the pocket of her gray skirt and tipped the porter. "Thank you, ma'am."

"They're still serving lunch in the diner," Jill said. "Would you like me to take you there?"

"I'd like to get settled in first," Mrs. Tatum said, leaning her white cane against the wall. "I'll find my way to the dining car in a little while."

Jill followed the porter back to the vestibule, where a burly, balding man in a brown suit was boarding the train. He had a ticket in his right hand and a battered brown valise in his left. He flashed the ticket at the porter.

"You're in roomette number ten, sir," Frank Nathan said. "Right this way."

The man shoved his valise at the porter. "Put the bag in the roomette, boy," he barked in a gruff bass. "I'll be in the lounge."

"Yes, sir." Frank Nathan took the bag. The man turned, jostling Jill as he left the vestibule. The conductor walked by, calling, "All aboard." Frank Nathan set the valise on the floor of the vestibule. He closed and locked the doors. Then the engineer blew the horn and the *California Zephyr* pulled out of the Sacramento station.

Chapter Six

JILL WALKED THROUGH the cars, giving change and receipts to the people who'd asked her to send telegrams. The last of these was Mr. Finch, in the Silver Solarium. The Finches were just returning to the observation car after having lunch in the diner.

"Excellent meal," Mr. Finch said. "I'm always pleased with the food on the *Zephyr*. Thank you for sending the wire, Miss McLeod."

"When do we get to the Feather River Canyon?" Mrs. Finch asked.

Jill consulted her watch. "We'll be in Marysville at one thirty-eight, and Oroville at two-eleven. I'll make an announcement when we start up the canyon."

"We went through there two years ago, during the summer. It was so beautiful. I'm looking forward to seeing it during the winter."

The Finches' two daughters climbed the stairs up to the Vista-Dome. In the lounge at the rear of the car, Mrs. Constanza was knitting while her husband read *The Lady in the Lake* by Raymond Chandler. He set his book aside and glanced up at Mr. Finch. "Tell me, do you and your wife play bridge?"

"Oh, we're rabid players," Mrs. Finch said with a smile. "Shall we have a few rubbers? Do you have cards, Porter?"

"Sure do, ma'am," Mr. Parsons said. "If you would care to move to the buffet, there is a booth for four."

As Jill left the car, her stomach growled. It was past time for lunch. She walked forward through the sleeper cars, pausing to answer questions from passengers. In the Silver Palisade, Dr.

Kovacs was in his roomette, amid his books and papers. He looked up and smiled as she passed.

When Jill reached the bedrooms, Mrs. Tatum stepped out into the corridor, tapping her surroundings with her white cane.

"Hello, Mrs. Tatum, it's Miss McLeod. Are you going to the dining car? I'm headed that way myself, because I haven't had lunch yet."

Mrs. Tatum smiled. "In that case, let's away to the diner."

When they reached the dining car, Mr. Gridley, the dining car steward, beckoned to them. "Ready for lunch now, Miss McLeod?"

"I certainly am, thanks."

He directed them to a table that had just been cleared and reset with a clean white linen tablecloth. Each place setting had heavy silverware and Western Pacific china decorated with a rim of feathers denoting the railroad's Feather River Route. Completing the table setting were folded napkins, the bud vase with its holly and carnation, and a menu in an upright silver holder.

When she and Mrs. Tatum were seated, Jill poured water for both of them from the bottle on the table. Then she pulled the luncheon menu from its stand and opened it.

"The soup today is split pea," Jill said. "That's one of my favorites."

"Mine, too," Mrs. Tatum said. "I'll have a cup of that. What are the entrées and sandwiches?"

Jill read through the items and prices on the menu and they both decided to have the chicken salad sandwich. Jill noted their selections on the table checks and handed them to the waiter. In a moment, he returned with two cups of soup. They picked up their spoons and ate in companionable silence. When Mrs. Tatum finished her soup, she took a sip of water, careful not to spill any as she raised the glass to her lips.

"How long have you been a Zephyrette?"

"Nearly two years." Jill smiled at the waiter as he delivered their sandwiches and whisked away their empty soup cups.

"You must be on your feet all day," Mrs. Tatum said.

Jill laughed. "Yes, from the time we leave Oakland. I'm constantly walking through the train. It's good exercise. I do get some breaks, though. Mealtimes, like now. I go off duty at night, about ten, and I'm up before seven. And I'm on call at night, if anything should happen."

"How often do you make the journey?"

"I average three round trips a month."

"It seems like an interesting job for a young woman. I gather you enjoy it."

"I do," Jill said. "I've met all sorts of people. And I've traveled, not just on the *Zephyr*. I have passes from all three railroads, and I've used them to go other places."

"Are you based in Chicago or the Bay Area?"

"I live in Alameda with my family."

A boy and a girl, unaccompanied by an adult, rushed past their table, giggling and chattering. They nearly collided with the waiter who was approaching the table where Mrs. Tatum and Jill sat. He deftly sidestepped the children. "We sure do have a lot of young ones on the train this run," he said.

"We certainly do." Jill had already noted that for her trip report. "It's the holidays, folks traveling to be with their families for Christmas. The children roam through the train, looking for vacant seats in the Vista-Domes."

"Don't their parents keep track of them?" Mrs. Tatum asked. "I always did with my children."

"Some do and some don't," Jill said. "I think the parents sometimes view being on the train as their own holiday as well. We keep an eye on the children, make sure they don't get into mischief, or get hurt. I'm planning a Christmas party tomorrow afternoon, right here in the diner."

"That's right," the waiter said. "The chefs are baking a Christmas cake for the little ones. Now, are you ladies ready for dessert? We have pumpkin pie. I know that's one of your favorites, Miss McLeod."

"Thank you. Pumpkin pie sounds great, with whipped cream on top. And I would like coffee."

"Of course." The waiter turned to Mrs. Tatum. "What about you, ma'am? We also have apple pie, and I can put some ice cream on that, or a bit of cheese, if you prefer."

"Apple," Mrs. Tatum said. "With ice cream."

"What about you?" Jill asked Mrs. Tatum as the waiter stepped away. "Are you from Sacramento?"

"I've lived there nearly twenty-five years. My husband was an engineer for the California Department of Transportation. I taught grade school, until I started losing my sight. So I retired. Mr. Tatum died a few years ago, but my son and his wife are in Sacramento. He owns a business downtown. This year I'm spending Christmas with my daughter and her family in Grand Junction. I'm originally from Colorado. The town of Gunnison. Do you know where that is?"

"Oh, yes. My mother's hometown is Denver. We lived there with my grandmother, during the war, while my father was in the Navy. My cousin David went to school in Gunnison, at Western State College."

Mrs. Tatum smiled. "They didn't call it that until the 'twenties. Back in my day it was called the Colorado State Normal School for Children. That's where I learned how to be a teacher. What did your father do in the Navy?"

"He's a doctor. He was in the Pacific during the war. Then he worked at the Navy hospital in Oakland. He's in private practice now."

The *Zephyr*'s horn blew as the train approached a grade crossing. They were coming into Marysville now. The train slowed, then stopped briefly. Jill and Mrs. Tatum finished their pie and paid their checks. Jill escorted Mrs. Tatum back to her compartment in the Silver Palisade. Then she walked back through the diner to the Silver Hostel. Past the door to the crew's dormitory were the stairs that led up to the Vista-Dome. Just then a middle-aged man with a receding hairline stepped out of the lounge. It was Mr. Washburn, the man who'd removed his wedding ring before boarding the train. She hadn't seen him since his attempt to flirt with her at the Oakland Mole.

Jill backed against the corridor wall, to let Mr. Washburn pass. But he didn't. Instead he leaned forward, putting his left hand against the wall, just above her right shoulder, blocking her from moving in that direction. She smelled liquor on his breath.

"Well, well, if it isn't that pretty Zephyrette. C'mon, honey. Have a drink with me."

There's one on every trip, Jill thought.

Jill moved to her left, away from his encroaching arm, and glanced to her right, over his shoulder, hoping one of the stewards or another passenger would appear.

"I'm sorry, sir," Jill said. "I'm not supposed to drink while I'm on duty."

"I can wait," Mr. Washburn said, a leer spreading across his face. "Tonight would be even better. What time do you get off duty, honey? I've got some fine old bourbon. We can have a party in my compartment."

"I'm on duty until we get to Chicago," Jill said. That was the truth but she didn't think it would deter this would-be playboy.

"Chicago?" The man looked befuddled, then his voice took on a wheedling tone. "What the hell. That doesn't work. I'm getting off the train in Omaha. C'mon, honey, have a drink with me. What's the harm in having just one little drink?"

He reached for her arm and she quickly moved farther to her left, putting some distance between them. "You wouldn't want me to lose my job, sir."

"She doesn't want to have a drink with you."

Jill turned to see who had spoken. It was Mrs. Tidsdale, one hand on her hip in her bright red dress, a steely look in her blue eyes.

Mr. Washburn screwed up his face, looking like a petulant kid who'd been thwarted. "But I wanna have another drink."

"I'll have a drink with you," Mrs. Tidsdale said. She stepped past Jill and took the drunk's arm. "My name's Tidsy. What's yours?"

As Tidsy led the man into the lounge, Jill turned and went back through the diner and the Silver Gull to the Silver Palisade. She tapped on the door of bedroom A. "Emily? It's Miss McLeod." There was no answer. Jill opened the door a crack and saw Emily stretched out on the bench seat, arm around her teddy bear. The little girl was asleep.

Jill shut the door, just as Frank Nathan rounded the corner. "Just checking on Emily. She's napping."

"I saw Mrs. Tidsdale leave a few minutes ago," he said.

"She's in the lounge, having a drink."

Billy Benson came barreling out of bedroom E, followed by his younger brother, Chip. They ran down the passageway and stopped, looking up at Jill and the porter.

"Train robbers," Chip said.

"Does this train ever get robbed?" Billy asked. "In the movies train robbers hide in the mountains and come down on the train and make people give them money and jewelry."

Frank Nathan laughed. "I don't think we've had a train robbery on the *California Zephyr*. Have you heard about any robbers these days, Miss McLeod?"

"Back in the olden days," she said, smiling as she recalled tales of California's past, like Black Bart holding up stagecoaches before the advent of the railroad. "But we haven't had any robberies on this train. You see, we have special agents. Those Western Pacific agents are very good about preventing things like train robberies."

Billy seemed satisfied with the answers. He pounded on the door of bedroom A. Emily opened the door, teddy bear clutched in one hand. "Hey, Emily, you want to play games? We got cards and dominoes and checkers."

"Okay." Emily stepped out of the bedroom and shut the door.

"What's your teddy's name?" Jill asked.

"Benny," Emily said. "Benny the Bear."

"I got a bear named Max," Billy told her.

"I'll tell Mrs. Tidsdale where you are," Jill said. Emily nodded and followed Billy into the Bensons' bedroom.

Jill walked back to the lounge car and saw Mrs. Tidsdale seated alone at one of the tables, a glass of amber liquid in front of her. She was smoking a cigarette as she leaned back in her seat, eyes half-closed.

"You're alone."

"The wolf went back to his lair. He'd already had one little drinkie too many." Mrs. Tidsdale stubbed out her cigarette in the ashtray and picked up the glass, swirling the ice cubes before she raised it to her lips.

"Thank you for taking him off my hands," Jill said.

Mrs. Tidsdale winked at her. "Us girls got to stick together."

"I came to tell you Emily is playing games with the Benson boys."

"Thanks. I'll look in on her in a while." Mrs Tidsdale knocked back the rest of her drink and waved her hand to summon the steward. "Another Scotch on the rocks, please. Well, Emily can't get into much trouble on a train. Still...I suspect Mrs. Benson's far better equipped to look after a bunch of kids than I am."

Jill didn't respond but privately she agreed.

Mrs. Tidsdale smiled and changed the subject. ""How come you're riding the rails, fending off wolves, instead of settling down and getting married?"

There it was again, that pang of loss. Would it ever go away? "I was engaged," Jill said. "He was killed in Korea, two years ago."

"Ah. I'm sorry." Mrs. Tidsdale paused as the steward delivered her drink. She picked it up and took a sip. The whistle blew its warning as they headed past a grade crossing. "Where are we now?"

Jill looked out the window, seeing cars stopped, waiting for the train to pass. Beyond that were grain elevators, commercial buildings, houses. She recognized the plateau called South Table Mountain. They were at the eastern rim of California's great Central Valley. Soon the train would leave the plain and climb into the mountains looming in the distance.

"We're coming into Oroville."

Chapter Seven ————————————————

THE *CALIFORNIA ZEPHYR* slowed as it headed into Oroville. Jill walked through the train, collecting a few letters and post-cards to mail. She was in the vestibule of the Silver Saddle, the third coach car, as the train pulled into the station.

A young sailor, wearing a heavy pea coat over his dress blue uniform, hoisted his duffel bag to his shoulder. He stepped down from the vestibule and scanned the platform, his gaze alighting on an older man and woman standing near the station entrance, bundled against the December cold. They spied him at the same time and rushed toward him. The sailor set the duffel bag on the platform and threw his arms around both of them. "Merry Christmas, Mama, Papa. I'm home."

Tears glistened on the woman's face as she embraced her son, while the man grinned. "How long can you stay?"

"I got leave for a whole week," the sailor said. "I hope you're fixing a big turkey, Mama, and a bunch of pies. They feed us all right on the ship, but I sure miss your home cooking."

"I've been baking for days," the mother said as the father picked up his son's duffel bag. "Aunt Polly's here from Susanville and Uncle Clyde brought a twenty-five-pound turkey from his farm." The woman's voice trailed off as the family walked away.

Jill dropped the postcards and letters into the nearby mailbox and headed back toward the train. She glanced toward the baggage car as the baggage man maneuvered a flag-covered coffin onto a cart. Another serviceman had arrived home, but there was no one here to greet him, except the man in a dark suit, ready to load the coffin into the waiting hearse.

At the vestibule of the Silver Gull, Si Lovell and a young man in a worn brown leather jacket were helping an old man out of a wheelchair. "I'll bring the chair," the young man said. "You just get Gramps settled into the compartment."

Jill quickened her pace and joined them. "Can I help?"

"I got it, Miss McLeod," the porter said. "Now, Mr. Scolari, just put your arm around my shoulder."

The old man looked so small and frail that a breeze might blow him away. He looped his arms around Mr. Lovell's neck as the porter put his arm under the old man's legs and carried him up the steps to the vestibule.

The young man was a few years older and several inches taller than Jill, with curly dark hair framing an olive-skinned face. He smiled at Jill and held out his hand. "Miss McLeod, huh? You're the Zephyrette. I'm Mike Scolari and that's my grandfather. We're going to Denver for Christmas."

She took his hand. He had a firm handshake. And nice eyes, a warm brown, with laugh lines crinkling the corners. "Do you live here in Oroville, Mr. Scolari?"

He shook his head as he released her hand. "We came up a few days ago to visit my aunt here in Oroville. We're from San Francisco, North Beach. What about you? You based in Chicago or the Bay Area?"

"The Bay Area," Jill said.

"Good." He smiled again.

"I hope you enjoy the trip."

"I plan to. Well, I'd better see about Gramps." Mr. Scolari folded the wheelchair and carried it onto the train.

Jill's attention was drawn to a flurry of activity at the front of the train. Oroville was a crew change stop, for both the train and the engine crews. The train crew—conductor, brakeman, switchman—would ride the train from Oroville to Winnemucca, Nevada. The engine crew—engineer and fireman—would change out earlier, in Gerlach, Nevada. Now Mr. Wylie, the conductor who'd boarded in Oakland, was talking with the new conductor near the vestibule of the Silver Palace. When Mr. Wylie waved and headed for the station, Jill got her first look at the new conductor. She beamed and walked quickly up to greet him.

"Merry Christmas, Mr. Haggerty. It's so good to see you. I hope your family is well."

Steve's Uncle Pat grinned back at her. "Merry Christmas, Miss McLeod. Good to see you. My family's fine. Hope yours is, too. How are things on this run?"

"Very busy. We do have a full train, even this close to Christmas. Lots of kids running up and down the aisles."

"That's to be expected, this time of year. I'm with you till Winnemucca. You know Brian Keller, don't you?" Pat pointed a thumb back at the young, sandy-haired brakeman behind him.

"We've met," Jill said. "A couple of months ago, wasn't it? Nice to see you again, Mr. Keller."

"October," Brian Keller said with a lopsided grin. "Good to see you, Miss McLeod."

Pat Haggerty pulled his pocket watch from his vest. "Time to go. See you on board." He walked along the platform, calling, "All aboard."

Jill climbed into the Silver Pony vestibule. The *California Zephyr* pulled out of the Oroville station, moving slowly away from the downtown and through the outskirts. The view from the windows changed from houses to hillsides as the train moved toward another plateau, North Table Mountain. Ahead were the rising slopes of the Sierra Nevada. The train was now traveling up the North Fork of the Feather River, crisscrossing the river on a route that had been carved out of solid granite cliffs, with a series of tunnels that had been pummeled through rock.

Jill was already familiar with the canyon's history before becoming a Zephyrette. After all, she'd majored in American history and was knowledgeable about California history. She enjoyed telling the passengers about the places they saw as the train wound its way up the canyon. She walked to the dining car and lifted the microphone from its holder on the public address system.

"We're now in the famous Feather River Canyon. The Feather River received its name from Don Arguello, the Spanish conquistador who discovered it in eighteen-twenty. He was intrigued by the vast number of wild pigeon feathers that floated on its ripples. *Rio de las Plumas*, he called it in Castilian, River of the Feathers.

"Before the Gold Rush, Jim Beckwourth, a trail blazer of the Old West, found the pass through the Sierra Nevada Mountains that still bears his name. It was a better place to cross the ridge than the route the emigrant wagon trains were using, because it was about two thousand feet lower, but the country on the west side of the pass was very rugged, and it was not until the 'sixties that pioneer Arthur W. Keddie surveyed a practical railway line down the various forks of the Feather River. A line, however, was not built until nineteen-nine, when the Western Pacific Raiload was completed.

"Gold was discovered at Bidwell's Bar on the fourth of July, eighteen forty-eight, only a few months after James Marshall made the strike that started the big rush to California, and millions were panned from the shining sands of the Feather River. There's still gold there, too. Most likely you'll see a prospector or two today, working down at the river's edge.

"In the lower half of the Feather River Canyon, you will see four Pacific Gas and Electric Company power plants. PG and E serves Northern and Central California with electricity from seventy-three power houses.

"I won't bore you by talking about the scenery," Jill concluded, "because I couldn't do it justice. And anyway, you're going to see it for yourself. I'll just say it's some of the most gorgeous I've ever seen. And three hours from now, I think you will agree with me."

Jill hung up the mike and walked forward to the Silver Hostel. The Finch girls, Nan and Cathy, climbed the stairs to the Vista-Dome, accompanied by George Neeley, the boy she'd seen earlier, traveling with his family in the Silver Pine. "Keep an eye out for the Pulga Bridges," she told the children. "There's a highway bridge that crosses over a railroad bridge. And there's another set of bridges farther on, called the Tobin Bridges. But it's reversed, the railroad bridge crosses over the top of the highway bridge."

As the children headed through the car, Jill went to her compartment. She retrieved a binder containing cards, then walked back through the sleeper cars to the Silver Solarium. There was no response when she knocked on the door to bedroom A. It was the same with bedroom B. She heard the sound of the typewriter coming from bedroom C. At Jill's knock, Miss Stafford called, "Come in."

Jill opened the door and saw Miss Stafford raise her hands from the typewriter keys, flexing her fingers. "I hope you're getting a lot of work done."

"I am," Miss Stafford said. "Though I think I'll take a break and go up to the Vista-Dome as we head up the canyon."

"Your novel about the Gold Rush," Jill said. "Part of it took place here."

The writer nodded. "Yes. I'm well read on the history of this particular canyon. And I stayed up here. A friend who works for the Western Pacific has a cabin near Quincy. I'm working on a sequel to that book." She waved at the growing pile of pages next to the typewriter.

"Wonderful. I look forward to reading it." Jill opened the binder she carried. "I'm here about dinner reservations. Our seatings are at six, seven, and eight o'clock."

"Seven for me, thanks." Miss Stafford stood and stretched as Jill noted the reservation in her binder. She filled out a color-coded reminder card that designated which seating, in this case a white card for Miss Stafford's 7 P.M. reservation. On the card, she wrote "18/1," denoting the train number and the first day of the run.

"Here you are. Enjoy your dinner."

"Thanks, I'm sure I will."

As they left the bedroom, Jill stepped aside and let Miss Stafford walk ahead of her, down the steps to the lower level that held the buffet. Miss Stafford continued back toward the stairs leading up to the Vista-Dome, while Jill stopped and looked through the glass panel at the buffet. The Finches and Constanzas were in the booth, finishing a hand of bridge.

"Oh, Miss McLeod, have you seen my girls?" Mrs. Finch asked.

"Yes, they're in the lounge car Vista-Dome."

"Please let us know if they get in the way," Mr. Finch said as he gathered the cards and shuffled them.

"They're no trouble at all," Jill said. "We're used to having

children on the train. Would you like to make dinner reserva-
tions for the dining car? We have seatings at six, seven, and eight.
We also have the Chef's Early Dinner, for families with children.
Those seatings are at four-fifteen and five."

Mrs. Finch smiled. "Our girls are old enough to eat with the
grown-ups. Still, I think we'd prefer early rather than late. Shall
we have dinner at six, dear?" She glanced at her husband, who
nodded in the affirmative and dealt another hand.

Mrs. Constanza consulted with her husband, then said, "We
would prefer eight o'clock. In Italy, we are accustomed to eating
later in the evening."

Jill then went back to the lounge, where every seat on the
lower level was full. She made dinner reservations there and up
in the Vista-Dome, then she headed through the sleeper cars, the
Silver Rapids and the Silver Pine. As she made reservations and
handed out cards, she kept track of the numbers and the times
in her binder, holding back reservations for the coach passengers.

When she got to the Silver Palisade, the door to one of the
bedrooms occupied by the Bensons opened and the two boys
charged out into the passageway.

"They're a lively pair," Jill said as Billy and Chip rounded the
corner, heading forward, to the roomette section of the car

Mrs. Benson laughed. "You're telling me. I was hoping they'd
nap this afternoon. But they're too keyed up about the trip. Eventually they'll wear themselves out."

"I thought Emily was playing with them."

"She went back to her bedroom," Mrs. Benson said. "My boys
are a little young for her, and too boisterous. She's a quiet little
thing. Is that her mother she's traveling with?"

Jill shook her head. "No. Mrs. Tidsdale is escorting Emily to
Denver. Emily's parents are dead, her mother some years back and
her father just a month ago. She's going to live with her grandmother."

"That's rough," Mrs. Benson said. "Poor girl. No wonder she's
quiet."

Jill told them about the dining car seatings. "Dinner at five,
Ed?" Mrs. Benson called over her shoulder.

"Yep, five's great." Mr. Benson said. "I hear the food's wonderful on these trains."

"We pride ourselves on the food," Jill said. She wrote the reservation in her notebook and gave Mrs. Benson a brown card for the Chef's Early Dinner.

Just then Billy rounded the corner, heading back from the forward section. "There's empty rooms," he told his mother. "We went inside. Those rooms are a lot smaller than ours."

"You're not supposed to go in those rooms," Mrs. Benson told him. "Where's Chip?"

"He's coming," Billy said. "The doors of those rooms were open, and there wasn't anybody inside."

"All the same, I'd rather you didn't do that," Mrs. Benson said. "Those rooms might be empty now but other passengers might be staying in them later. And if you looked inside then, you'd be bothering other people. Now you go find Chip and bring him back here."

Suddenly they heard a loud voice, and Chip ran around the corner. Behind him was the balding man who'd gotten on the train in Sacramento. "You keep out of my room, you little brat, or I'll—"

Chip slipped past Jill and ran to his mother, hiding behind her. The burly man made as if to follow. Mrs. Benson called, "Ed."

Mr. Benson stepped out of bedroom E and faced the other man. "What's the problem?"

"Keep your goddamn kid out of my room," the burly man bellowed, shaking his fist. Mrs. Tatum and Mrs. Clive opened their doors.

"No need to yell," Ed Benson said. "I'll deal with it."

"You better deal with it, or I will." The other man turned, nearly bumping into Frank Nathan, who had come to investigate. "Get out of my way, boy." The porter stepped aside, letting the man pass.

"Well, really," Mrs. Tatum said. "There's no need for him to be so unpleasant."

Mrs. Clive sniffed, then called to Jill. "Are you making dinner reservations? I want an eight o'clock seating."

"Certainly," Jill said. She quickly filled out a blue card and gave it to Mrs. Clive.

By now both the Benson boys were hugging their mother, frightened tears rolling down Chip's cheeks. Mr. Benson knelt and brushed the tears away with his hand. "It's all right. I'm not going to let that man hurt you. But I don't want you going into other people's rooms. It's not polite. And it could get you into trouble. Do you understand me?"

Billy and Chip both nodded. Mr. Benson straightened and took his sons by their hands. "I'm going to get my camera. We'll go back to the Silver Solarium and go up to the Vista-Dome so we can get a good look at the mountains and the river. I should be able to get some good pictures, even if the train is moving. I'm using a fast film."

Jill knocked on the door of bedroom C. "Mrs. Tatum, it's Jill McLeod. Would you like a dinner reservation?"

Mrs. Tatum opened the door. "Goodness, what a to-do. Just children and their high spirits. No need for that man to be so grumpy. But some people are just like that. Yes, I think I'll have dinner at six o'clock. I plan to retire early. And please don't worry about getting me to the diner. I can find my way."

Jill marked a red card for Mrs. Tatum. Then she tapped on the door of bedroom B. She'd met the passenger, Mrs. Loomis, earlier when she'd boarded the train in Stockton. There was no response. She moved to bedroom A. No response here, either. Then Mrs. Loomis, a tall brunette in her thirties, rounded the corner, coming from the front of the train. "Hi, Miss McLeod. If you're looking for that woman, what's her name...? Mrs. Tidsdale, that's it. Anyway, she and her little girl, I just saw them in the lounge. They're playing cards."

"Thank you. Actually, I'm making dinner reservations." When Jill completed a white card for Mrs. Loomis's seven o'clock reservation, she rounded the corner and started on the roomettes. Number 10 was just past the soiled linen locker in the middle of the car, on her right as she headed forward. The door was closed. She tapped lightly. No response. She turned to go, then the door opened. She found herself face-to-face with the man who had just yelled at Chip. Up close he had a jowly face with pitted acne scars and a hint of black stubble across his jaw. He stared at her with hard brown eyes that reminded her pebbles. "What do you want?"

"I'm sorry to disturb you, sir," Jill said, smiling at him. "I'm taking dinner reservations, if you'd care to make one. We have seatings at—"

"I don't want to eat in the diner. Have the boy bring something to me."

"Certainly, sir. There is an additional charge of fifty cents for dinner served in your roomette. I'll see that you get a menu. What is your name, sir?"

"Smith," the man said, narrowing his eyes.

"What time would you—"

"Seven." Mr. Smith shut the door in her face.

Jill sighed. All in a day's work. Usually the passengers were polite, even if some of them could be quite demanding. But there were a few rude ones on every trip. And it seemed Mr. Smith was one of those. She tried not to let them get to her. She made a mental note to herself to see that Mr. Smith got a menu.

"He's a piece of work, isn't he?"

The voice came from behind her. Jill turned and found herself face to face with the occupant of roomette nine, a stout, middle-aged woman with brown hair turning gray.

"I introduced myself when he got on the train," the woman continued, "and he just about snapped my head off. Now, I pride myself on being friendly to everyone, but people like that are just a trial."

Jill smiled, privately agreeing with the woman. "I'm making dinner reservations. Would you like one, Mrs....?"

"Mrs. Barlow. And yes, I do want a reservation. For six o'clock. It's just me, but I'm sure to have some interesting dining companions. I do enjoy talking with people on the train."

Jill filled out a red card and gave it to Mrs. Barlow. She moved to the next roomette. When she got to the end of the aisle, she found Dr. Kovacs dozing in his roomette, head back against the seat, eyes closed under the lenses of his glasses, a file folder on his lap. As she peered in through the half-closed door, he woke with a start. The file folder slipped from his lap and fell to the floor. He leaned over and grabbed it.

"I didn't mean to wake you, Professor Kovacs," Jill said. "But I'm taking dinner reservations."

"Not to worry," he said. "I am a light sleeper. But I must say, the rhythm of the train, it lulls one to nap. Dinner reservations, you say?"

"Yes. We have seatings at six, seven, and eight."

He nodded. " I would prefer seven o'clock."

She filled out a white card and handed it to him. Then she continued forward to the Silver Gull, working her way down the row of bedrooms and compartments. When she knocked on the door of compartment F, Mike Scolari opened the door. "Gramps has trouble walking." He glanced over his shoulder at the elderly man on the bench seat. "He can't make it to the dining car. We'll need to eat here in the compartment."

"I thought as much," Jill said. "Mr. Lovell, the porter, can bring your dinner to you. Because of your grandfather's condition, there's no additional charge for that. I'll see that you get a menu."

Loud voices came from compartment B. It sounded as though Mr. and Mrs. Cole were arguing. Jill knocked. Mrs. Cole opened the door, the expression on her face changing quickly from tense to pleasant as Jill explained why she was there and listed the available times for dinner reservations.

"Let's eat at eight o'clock, darling," Mrs. Cole said, all smiles again as she reached for her husband's hand. Jill gave them a blue card. Mr. Cole smiled and thanked her. But the upturned mouth didn't match the expression in his eyes. The newlyweds were evidently having a spat, Jill thought, and she'd interrupted the exchange.

When she knocked on the door to bedroom J, Mr. Washburn opened the door, a glass of amber liquid in his hand. He leered down at her. "Hey, honey. Have a drink with me. Got some really good bourbon here."

Jill glanced past him. An empty bottle lay on the bedroom

floor. Mr. Washburn had already consumed a great deal of bourbon. He was weaving from side to side. She held up the binder,
inadequate protection. "What time would you like to have dinner, sir?"

"What time are you gonna have dinner? We could eat together. And then come back here for a drink."

"I don't know when I'll have dinner, sir. Let's see, I could seat
you at seven o'clock." She filled out a reservation card and handed it to Mr. Washburn. He took the card, then grabbed her hand.
She pulled it free.

"Can I be of some assistance?" Si Lovell, the porter, appeared,
coming from the direction of the linen lockers. He carried an arm-
load of towels. "Do you need fresh towels, sir?"

"No, s'all good, ever'thing fine." Mr. Washburn backed away
and shut the door.

Jill turned and moved toward the porter's seat and the linen
lockers. Mr. Lovell followed, speaking in a low voice. "Is that man
bothering you, Miss McLeod? I know sometimes the men passengers get ideas about you young ladies."

"Thank you for your concern, Mr. Lovell. I can handle it."
She could, but Mr. Washburn was being persistent. "If I need your
help... Well, thanks."

"If you say so." The porter frowned and stared at the door to
bedroom J. "That fellow brought several bottles on board with
him. He's been drinking quite a bit. Both here and in the lounge.
I'll keep an eye on him."

Mr. Lovell headed back toward the bedrooms. Jill sighed and
continued forward, through the dining car, quiet for the moment
in the middle of the afternoon. In the Silver Hostel, Mrs. Tidsdale
and Emily were in the lounge, seated near the window. Benny,
Emily's brown corduroy teddy bear, perched on the window ledge,
his back to the scenery. The ashtray on the table in front of them
contained several cigarette butts stained with lipstick. Both Tidsy
and Emily had full glasses at their elbows. Emily's glass contained
lemonade, while Mrs. Tidsdale was sipping an amber liquid that
looked like Scotch. They each had three stacks of coins—pennies,
nickels, and dimes. Tidsy pulled a pack of cards from their box.

Emily watched, fascinated, as Tidsy shuffled like a Las Vegas dealer, cards fluttering in her hands.

"The name of this game is seven-card stud. First we each put a penny in the pot. That's our ante." Tidsy held the cards with her left hand and tossed a penny into the center of the table. Emily followed suit. "Tidsy's gonna deal two cards face down. These are called hole cards. You look at your hole cards, but you don't let me or Benny the Bear or anyone else see them." Emily picked up each card by its corner and looked. "Now, I deal one card up. You think about how that fits with your hole cards to make up a poker hand. We both bet on what we have. Then I deal more cards. Remember what I told you about poker hands, sweetie. Two pair beats one pair. And...?"

Emily nodded. "Three of a kind beats two pair, a straight beats three of a kind, and a flush beats a straight."

"That's right." Tidsy dealt the cards. "Ace of hearts to you, three of clubs to me. You have the high card. So bet your ace, sweetie."

Emily consulted her hole cards again. Then she pulled a penny from her pile of coins and tossed it into the pot. Tidsy did the same. "Call." She dealt two more cards up. "Seven of hearts to you, possible flush. Deuce of diamonds to me."

Emily seemed to pick up the nuances of poker quickly. She won the first hand with three eights that outranked Mrs. Tidsdale's two pair. As the little girl raked in the pot of coins, she grinned. It was the first time Jill had seen the child smile since the trip began.

Mrs. Tidsdale picked up the cards and shuffled them, giving Jill a sidelong glance. "Did you need something, Miss McLeod?"

"I'm making dinner reservations, Mrs. Tidsdale. There's a Chef's Special Dinner for families traveling with children, with seatings at four-fifteen and at five. Regular dinner seatings start at six."

Tidsy grimaced. "I can't possibly eat dinner at four-fifteen or five. I usually eat at seven, but in this case I think six o'clock would do. After dinner I can get Emily all tucked in bed. What time do you usually go to bed, sweetie?"

Emily, who was dividing her coins into stacks, looked up. "Eight. But if it's not a school night, Stella would let me stay up till nine."

"Let's split the difference and say bedtime at eight-thirty." Tidsy shuffled the cards one last time and set them on the table, reaching for another cigarette from the pack tucked into her nearby purse. She stuck a cigarette into her red-lipsticked mouth and opened the matchbook on the table. "Oh, bother, I'm out of matches."

"Use my lighter," said a man's voice.

Jill, who'd been filling out dinner reservation cards for Mrs. Tidsdale and Emily, looked up from her binder, and saw Mr. Paynter, the dark-haired man traveling on the Silver Gull. He held out his Zippo, the top flipped open, its flame burning brightly. Mrs. Tidsdale smiled, a predatory look in her wide blue eyes. She took his hand and pulled it toward her, igniting the end of her cigarette. She inhaled and then expelled smoke.

"Thanks. I'm Grace Tidsdale."

"Neal Paynter," he said, returning her smile.

Tidsy leaned back in her chair and ran one hand through her blond curls. "Join us, Mr. Paynter. Do you play poker?"

"Usually for higher stakes than pocket change." He sat down next to Mrs. Tidsdale. "Looks like your daughter is winning, Mrs. Tidsdale."

"She's not my daughter." Tidsy crossed her legs, showing a shapely calf. "Emily and I are traveling together, in the Silver Palisade. I'm instructing her in the fine art of seven-card stud. What car are you in, Mr. Paynter? And who are you traveling with?"

"The Silver Gull," he said, lighting a cigarette of his own. He inhaled and then blew out a stream of smoke. "Bedroom A. I'm traveling by myself."

Mrs. Tidsdale laughed, a silvery tinkle. "Indeed. Shall I deal you in?"

"Perhaps later. After Emily's tucked in bed." Mr. Paynter signaled the steward with one hand, smiling at Jill. "I'll have another gin and tonic. I'd like a dinner reservation, too. Seven o'clock would be fine."

Jill made note of the reservations and gave out the cards. She heard voices and footsteps coming down from the Vista-Dome, then the Finch girls and George Neeley entered the lounge, clustering around Mrs. Tidsdale and Emily.

"Can we play cards?" George asked.

Mrs. Tidsdale took a drag from her cigarette. "You know how to play poker?"

"Sure I do," George said. "My brother taught me."

"How about you girls?" Mrs. Tidsdale asked.

"I can pick up anything fast," Nan said. "My sister, too. My mother is teaching us how to play bridge."

"Fine, I'll instruct you in the fine art of poker. What's your name, sweetie?"

"I'm Nan, and this is my sister, Cathy."

"I'm George," the boy chimed in.

"Great. You kids got any money on you?" Mrs. Tidsdale asked.

"Cathy and I have some quarters," Nan said.

George shook his head. "I don't have any but I could ask my dad."

"Never mind. I'll give you a stake." Mrs. Tidsdale stubbed out her cigarette and pulled some singles from her purse, then signaled to the steward. "Bring us more change, please, and a round of lemonade for the kids. We need a bigger table. Grab that booth over there."

Three people had just vacated the booth on the opposite side of the lounge. Nan, Cathy, and George claimed it as the steward picked up empty glasses and wiped off the table. He took Mrs. Tidsdale's bills and headed back to the bar. Mrs. Tidsdale and Emily transferred the cards and their coins. They settled in as the steward delivered the gin and tonic to Mr. Paynter, who'd claimed the seat Mrs. Tidsdale had just vacated. Then the steward brought change and lemonade for the children. Mrs. Tidsdale began shuffling the cards. "Okay, the name of this game is seven-card stud. Everybody ante up a penny."

Mrs. Clive swept into the lounge, heading for the bar. Then she stopped and looked down her nose at the group clustered around the table. "Are you teaching those children to gamble? With money? That's disgraceful."

"Put a lid on it, sister. Mind your own damn business."

Mrs. Clive turned red and clamped her mouth into a tight, indignant line. She sniffed, and drew herself up like a snake about to strike. Then she did an about-face and left the lounge.

Mr. Paynter, nursing his gin and tonic, threw back his head and laughed. "I guess you told her."

"She needed telling. Damn busybody." Without missing a beat, Tidsy began dealing the cards. "Okay, let's play poker. Ten for Nan, deuce for Cathy, trey for George, Emily gets a jack, Tidsy gets a seven. Emily, you've got the high card. Bet your jack."

"I bet a nickel," Emily said. With a flourish, she tossed her coin in the center of the table.

Chapter Eight —————————

JILL LEFT THE Silver Hostel and continued forward, making dinner reservations in all the chair cars. Then she walked back to the dining car and gave the steward the count of passengers who would be eating dinner in the diner. After she was finished, she returned the binder to her compartment and walked back through the train to the Silver Solarium.

The lounge was full of passengers, looking out at the canyon and the river below. She went up the stairs to the Vista-Dome. Every seat was taken. Mr. and Mrs. Cole sat close together in one pair of seats, holding hands. If that was an argument Jill had interrupted earlier, the couple's spat had evidently been short-lived. At the very front of the Dome, Mrs. Benson sat on the left, with Chip and Emily Charlton, while on the right, Mr. Benson and Billy leaned forward, looking down at the snow-covered slopes and the river, flowing between icy banks.

"Hey, kids, look at those bridges." Mr. Benson pointed. "The railroad bridge goes over the river, and the highway bridge goes over both. How high is that?"

"The highway bridge is about two hundred feet above the bridge we're on," Jill said as the first engine rumbled onto the span.

Jill stayed in the Vista-Dome until the train passed the second set of bridges. Then she went downstairs to the lounge where Dr. Kovacs stood with the Constanzas. "I enjoyed your performance in *Cavalleria Rusticana*," the professor said. "And *La Traviata*, of course. I'll be in Chicago for a week after New Year's. Will you be performing there?"

"I'm giving a concert at the Civic Opera House," Mr. Constanza said. "The first Saturday in January."

"Wonderful. I'll put that on my calendar." Dr. Kovacs took out a slim leather-bound notebook and reached for a pencil from the nearby writing desk.

"I'm so glad we took the train," Mrs. Constanza told Jill. "These Sierra Nevada Mountains are beautiful."

"Wait till you see the Rockies," Jill said.

She heard two excited voices talking at once and looked up. Billy and Chip Benson were coming down the steps from the Vista-Dome, their parents behind them. "Slow down," Ed Benson said, "and don't jump." But Billy, a few steps from the lower level, had already launched himself, landing with a thump on the floor. Chip followed, emulating his older brother, but he stumbled and fell. He screwed up his face, getting ready to cry.

The professor leaned down and picked up the little boy, setting him on his feet. "There you are, young man. No harm done."

"I told you not to jump, sport." Mr. Benson knelt and put his arm around his younger son. "Are you hurt?" Chip shook his head. "Okay, then, no need to cry."

Norma Benson ruffled Chip's dark hair and wagged a finger at her elder son. "Billy, don't do that again. Chip wants to do everything you do, and I don't want him to get hurt."

Ed Benson straightened and turned to the professor. "You're Dr. Laszlo Kovacs, right?"

"Yes, that's my name," the professor said. "Have we met?"

"We have, but you probably don't remember me. Staff Sergeant Ed Benson. I worked on the Hill during the war. So did my wife. Only she wasn't my wife in those days."

Mrs. Benson smiled and stepped away from the stairs. "I was Private Norma Sanchez, a WAC, working in the motor pool. I drove you to Santa Fe and back a few times."

"I'm sorry," Dr. Kovacs said. "I don't remember either of you. It was such a busy time, and so many people there on the Hill."

The professor glanced up, his features tightening as he saw Rita and Clifford Cole descending the stairs from the Vista-Dome. Arms entwined, the Coles walked to the rear of the lounge car and stood looking out the windows at the back. Dr. Kovacs gazed at them for a few seconds and frowned. Then he turned and nodded to Jill and the Bensons. "If you'll excuse me." He left the lounge, walking forward toward the sleeper cars.

"He's an odd bird," Mr. Benson said. "But so were a lot of them up on the Hill."

"The Hill?" Jill asked. "Do you mean Los Alamos? The Manhattan Project? I know Dr. Kovacs was there. He's a physicist. When I was going to school at Cal I heard him give a talk about his work on the project."

"'Lost Almost.' That's what we called it. Because it was at the backside of beyond. But that's where I met Norma." Mr. Benson gave his wife's hand a squeeze.

"Little Norma Sanchez from Española. I joined the army and thought I'd get out of New Mexico, go somewhere I hadn't been before. My chance to travel." She laughed. "No such luck. They sent me to the Hill. I grew up in that area, so I'd been to Los Alamos before, over to Bandelier National Monument and Jemez Springs. Not much up there back then, except ranches and that boys' school. That changed when they started building the lab in the spring of 'forty-three. I spent two years driving up and down that road. Back and forth, from the train station at Lamy, to Santa Fe, then up to the Hill, more times than I can count. My word, it was steep. At least they paved it."

"I was with the MPs, the military police," Ed Benson added. "Got there when they started construction. I was at Oak Ridge before that. The place was classified and security was tight. Down in Santa Fe, if you asked a question about the place, they'd deny it even existed."

"It must have been fascinating," Jill said.

"We didn't think of it like that," Mrs. Benson said. "We knew they were working on something big, and secret. But for people like us, it was just a job. Anyway, I met Ed and we kept company up there on the Hill. When we could get some leave, we'd go down to Santa Fe, or to Española to see my folks. We got married right after the war and came out to San Francisco. That's where Ed grew up."

"Yep, born and raised in the Mission District. I'm in insurance now. And Norma's got her hands full with these two boys of ours." Mr. Benson turned to his wife. "Say, you remember that redhead Kovacs was married to? That's her, that came down the stairs just now." He tilted his head toward the rear of the car. Mr. and Mrs. Cole had turned from the window and they were walking this way.

Mrs. Benson looked toward the couple and nodded, but she didn't speak until the Coles had passed them, heading forward toward the sleeper cars. "Yes, I recognize her. She looks about the same, though she wears her hair different. Now her husband, I've seen him before, I'm sure of it. In New Mexico."

"That's odd," Jill said. "I heard Mr. Cole say he'd never been to New Mexico."

Norma Benson shrugged. "Could be I don't have the right face. I saw a lot of faces in those two years I was on the Hill. Not surprising the professor's marriage didn't last. Living up on the Hill was hard on all of us, especially the families. They had more people than they had housing, with folks shoehorned into flimsy apartments. The water was bad and in short supply and the food was terrible. And the isolation. The military people were stuck there for the duration, but there were more than a few wives who couldn't take the place and left."

"What interesting stories," Jill said. "I'd love to hear more. But we're getting close to the Keddie Wye. You'll want to see that."

"What is it?" Billy asked.

"Let's go up to the Vista-Dome and I'll show you."

Jill led the way up the stairs. As the train rumbled toward the split bridge that rose over Spanish Creek, passengers pressed toward the windows. Two sections of the Wye stood on high steel trestles, while a third tunneled through a hillside. One side of the split headed north through the trees, to connect with the Great Northern Line. The *California Zephyr* stayed on the other section of the Y-shaped bridge, known as the mainline.

"Western Pacific had a last-spike ceremony here in nineteen-oh-nine, when the track was completed." Jill glanced at her watch. "We'll be coming into the town of Keddie soon. Both the town and the Wye are named after Arthur Keddie. He's the original surveyor of the railroad route through the Feather River Canyon."

The *Zephyr* stopped briefly in Keddie, then continued east

past Quincy Junction. Dusk darkened the sky, blurring landmarks as the train curved into the Williams Loop, a complete circle designed to provide the train with a one-percent grade as it continued up the canyon. As the *Zephyr* gained elevation, it crossed over itself on the trestle. Had it been summer, the passengers might have been able to see the first and last cars, looking as though they were traveling in opposite directions. But it was December, with the shortest daylight of the year. By the time the train emerged from the Loop it was dark. The *Zephyr* entered the tunnel at Spring Garden that took the tracks from the North Fork of the Feather River to the Middle Fork. The Clio Trestle was next, over a thousand feet long, towering some 172 feet over the valley, its view over the valley obscured by night.

Jill retrieved her binder from her compartment. Most of the dinner reservations had been made earlier, but she always checked to see if there were any last-minute arrangements to be made. The next stop was Portola, at 5:25 P.M., and there might be passengers boarding there.

In the lounge, Mrs. Tidsdale sat in her usual spot, the table by the window, a tumbler of Scotch in front of her, a cigarette in her hand. She wasn't alone. Mr. Paynter sat next to her. Mrs. Tidsdale regarded him with a flirtatious smile. He leaned across the table, whispering something in her ear. Mrs. Tidsdale threw back her head and laughed. She recrossed her legs, showing them to advantage under the hem of her red dress.

"Miss McLeod, have you seen Emily? We're supposed to have dinner at six. Ungodly early hour to have dinner." Tidsy rolled her eyes for Mr. Paynter's benefit, and he chuckled.

"She's back in the Silver Solarium with the Finch girls."

"Guess I'd better see to my chaperone duties." Tidsy stubbed out her cigarette and downed the last of her Scotch. "See you later, Neal?"

"Certainly," Mr. Paynter said, flashing his easy smile. He watched as she stood up and left the lounge.

A man and a woman seated at a nearby table waved at Jill. "Is it too late to make a dinner reservation? For two?" the woman asked.

"Not at all." Jill consulted her binder. "The seven o'clock seating is full, but there are several seats available at six or eight."

The man glanced at his watch. "Six is too early. It's after five now. How about eight?" The woman nodded.

Jill filled out blue reservation cards for the eight o'clock seating and handed them to the passengers. Then she stepped into the passageway and headed forward, past the coffee shop, which was as crowded as the lounge. She walked through the third chair car, the Silver Saddle, making a last-minute dinner reservation. Then she headed into the second car, the Silver Palace.

The train's motion changed, the rhythm of wheels on tracks slowing. The *Zephyr* was heading into the little railroad town of Portola. The tracks, train station, and downtown district were on the south side of the Feather River. Jill saw the lights of the station and the train shed, and in the distance, the glow illuminating buildings along Commercial Street. If this were summer, the train and its cars would be washed here in Portola, running through a curved series of pipes spraying water to chase dust and grime from the Vista-Domes. But this was winter, and washing the train would cause ice to form. Even now, snow swirled out of the darkness into the pools of light from overhead poles.

Jill went to the vestibule as the train came to a stop at the Portola station. She shivered in the chill, peering out. A few people waited on the platform, some with luggage, others there to greet passengers who were getting off the train.

A tall, stringy man wearing a cowboy hat walked toward the train, the collar of his sheepskin coat pulled up around his neck, a barrier against the winter cold. He carried a small carpetbag in his left hand, a ticket in his right. "Goin' to Denver," he said in a low voice.

The porter checked the man's ticket. "Yes, sir. You're on this car. Your seat is a few rows back of the stairs leading up to the Vista-Dome. That's on the right, on the aisle."

"Thank you," the man said. He climbed into the vestibule, towering over Jill. He tipped his cowboy hat. "Evenin', ma'am."

"Good evening. I'm Miss McLeod, the Zephyrette. Please let me know if there's anything you need."

"I sure could use some dinner, ma'am," he said. "Do I need to put my name down on a list to eat a meal in the diner?"

"Yes, for dinner you do. Let's get you settled in your seat. Then I'll make a reservation for you."

Pat Haggerty, out on the platform, walked by, calling, "All aboard." The train whistle blew and the *California Zephyr* moved out of the Portola station.

She led the way into the chair car, where the man located his aisle seat. He nodded at the older man in the window seat and put his carpetbag and cowboy hat in the overhead rack. He removed his sheepskin jacket, revealing a red-and-black-checked flannel shirt. After taking a dog-eared paperback book from the pocket, he rolled up the jacket and stowed it in the rack. Then he sat down, stretching out long legs in faded jeans, over a pair of battered cowboy boots.

Jill opened her binder of dinner reservations. "I can seat you at six o'clock or eight o'clock."

"Six would do me just fine, ma'am," he said.

Jill filled out a red card. "Just give this to the dining car steward and he'll seat you. By the way, you don't need reservations for breakfast or lunch. That's first-come, first-served."

"Thank you kindly, ma'am," he said, taking the card. He tucked it into the pocket of his flannel shirt.

The train moved away from the lights of Portola, traveling in darkness on the eastern slope of the Sierra Nevada now, moving east into the Sierra Valley, over five thousand feet in elevation, a passage between the steep mountains. It was here that the mountain man James Beckwourth built his trading post. There was still a tiny community that bore Beckwourth's name, and the train went through it in the blink of an eye. Farther east the train would go through a six-thousand-foot tunnel at a place called Chilcoot, coming out onto the Nevada desert, angling across the Great Basin to Gerlach, where the engine crew would change.

Jill made another dinner reservation in the first chair car, then she headed back to the buffet-lounge car. In her compartment, she sat for a moment, checking the binder. It looked like all the Pullman passengers had reservations. She closed the binder and left it on her berth. Her stomach rumbled as she left her compartment. Time to get some dinner herself.

Chapter Nine

IT WAS JUST after six when Jill entered the dining car. She saw Mrs. Tidsdale and Emily seated at a table in one of the semi-private nooks, with an older couple from the chair cars. The Finches, who also had a six-o'clock seating, were a few tables down. Then she spied Mrs. Tatum at a table, sitting next to Mrs. Barlow, who was traveling on the Silver Palisade. Across from Mrs. Tatum was the tall cowboy who'd boarded the train in Portola.

"Miss McLeod, please join us," Mrs. Tatum said.

"Yes, ma'am," the cowboy said. He was already on his feet, pulling out the chair next to him. Jill took a seat.

"This is Mrs. Barlow," Mrs. Tatum said.

"Yes, we met earlier, when I was making dinner reservations."

"When that man in the roomette across from me was rude to you," Mrs. Barlow said. "I just can't abide rude people."

"And this is Mr. Alvah Webb," Mrs. Tatum said. "He and I have discovered we have something in common. We're both from Gunnison, Colorado."

"Born there, anyway," Mr. Webb said, fingering the menu. "When I was growing up we lived all around that part of Colorado, over to Montrose and up to Delta, down toward Lake City and Creede."

"Where do you live now?" Mrs. Barlow asked.

"I work on a ranch at Beckwourth, ma'am," he said. "That's a little town just east of Portola. We went through it a while back. I been there two years now, since I got out of..."

He hesitated, as though he didn't want to say where he'd been. Maybe he'd gotten out of the army, Jill thought. But Mr.

Webb appeared to be in his fifties or sixties. That seemed a bit old to have been in the army. Maybe he wasn't as old as he looked. He had the leathery, seamed skin of a man who'd spent years working out of doors. The sun could age a man.

Jill took a menu from the rack on the table. "Where are you headed, Mrs. Barlow?"

"Akron, Colorado." The woman smiled. "I'm spending Christmas with my son and his family. I'm sure a lot of people on the train are doing the same. Except you, dear. You're on the train until it gets to Chicago on Christmas Eve. What a shame to be working on the holiday."

"I don't mind," Jill said. "I'm looking forward to some time off with my family when I get back to the Bay Area. We're having a Christmas party for the children tomorrow afternoon. That will be here in the diner. The chef is baking a cake."

"What fun," Mrs. Barlow said. "Mrs. Tatum tells me her daughter is in Grand Junction. What about you, Mr. Webb? Who will you be spending Christmas with?"

Again Mr. Webb hesitated before answering. "Got a daughter, ma'am. She's married, has two little kids. They live in a place called Arvada, Colorado. I guess that's outside of Denver."

"How lovely," Mrs. Barlow said. "How old are your grandchildren?"

"I don't rightly know, ma'am." Mr. Webb looked uncomfortable. "This'll be the first time I've seen them."

"I have quite an appetite," Mrs. Tatum said before Mrs. Barlow could respond. "What looks good on the menu, Miss McLeod?"

Jill read through the items and prices on the dinner menu. Mrs. Tatum considered for a moment, then chose the roast beef. Mrs. Barlow wanted a steak. Jill marked her own check indicating the pork loin. Mr. Webb stared at the menu as though he couldn't make up his mind. Then he marked his selection, fried chicken. At $3.30, it was the least expensive entrée on the menu. And nothing to go with it. Maybe he was being frugal, or maybe he just liked fried chicken with nothing on the side. If he was short of funds, the railroad had steps to deal with that. They didn't want passengers to go without food. In her nearly two years as a

Zephyrette, Jill had encountered the situation several times before, diplomatically inquiring to determine if there was a problem. Passengers who weren't eating might be sick, or they might be short of cash. If such situations arose, Jill reported the information to the conductor, who was authorized to sign chits in the diner for any passenger who was hungry.

"I'm going to have a glass of wine," Mrs. Barlow said. "Or we could share a bottle. How about the rest of you?"

Mr. Webb shook his head. "No, thank you. I don't drink."

"None for me," Jill said. "Not while I'm working."

"I'll share a bottle," Mrs. Tatum said.

She and Mrs. Barlow agreed on a cabernet. Mrs. Barlow was talkative, dominating the conversation during dinner. Mr. Webb hardly spoke at all, content to let the others talk. They finished their entrées and the waiter cleared away the dishes.

"How about some coffee and dessert?" he asked. "We've got chocolate cream pie tonight. And it's mighty good, I must say."

"Oh, that sounds delicious," Mrs. Barlow said. "I'll have a piece of that."

"What are the other choices?" Mrs. Tatum asked. "I certainly enjoyed that apple pie I had at lunch."

"We do have some of the apple pie left," the waiter said. "Pumpkin pie as well, and custard."

Mrs. Tatum chose the apple pie and so did Mr. Webb. Jill considered pumpkin then chose the chocolate. "I shouldn't, really."

"Oh, you get plenty of exercise walking up and down this train, I'm sure," Mrs. Barlow said. "You have a nice, trim figure, looking so professional in that uniform of yours."

Jill felt her cheeks grow pink. They ordered coffee all around. When they finished their desserts and got up to leave the diner, Mrs. Barlow excused herself, saying she was tired and wanted to make an early night of it. Mrs. Tatum turned to Mr. Webb. "Let's go to the coffee shop. I want to talk more about Colorado."

"That would be my pleasure, ma'am." The cowboy offered his arm.

"You, too, Miss McLeod. You told me earlier your mother's family has been in Colorado for years. I want to hear all about it."

"I'll join you later," Jill said. "I do a walk-through every couple of hours, so I think I'll head back to the sleepers."

She watched Mrs. Tatum and Mr. Webb go forward, past the steward's counter, where several passengers with seven o'clock reservations waited to be seated. As they made their way down the passage next to the kitchen and pantry, Jill turned and headed the other direction, toward the sleeper cars. Mr. and Mrs. Finch and their daughters had finished dinner and were walking back to their accommodations in the observation car. Nan and Cathy stopped at the table where Mrs. Tidsdale was drinking coffee while Emily polished off a piece of pumpkin pie.

"Come back to our car," Nan said.

Emily scraped up the last bit of pumpkin and whipped cream with her fork. "Okay."

Nan and Cathy caught up with their parents. Mrs. Tidsdale set her coffee cup in its saucer and checked the time on her wristwatch. "Don't you want to get ready for bed?"

Emily's face took on a stubborn look. "No. It's too early. You said I could stay up till eight-thirty."

Mrs. Tidsdale sighed. "So I did."

"You don't have to go with me." Emily wiped her mouth with her napkin. "If you want to go to the lounge, I can go to the observation car by myself."

Tidsy pursed her mouth, as though momentarily taken aback. Then she smiled across the table at her nine-year-old charge. "All right, sweetie. But first a quick stop in our bedroom."

Jill walked with them back to the sleeper cars. In the Silver Gull, Mr. Paynter was coming out of bedroom A. He nodded at them, his eyes lingering for a moment on Mrs. Tidsdale. Then he stepped past them, heading for the dining car.

Tidsy and Emily continued on their way. Jill stopped and tapped on the door to compartment F. When Mike Scolari answered, she said, "I'm just checking to make sure the porter brought dinner for you and your grandfather."

"Yes, he did," he told her. "He'll be back to collect the dishes. Everything's fine. Thanks for checking."

Jill headed back to the Silver Palisade. Dr. Kovacs came out of roomette 2, holding the white card for his seven o'clock dinner reservation. He smiled at her. "I was reading, and I nearly forgot about dinner. Until my stomach began to growl."

"Enjoy your dinner, Professor."

Jill walked down the aisle between the roomettes. When she rounded the corner at the linen locker in the center of the car, she came face to face with Mr. Smith, the man who was staying in roomette 10. He was looking down at something in his cupped hand. This was the first time she'd seen him since she'd tapped on his door while making dinner reservations. Had he been back to the observation car? But no, he wasn't very sociable. She couldn't see him mingling with the other passengers.

"May I help you with something, Mr. Smith?" Jill gave him her brightest smile.

He glared at her and tucked whatever he held in his trouser pocket. Then he brushed past her and turned right, heading for the roomettes.

Some people, she thought.

Billy and Chip Benson burst out of bedroom E, both dressed in red pajamas, laughing and yelling as they ran down the corridor with Mrs. Benson in pursuit. "You boys get back here. It's time for bed." She caught up with her sons and took each one by the arm.

Mrs. Clive opened the door of bedroom D and stepped out, her face red with indignation. "Really, the noise is intolerable. Can't you control those children?"

Norma Benson looked at her, with an apologetic smile. "I'm sorry, the boys are wound up, and excited about their first train trip. They're going to bed soon."

Mrs. Clive gave an annoyed sniff. "Honestly, children running wild all over the train. I had hoped this would be a relaxing trip." She went back in her bedroom and shut the door, a little harder than she needed to.

Mr. Smith or Mrs. Clive, Jill thought. It was a toss-up as to which passenger was more disagreeable.

Mrs. Benson shrugged and smiled at Jill. Then she shepherded the boys into their bedroom. "Into those bunks, you two. One story, and then lights out."

Jill walked past the two bedrooms where the Bensons were staying, then through to the Silver Pine, the sixteen-section sleeper where, later in the evening, the porter would convert the passengers' seats into berths, with curtains for privacy.

Things were already quiet in the Silver Rapids. Then Miss Wolford, the young Englishwoman, stepped out of her roomette and looked down at the floor.

"Are you looking for something?" Jill asked.

"As a matter of fact, I am," Miss Wolford said. "It's a little gold Biro, ballpoint pen, you call them here in the States. I knocked over my carry-all before I went to dinner. I thought I'd gathered up everything that came out, but the Biro's gone missing. My roomette door was open, so I thought it might have rolled out into the corridor."

"Was it open when you knocked over your bag? Or when you came back from dinner?"

"Both times," Miss Wolford said. "When I'm in the roomette I leave the door open a bit. I rather like seeing people come and go. And when I returned from dinner, it wasn't properly shut. I've noticed when we go round a curve the door sometimes comes open. Been meaning to speak to the porter about that. At any rate, I don't see the Biro. Perhaps the porter found it and picked it up."

Just then, the porter rounded the corner, coming from the bedroom section of the Silver Rapids. "Mr. Calvin," Jill said. "Have you found a pen? Miss Wolford seems to be missing one." She described the situation.

He shook his head. "No, ma'am, I haven't." After Miss Wolford described what had happened, he said, "You know, it might have rolled under that seat where you can't see it. If you'll step out, ma'am, I'll get down there and look for it."

But the pen was nowhere to be found. "Oh, bother," Miss Wolford said. "Now I'm wondering if I lost it somewhere else. I was back in the observation car before dinner, with my carry-all. Could have dropped it there. Maybe one of the other passengers found it."

"I'll keep a lookout, ma'am," Mr. Calvin said. "And check the latch on this door."

"And I will ask the porter in the observation car if he's seen your pen," Jill said. "Now, what does it look like?"

"It's real gold, you see," Miss Wolford said, "but it has more sentimental value, as it was a gift from my aunt. It's engraved with my initials, 'EFW.' About five inches long, I'd say."

In the Silver Solarium, Jill found the porter, Mr. Parsons, in the buffet and asked him to look for Miss Wolford's pen. Mr. and Mrs. Finch were playing bridge with the Constanzas, and in the lounge section each seat was taken by passengers. Mr. and Mrs. Cole sat together on one of the settees at the end of the car, their heads close together as they talked.

Jill went up the stairs to the Vista-Dome. The Finch girls and Emily sat in the very front seats. Nearby were George Neeley and his father. Now that the train had come out of the tunnel to the Great Basin of Nevada, the night sky was clear, stars twinkling in the blackness above. Mr. Neeley was an amateur astronomer, as it turned out, so he was pointing out constellations. "You can really see the stars without all the city lights around. Now over there, that's the Big Dipper."

When Jill returned to the Silver Hostel, she found Mrs. Tatum and Mr. Webb at a table in the coffee shop section, deep in conversation. Jill sat down and nodded when the steward asked if she'd like coffee.

"I remember it like it was yesterday," Mrs. Tatum said, "even though it's been more than thirty years."

Mr. Webb nodded. "Thirty-four years since then."

"Since when?" Jill asked as the steward brought her coffee.

"The Spanish Flu epidemic," Mrs. Tatum said. "Back in nineteen-eighteen."

"My mother lost her older brother to the flu," Jill said. "They lived in Denver. She says people were afraid to go out of their houses."

"It was terrible." Mr. Webb sipped his coffee. "We was living in Ouray at the time. That's a mining town in the San Juan Mountains, southwest Colorado. The folks that lived there, they set up what they called a 'shot gun' quarantine, to keep out the miners from Silverton and Telluride. But that sickness got there all the same. My cousin and his wife died, and their two little children."

"The flu didn't get to Gunnison," Mrs. Tatum said. "When the word got out about the flu and how bad it was, they quarantined the whole town."

"How could they do that?" Jill asked.

"If you're familiar with Colorado," Mrs. Tatum said, "then you know how isolated Gunnison is, with Monarch Pass to the east, and the Black Canyon to the west. There was already a ban on public gatherings. The city fathers decided to close off the town. The police blocked all the roads. They wouldn't even let passengers off the train at the station, said if anyone stepped down to the platform they'd be arrested. Two fellows from Nebraska tried to drive through the blockade and they threw them in jail. Seems harsh, but no one in Gunnison died of the flu." Mrs. Tatum sighed. "Now what are we doing? Sitting here just a few days from Christmas, talking about people dying."

Jill took a sip of coffee and set down the cup. It was too strong, as though it had been sitting at the bottom of the pot too long. "I lost someone, two years ago this month. My fiancé. He was killed in Korea."

Mrs. Tatum took Jill's hand. "Oh, my dear. I'm so sorry."

"I didn't mean to blurt that out. It's just that it's December. I think about him a lot in December."

"Of course you think about him."

Jill took a deep breath and let it out. "Let's talk about something else, then. You said you wanted to hear more about my mother's family. My great-grandfather came to Colorado back in eighteen fifty-nine, when they discovered gold in Central City."

She felt better as she told the family stories. The comfortable rhythm of the train clacked away the miles as the *California Zephyr* crossed the Nevada desert.

Chapter Ten

THE *ZEPHYR* PULLED OUT of Gerlach, Nevada at 7:42 P.M., right on schedule, with a new engine crew. The train now headed northeast, above Pyramid Lake, on the flat playa of the Black Rock Desert. If this were summer, Jill would have been able to see the stark landscape. But tonight winter darkness enveloped everything outside the train windows. Only the stars were visible, bright points of light above.

Jill left Mrs. Tatum and Mr. Webb in the coffee shop and walked forward to the dining car, where she saw Dr. Kovacs at a table, talking with his companions as they finished their meals. As passengers vacated their tables, the waiters quickly exchanged soiled linen for fresh, setting the tables again for passengers with eight o'clock reservations.

Dr. Kovacs got up from his table and walked back toward the sleepers, passing Mr. and Mrs. Cole, who were being seated by the dining car steward, and Mr. and Mrs. Constanza, who had just appeared at the door. Jill reached for the mike on the public address system and made her last announcement of the day. "This is Miss McLeod, your Zephyrette. Before retiring this evening, you may wish to set your watches ahead one hour, as we will be entering the Mountain Time Zone at Salt Lake City early in the morning. Thank you and good night."

Jill replaced the mike. When she turned from the PA, someone called her name. Pat Haggerty walked toward her, down the aisle between the tables. "We haven't had much time to catch up since I got on board. And I get off the train in Winnemucca. Let's have some pie and coffee." He glanced at the dining car steward. "Got a free table for us?"

The steward pointed to an unoccupied table in the nearby nook. "Take that one."

Once they were seated at the table, Pat pulled a meal check from the holder as the waiter approached with a coffeepot. "That chocolate pie I had with dinner was really good. Any more of that left?"

The waiter nodded and took the check Pat had marked. "Yes, sir, I'll bring you a piece. How about you, Miss McLeod? Would you like some pie to go with your coffee?"

Jill marked her own meal check and handed it to the waiter. "No coffee for me, Mr. Taylor. But I will have a dish of custard."

When the waiter had gone, Pat Haggerty doctored his coffee with cream and sugar and took a sip. "Did anyone find that gold pen?" he asked.

Jill had reported Miss Wolford's missing pen to the conductor and made a note for her trip report. "Not so far. I hope it turns up."

"It will. Too bad you have to be on a run during the holidays. Bet you wish you were home, with your family for Christmas."

Jill smiled. "It's all right. I don't mind. Mom was upset at the thought of me being away from home on Christmas Day. It's the first time. I didn't have to work the holiday run last year. But keeping busy, that's what's good for me."

The waiter returned from the kitchen and set their desserts in front of them. Pat picked up his fork and dug into the chocolate pie. "I know December's hard on you. The anniversary of Steve's death, and all. It's hard on Mick and Betty, too."

Jill dipped her spoon into the custard. "I miss him, of course. I guess I always will."

"You can't be a Zephyrette forever. Have you thought about what you want to do with the rest of your life?"

It was a logical question. The tenure of a Zephyrette seemed to be two or three years, and Jill was approaching her second anniversary with the railroad. The Zephyrettes moved on to other jobs. Or a Zephyrette left because she was getting married, often to someone she'd met on the train, either a crew member or a passenger. Fran Ellis, the Zephyrette who had trained Jill, was engaged to a Denver and Rio Grande Western fireman. One of the Chicago-based Zephyrettes had married the previous summer, to a passenger she'd met on a run.

"I like being a Zephyrette. It's a good job for me right now. I'm not ready to settle down just yet."

"You and Steve were going to settle down."

"I know, but that was two years ago. And Steve's dead." Jill took a deep breath. "You know, I really don't feel comfortable talking about this. We're supposed to keep things on a professional level."

"I know," Pat said. "It's because I'm Steve's uncle. If the two of you had gotten married, I'd be your uncle, too. Even though Steve's gone, it still feels like you're part of the family."

"I appreciate that you're concerned about me." Jill toyed with her spoon.

"You're right, it's none of my business. I won't bring it up again. Except to tell you that brakeman, Brian Keller, he'd like to get to know you better."

Jill smiled. "I figured that out on my own."

The train whistle blew a crossing warning. Outside, the darkness was pierced by a single light in the distance. Pat pulled his watch from his vest pocket. "That's Jungo. One of those little towns that grew up along the Western Pacific line. It's practically a ghost town now, been that way since the 'forties. We'll be in Winnemucca soon. I'll spend the night there and be on the westbound *Zephyr* a little after four tomorrow morning. That will get me home to Oroville before noon, in time to help with the Christmas preparations."

They left the diner and walked forward to the Silver Palace, where Pat Haggerty stepped into the conductor's office to prepare for the train's arrival in Winnemucca. Jill continued forward to the Silver Pony and climbed up to the Vista-Dome. She looked out at the darkness, thinking about her conversation with Pat.

What she'd said was true. She liked being a Zephyrette, traveling on the rails. Besides, what else would she do? Teach? Work in her father's office? At some point she wanted marriage and a family. But at present there were no men on her horizon.

In the distance she saw a glow of lights. The *Zephyr* was coming into Winnemucca. There was a train crew change here, a new conductor to take Pat's place. The new train crew would ride all the way to Salt Lake City, where the *California Zephyr* would be handed off to employees of the Denver and Rio Grande Western Railroad.

The train blew a grade crossing warning as it approached a country road. A lone pickup truck waited at the crossing, then disappeared from view. The lights of Winnemucca got brighter as the *Zephyr* narrowed the distance. Jill went downstairs and walked back to the Silver Palace. In the conductor's office, Pat Haggerty reached for his bag and stepped out to the corridor. He and Jill walked to the vestibule, where the car porter waited. The train slowed, whistle blowing, as it came into the station at Winnemucca.

"Nine-ten," Pat said, looking at his pocket watch. "On time."

The train would be here seven minutes, while the new train crew boarded, then the *California Zephyr* would depart at 9:17 P.M. The porter opened the vestibule door. Pat peered out at the conductor who would replace him.

"Loren Bullis will be with you to Salt Lake City," Pat said. "Merry Christmas, Miss McLeod. Hope the rest of your run is uneventful."

"Merry Christmas, Mr. Haggerty," Jill said. "Give my best to your family."

He patted her arm and stepped down to the platform, stopping to talk with Mr. Bullis. There were just a few people on the platform here in Winnemucca this cold December evening, some of them waiting for passengers who were getting off the train. Others were boarding. A few minutes later, the new conductor called, "All aboard." At 9:17 P.M., the *Zephyr* blew its whistle and moved slowly out of the Winnemucca station.

Jill greeted Mr. Bullis, the new conductor. "The trip's been uneventful so far. We have a lot of children on board."

"Sure do," the car porter said. "They're roaming the aisles, getting into mischief, while their parents take a vacation from being parents."

Mr. Bullis grinned and rubbed his nose. "Kids always do. Roam the aisles, I mean. Mom and Dad seem to think we're the babysitters. But the kids don't usually cause too much trouble. This time of night most folks will be sleeping, young or old. Weather's cold and clear, all the way to Salt Lake. Which is where I get off, so I won't see you in the morning, Miss McLeod. Unless you're up and about at five-twenty."

"I don't plan to be," Jill said, "not that early. Have a good run, Mr. Bullis. And a Merry Christmas."

The train picked up speed, moving eastward through the night. The next scheduled passenger stop, which was also an engine crew change, would be at Elko, Nevada, at 11:19 P.M. Jill left the Silver Palace vestibule and walked back through the Silver Saddle. It was not yet nine-thirty. Some passengers read or talked among themselves, illuminated by the lamps over their seats. Others had extinguished the lights above. They slept, lulled by the darkness outside and the rhythm of the train.

In the Silver Hostel, the passengers in the coffee shop section had thinned out, since it was nine-thirty. Food service stopped at ten o'clock. Alvah Webb was alone, with a cup of coffee and his battered paperback in front of him. He looked up. "Mrs. Tatum was tired. I walked her back to her car."

Jill glanced at the book's title, *Destry Rides Again*. "Max Brand is one of my dad's favorite writers."

Mr. Webb smiled. "He writes a good story. Him and Zane Grey. I like to read a bit before I turn in."

"So do I," Jill said. "I have the new Agatha Christie book waiting for me. I hope you sleep well. I do, on trains."

"Guess you'd have to, doing this kind of work. How long have you been a...what do you call it? Zephyrette?"

"Almost two years," Jill said. "May I sit down?"

"Oh, please do, ma'am. Would you like a cup of coffee?"

Jill shook her head. "I'd better not. If I drink coffee this late in the evening, it would keep me awake."

"Don't seem to affect me," he said, looking down at his cup, half-filled with dark brew.

"Something else keeping you up, then?" Jill asked.

He hesitated again, with that look on his face, the same one she'd seen earlier in the dining car, as though he was afraid to reveal too much of himself. He seemed to be troubled by something, and she was curious.

"I'm sorry," she said. "I shouldn't pry."

But she'd learned in the past two years that sometimes people needed to talk. Passengers often felt safe talking with someone they might not see again, such as the Zephyrette.

He put the book aside. "You ain't prying. You seem like a nice lady, Miss McLeod. I bet you hear a lot of stories."

"I do, Mr. Webb. Do you feel like telling me your story?"

He took a deep breath. "There is something keeping me up. It's about my daughter."

"I imagine you're looking forward to spending Christmas with her and the family."

"I'm nervous about it, and it shows. I don't rightly know what to expect." He reached for his wallet and opened it, taking out a color snapshot. It showed a young woman with a cloud of curly dark hair. She was in her twenties, and so was the young man seated next to her. The woman had a little girl, a baby about a year old, on her lap. The man held a small boy, a toddler.

"That's my daughter. Her name's Carol."

"She's very pretty," Jill said. "And she looks like you."

"Yes, real pretty. She does favor me a bit, in the eyes and the set of her mouth. That dark hair she gets from her mama."

"Why are you nervous about seeing her?"

Mr. Webb put the snapshot on the table. "I left Carol and her mama, when the war started. Never went back. I ain't seen Carol since January of 'forty-two. Almost eleven years. She was thirteen when I left. So she's twenty-four now."

"Did you leave because of the war?" Jill asked.

He sipped his coffee. "That was part of it. But not the whole story. I was working on a ranch in Paonia, Colorado. Wasn't getting along with my wife, for a lot of reasons, including my drinking. After Pearl Harbor I enlisted in the army. A month later I was in basic training. Saw fighting in North Africa, Italy, and Germany. I made sure the army sent most of my pay to my wife. But it ain't the same as being there."

"No, it isn't," Jill said. "But during wartime, people do what they have to do. My father's a doctor. He was in the Navy, out in the Pacific. He was away for three years."

"But he came home, didn't he?"

"Yes, he did."

"I didn't. I stayed away. I knew when I left I wasn't coming back." He sighed. "Carol, she wrote me letters while I was in the army. But I didn't answer them. I didn't know what to say to her. Eventually the letters stopped coming. Once I got out I didn't go back to Colorado. I drifted, just goin' from job to job."

"That's how you wound up in California?"

"Yes, ma'am. Worked a spell in New Mexico, then headed west. Arizona, then California." He sipped his coffee. "I was a drinker before the war, like I said. That was a bone of contention with me and my wife. I sure did some drinking while I was in the army, drinking too much, and I kept at it after the war. That's one reason I kept moving. I got fired a time or two, because of the booze."

"Then at some point you reconnected with your daughter?" Jill asked.

He nodded. "It was the Red Cross, you see. I'm a veteran, so from time to time I'll go see a doctor at one of them veteran's hospitals or clinics, if there was one near where I was workin'. So that left a trail about where I'd been. Four years ago the Red Cross tracked me down, gave me a letter from my daughter. My wife had died, and Carol was in Denver, livin' with my wife's sister. Said she was engaged to be married, to this fella in the picture." He tapped the young man's image. "So I wrote to her, finally. Told her I was glad she was gettin' married and I hoped she'd be happy. Happier than me and her mama. I didn't put that last bit in the letter, though. Carol wrote back and invited me to her wedding."

Jill smiled. "Did you go? But no, you said you hadn't seen her in eleven years."

Mr. Webb shook his head. "I didn't go. Because...I was working on a ranch up in Tehama County. One night after I got that wedding invitation, I got drunk in a bar in Red Bluff. I clobbered some guy with a pool cue. Hurt him bad. Lucky I didn't kill him. They sent me to prison in Folsom. I wrote to Carol, told her why

I couldn't come to her wedding. Told her she'd be better off without an old drunk like me."

Now tears glistened in his eyes. "She wrote me, every week while I was in prison. Those letters kept me going, the whole time I was locked up. She sent me pictures of the wedding and of the babies when they came. I got sober in prison. They had an Alcoholics Anonymous group. When I got out of prison six months ago, someone from the group helped me find a job on a ranch at Beckwourth, over by Portola. I kept up with the AA and stayed sober. Carol invited me to come spend Christmas with her and her husband, to see my grandkids. She even sent me the money for this train ticket. I don't know what it's going to be like, seeing her again, after everything that's happened."

"She really wants to see you, Mr. Webb. I think it will be fine."

"You know anything about AA, Alcoholics Anonymous?" he asked.

"A little bit." More than a little bit, she thought. Her cousin down in Van Nuys had struggled with alcohol and finally got sober through AA.

"There's a part in there about making amends. I've tried to make amends with Carol in my letters to her, but I need to do it in person."

"I understand. I hope it works out for you."

Suddenly Jill felt tired. "Excuse me. I think it's time for bed." She stood and left the coffee shop section. The lounge was open, serving beverages until midnight, and there were several passengers there having nightcaps, including the Coles and Mrs. Tidsdale. As Jill paused in the doorway, Mrs. Tidsdale picked up her glass and knocked back the rest of her Scotch. The Coles, at a nearby table, stared at Mrs. Tidsdale as she stood, unsteady on her feet, slowly making her way to the passage.

"Good evening, Mrs. Tidsdale," Jill said.

"Good night, you mean." Mrs. Tidsdale giggled. "Had a lot of drinkies. Now I'm going to bed. Emily's already in bed. Got her tucked in the upper berth."

"Do you want me to go with you to your car?"

Mrs. Tidsdale drew herself up to her full height. "Don't worry about me, honey. I can find my way."

She stepped out of the lounge and pivoted on her high heels, pointing herself in the direction of the chair cars instead of the sleepers. She walked forward and started to sing.

"'Show me the way to go home, I'm tired and I wanna go to bed. I had a little drink about an hour ago, and it went right to my head.'" Mrs. Tidsdale hiccupped and giggled. The train swayed as it moved into a curve, and the woman swayed with it. "...had a li'l drink 'bout an hour ago, and it went right to my head. Certainly did." She laughed. The passengers in the lounge laughed as well, and whispered among themselves. Tidsy launched into the song again. "'Wherever I may roam, on land or sea or foam, you'll always hear me singing this song, show me the way to go home.'"

Mrs. Tidsdale stumbled on the two steps leading up to the coffee shop, then she righted herself. Alvah Webb got up from the table where he'd been sitting, and came down the steps. He towered over her.

"Oopsie," Mrs. Tidsdale said. "Head-on collision. Better put that train on a siding, cowboy."

Jill looked at Mr. Webb over Mrs. Tidsdale's shoulder. "She's going the wrong way. The sleeper cars are to the rear. She's been drinking, and I think she's had too much."

"Has she, now?" Mr. Webb's face held a curious look, as he examined Mrs. Tidsdale. Then he held out his arm. "You need to back up to the station, ma'am. You're headed in the wrong direction."

"Oopsie. That's gonna put us off schedule." Mrs. Tidsdale took his arm and steadied herself as she did an about-face. "Right direction now."

"Yes, ma'am," Mr. Webb said. "You want me to go with you?"

"I'm perfectly all right," Mrs. Tidsdale said. "I can find my way."

Mr. Webb inclined his head. "Then I'll say good night, ma'am. Miss McLeod." He released Mrs. Tidsdale's arm and walked away, heading forward to the chair cars.

Mrs. Tidsdale launched into her song again as she walked past the lounge. She managed the steps to the upper level and walked slowly past the crew's dormitory. Jill followed her, watching as the woman navigated her way through the sleeper cars, putting out both hands to steady herself as she headed down the corridor.

In the Silver Palisade, Frank Nathan appeared, his voice soft. "You need some help, Mrs. Tidsdale?"

She waved her finger in front of her mouth. "Shh, you'll wake everybody up. I'm perfectly fine." She opened the door of bedroom A and waggled her fingers. "Nighty-night."

Once Mrs. Tidsdale was safely inside, Jill turned to the porter. "I'm going to bed. I hope you have a quiet night, Mr. Nathan."

"Same to you, Miss McLeod."

Chapter Eleven

JILL RETURNED to the Silver Hostel, entered her compartment, and locked the door. Yawning, she glanced at her watch. By now it was past ten. She leaned over, peering out the small window above her berth. Outside all was in darkness, punctuated by the occasional lights, from cars on country roads or ranches, distant outposts spread out on Nevada's Great Basin. Jill closed the curtains. The compartment was barely big enough to turn around in, but by now she was used to it. She kicked off her shoes and removed her nylons, rolling them up and tucking them into her shoes. Then she took off her clothes and put her uniform on a hanger. She put on soft, comfortable red-and-green-flannel pajamas. She hoped there wouldn't be any middle-of-the-night calls for her services. If there were, she'd have to get dressed again before going out to deal with whatever situation had arisen. Zephyrettes didn't respond to emergencies in their PJs.

Jill pulled the sink down from the wall, then washed her face and brushed her teeth. After pushing the sink back up to the wall, she lowered the back of the bench seat, transforming it into her bed. She switched on the light above her berth and turned off the overhead light. It felt good to get off her feet and tuck herself into the berth under the warm blankets. Now she propped herself up with her pillow and set her watch forward one hour. She'd set her notebook, pencil, and her book on the toilet lid. Now she reached for the notebook and pencil and went over the notes she'd made for her trip report. All in all, this first day out had been routine. She hoped tomorrow would be as well.

With another yawn, Jill set aside her notebook, reaching for the Agatha Christie novel her sister and brother had given her that morning. It was called *Murder with Mirrors*. She opened the hardbound book and turned to chapter one, ready to escape into another case featuring the redoubtable Miss Jane Marple of St. Mary Mead. But it had been a long day, and she was tired. Sleep tugged at her eyelids as she came to the end of the first chapter. She tucked a bookmark between the pages, turned off the reading light, and snuggled down under the covers. She fell asleep almost immediately, lulled by the familiar soothing *clickety-clack* of wheels on the rails.

Jill woke up again as the train pulled into the station at Elko. She glanced at her watch. Eleven-twenty, right on schedule. There was another engine crew change here. She heard voices outside the train, propped herself up and looked out the window. Snow blanketed the platform. A moment later the train moved, pulling out of the station. *Clickety-clack* again on the rails as the *Zephyr* picked up speed, heading northeast to Wells, then southeast to Wendover on the Nevada–Utah border. After that it would be a fairly straight eastbound run across the flat terrain of the Great Salt Desert, skirting the southern shore of the Great Salt Lake. She fell asleep again, her slumber undisturbed until the train pulled into the station at Salt Lake City at five-twenty.

Salt Lake City was a longer stop, with passengers getting off the train and others boarding. This was the changeover stop as well, where the train's Western Pacific crew put the *California Zephyr* into the hands of the Denver and Rio Grande Western crew. The orange WP locomotives were switched out for the yellow of the D&RGW, which advertised itself as "The Main Line Through the Rockies." Five powerful diesel engines would pull the train over the high reaches of the Rocky Mountains.

It was too early to get up, though. Jill turned over and dozed again. Next time she woke up, the train was pulling into Provo, southeast of Salt Lake City. It was still dark outside. She looked at her watch. Six-thirty, the morning of December 23rd. She stretched her arms over her head and yawned. Her stomach rumbled and she needed coffee. She threw back the covers and swung her legs over the edge of her berth. Though there was a shower in the dormitory section, that was used only by the male crew members. There would be no hot shower for Jill until she got to the Chicago hotel where she would spend her layover before returning to California on the westbound *Zephyr*. She made do with a washcloth and water in the sink. Once she was dressed, she put on her makeup with quick, practiced gestures and left her compartment.

It was still dark outside on this winter morning. The kitchen and dining car staff had been up far earlier than Jill, preparing to cook and serve breakfast to passengers. But at a quarter to seven, the tables in the diner weren't crowded. There were just a few passengers, early risers like Jill, outnumbered by the waiters. She saw Mr. Webb at a table with a man and a woman she recognized, passengers in the same car. He smiled at her as the waiter delivered plates of ham and eggs.

The dining car steward directed her to a vacant table. A waiter brought Jill a pot of coffee as soon as she sat down, pouring a cup for her. "How are you this morning, Miss McLeod?"

"Fine, thanks. I'll be a lot better once I get some coffee in me." She took a restorative sip of the dark brew and pulled a menu from the stand. She didn't really need to look, though. She always had the same thing for breakfast when she was on the road. She marked her meal check—orange juice, French toast with syrup, bacon—and handed the check to the waiter when he came back to her table.

The Denver and Rio Grande Western conductor who'd boarded the train in Salt Lake City entered the diner. He was a thin man with salt-and-pepper hair, a pair of round wire-rimmed glasses perched on his long nose. The conductor's uniform was similar to those worn by the WP conductors, but his badge showed the railroad's insignia—a snowcapped mountain peak, and the words MAIN LINE THRU THE ROCKIES surrounding RIO GRANDE.

The conductor scanned the car and walked to her table. "Homer Wilson. You must be Miss McLeod. May I join you?"

"Certainly," Jill said with a smile.

He pulled out a chair and sat down, then reached for a meal check. "Don't even need to look at the menu. I always have the

same thing. Corned beef hash and eggs, over easy." The waiter
brought another pot of coffee and took Mr. Wilson's check.

"We're both creatures of habit," Jill said. "I always get the
French toast."

Mr. Wilson took a sip of his coffee. "How's the run so far?"

"Uneventful. Though we have a missing item." She told him
about the gold pen. "I hope we find it. There are quite a few children on board. I'm having a Christmas party in the diner this
afternoon. What do the train orders say about the weather?"

"Wet weather, and be on the lookout for loose and falling
rocks in the canyons," Mr. Wilson said. "We've had snow all over
southeast Utah these past few days. Western Colorado, too. The
forecast is several inches of snow in the Rockies. We'll do our
best to make sure we don't have any delays. Since it's so close
to Christmas, people will want to arrive in Denver on schedule.
Barring any unforeseen complications, we should get into Union
Station on time, at seven o'clock this evening."

"We have lots of passengers getting off in Denver," Jill said.

"Probably not as many getting on there. I expect the passenger count will be lighter from Denver to Chicago."

The waiter brought their breakfasts. Jill poured maple syrup
on her French toast and picked up her fork. It was after seven now.
The dining car gradually filled, as passengers in the chair cars and
sleepers awakened, needing coffee and food for this second day of
the journey. Dr. Kovacs appeared, escorting Mrs. Tatum and the
woman in the bedroom next to her, Mrs. Loomis. They were soon
seated at a nearby table.

She and the conductor chatted as they ate. Mr. Wilson lived
in Grand Junction, he told her, with his wife and three children,
and he'd been with the Denver and Rio Grande Western for nearly twenty years, with a break during the war when he was in the
army.

Jill saw a faint red glow to the east, growing brighter as the
sun came up. Sunlight soon sparked crystals in the snow that
blanketed the landscape on either side of the train. Jill finished
her breakfast and looked at her watch. They were nearing a place
called Soldier Summit, and it was time for her to make her first

announcement of the day. She finished her coffee and excused herself. As she stood up, the Finches and Mrs. and Mrs. Constanza arrived from the sleeper section. A few steps behind them were Mrs. Tidsdale and Emily. Jill stopped to talk as the dining car steward seated the Finches, then came back to assist the Constanzas.

Mrs. Tidsdale looked as though she wasn't quite awake. Not surprising, since she'd still been drinking in the lounge last night till Jill went to bed.

"God, I need coffee, and plenty of it," she said, in response to Jill's greeting.

"We have really good French toast," Jill told Emily. "You should try it."

Mrs. Tidsdale blanched. "Can I get a Bloody Mary instead?"

"You'll have to go to the lounge for that."

"Don't worry, I will. As soon as we get some breakfast. Come to think of it, I could make the acquaintance of some ham and eggs." Mrs. Tidsdale looked down at Emily. "Does that sound good, sweetie?"

Emily looked dubious. "I like French toast. With bacon."

"Then French toast and bacon for you, ham and eggs for me," Mrs. Tidsdale said. The dining car steward directed them to a table. The Bensons arrived, with Billy and Chip bouncing up and down. "Bacon and eggs, bacon and eggs," Chip sang, to the tune of "Three Blind Mice."

"Coffee, black, and lots of it," his father said.

Jill laughed and headed for the public address system. "Good morning, ladies and gentlemen. This is your Zephyrette, Miss McLeod, welcoming you to Utah and the Denver and Rio Grande Western Railroad, the Main Line Through the Rockies.

"A variety of scenic wonders will be yours to see today. Beautiful rock formations such as Castle Gate. The bleak, forbidding, and yet beautiful Utah desert. Industry and agriculture will be side by side at Helper and Price, Utah. Colorado's famous peach-producing area at Grand Junction and Palisade. Once little-known but now famous Rifle, Colorado, where oil is being extracted from shale at a government experimental plant. The marvelous canyons of the Colorado River, including the Glenwood Canyon, inspiration for the Vista-Dome car. The high spot of today's trip will be when we are in the Moffat Tunnel. That's nine thousand two hundred thirty-nine feet above sea level. Your 'Vista-Dome Views' booklet tells you when and where to look. Don't miss any of these western wonders, for this is a travel day you'll long remember."

By the time Jill finished the announcement and turned off the mike, the Bensons were seated in one of the semi-private nooks and the waiter was delivering their food. Both boys quieted as they forked up bacon and eggs. Mr. Benson looked livelier now that he had a cup of coffee in front of him.

The train headed down the eastern side of the Wasatch Plateau. This was a steep grade, and the next town on the route, Helper, Utah, was named after the helper engines that would assist the westbound trains in making the climb to the summit. The train also stopped in Price, which was just seven miles from Helper. After that, it was another hour to Green River.

After the train pulled out of the Price station, Jill walked back through the Silver Hostel. There were people in the coffee shop section, which also served breakfast. In the lounge, she saw Mrs. Tidsdale at her usual spot near the bar, a drink in front of her. Mr. Paynter was with her. Tidsy smiled flirtatiously as she pulled out a cigarette and he lit it with his Zippo.

Jill headed back to the Silver Gull. She passed the porter's seat, but didn't see Si Lovell. He must be in one of the compartments, she thought. At the other end of the car, she saw Mr. Smith, the gruff, unpleasant man who was traveling on the Silver Palisade. He walked forward, as though headed for the dining car. They both neared the middle section of the car. Then Si Lovell, carrying a tray of breakfast dishes, stepped out of compartment F. The porter stopped, but not before he bumped into Smith.

"Watch where you're going, boy," Smith snarled. "You damn near spilled that coffee on me."

"I'm sorry, sir." Mr. Lovell drew back against the window opposite the compartment door, leaving room for Smith to pass.

Now Mike Scolari appeared in the compartment doorway.

"It was an accident. No harm done, and no need to blame the porter."

Smith turned to him, mouth twisting. "Mind your own damn business."

"Good morning, Mr. Smith, Mr. Scolari," Jill said, hoping to defuse the situation. "Can I be of any assistance?"

Smith glared at all of them. "Stupid damn nig—"

"Watch your language in front of the lady," Mike Scolari said.

"Is there a problem?" The voice came from behind Jill. She turned to look and saw Mr. Cole in the doorway of compartment B. "I'd appreciate it if you'd keep the noise down. My wife's still asleep."

Smith growled, deep in his throat, then he shouldered his way past Jill, heading for the front of the car. Jill turned to Mr. Lovell, who stood holding the breakfast tray. On first glance, his face was impassive but Jill noticed a tightness around his mouth. It bothered her when the passengers verbally abused the porters, or called them "boy" or worse instead of their names. She knew that porters traveling in the Southern states often had a rough time from the passengers. Mr. Smith was particularly unpleasant and it was clear he didn't like Negroes. She wondered if he was from the South, but he didn't have an accent.

"I'm so sorry, Mr. Lovell," she said.

"Me, too," Mike Scolari added. "That guy's a jerk."

Mr. Lovell let out a sigh, as though he'd been holding his breath. "Don't worry about it, sir. It happens." He turned and walked forward, taking the tray of dishes back to the kitchen.

"It happens, all the time, but it shouldn't," Scolari said. "Mr. Lovell will get a big tip from me when we get to Denver. Not that it takes the sting out of bigots like that and their race prejudice. I'm Italian. All the time I was in the service, they called me names, too. You must see lots of jerks on the train."

"Sometimes. But I meet lots of nice people, too. There are more of them than the unpleasant people, so I try not to let the other ones bother me."

He smiled at her. "That's a good attitude to have."

He went back into the compartment and shut the door. Suddenly Jill heard loud voices, coming from one of the compartments behind her. She turned. The raised voices were coming from compartment B. It sounded as though Mr. and Mrs. Cole were arguing. But hadn't Mr. Cole said his wife was asleep?

"...make our move soon," Mrs. Cole said, sounding so close that she must be standing just the other side of the door.

Jill backed away. She really shouldn't be eavesdropping. Now she walked the way she'd originally been headed, toward the rear of the train. Still, she couldn't help wondering.

"Make our move soon." What did Mrs. Cole mean by that?

Chapter Twelve

THE *CALIFORNIA ZEPHYR* pulled out of Green River, Utah at 9:53 A.M. The next scheduled stop was Grand Junction, Colorado, at 11:43 A.M., just under two hours. Jill walked back to the Silver Solarium, where she saw Mrs. Clive climbing the stairs to the Vista-Dome. The Finches and the Constanzas sat in the lounge, next to Mr. and Mrs. Cole. Across from them, Ed and Norma Benson were chatting with Mrs. Tatum. Jill heard voices from above, passengers in the Vista-Dome. The area around Green River was high desert, its wide-open landscape covered with snow. To the east loomed the Rocky Mountains.

A group of children, radiating pent-up energy, gathered at the rounded back of the car. The Finch girls, Nan and Cathy, were at the center of the group, which included Emily and Billy and Chip Benson. Tina Moreno, the little girl who'd scraped her knee the day before, was there. So was George Neeley.

Mrs. Finch looked up and smiled. "Oh, Miss McLeod, there you are. The girls tell me they're bored. I'm afraid they have already read all the books they brought with them. I know you're having a Christmas party later on, but any ideas for keeping them occupied right now?"

"How about a game?" Jill suggested.

The children swirled around her, seconding the notion with enthusiasm. "That sounds like fun," Nan said.

"A card game?" Mrs. Finch smiled at her daughters. "I've been teaching the girls how to play bridge."

"Mrs. Tidsdale taught us how to play poker, a game called seven-card stud," Emily said.

"Did she indeed?" Mrs. Finch raised an eyebrow. "Looks like I may need to have a word with Mrs. Tidsdale."

"A lady in the lounge car had a word with Mrs. Tidsdale," Emily said. "Mrs. Tidsdale told her to put a lid on it and mind her own darn business. Only she didn't say darn."

Ed Benson laughed and the other men joined in. "I'd pay money to see that," Mr. Finch said over his wife's exasperated sigh. "Now, Margaret, poker's a good game to learn, like bridge."

"Poker's all right," Norma Benson said. "My brother taught Billy how to play the last time he came for a visit."

Mr. Finch nodded. "No harm in playing a friendly game of nickel-dime-quarter around the kitchen table. I did it all the time when I was growing up."

"So did I," Mrs. Tatum said, chuckling.

"It was pennies, nickels, and dimes," Cathy said. "I won thirty-seven cents."

"I'd rather the children didn't learn to gamble just yet," Mrs. Finch said. "Even if it was pennies. Thirty-seven cents, indeed."

"I don't want to play cards," Nan said. "We're all tired of sitting. We want to move around the train."

"It's all right to walk from car to car," her mother said. "Make sure you don't get in the way of Miss McLeod and the rest of the crew. They have their jobs to do. And don't bother the other passengers."

Nan grinned, a mischievous light flashing in her eyes. "Let's play a mystery game. I'll be Nancy Drew. Cathy can be Bess and Emily can be George."

"I'm already George," the boy from the Silver Pine said.

"I'll just be myself," Emily said.

"I want to play, too," Billy said.

"Me, too," Chip chimed in.

"You're a bit young, sport," Ed Benson told Chip.

The Benson boys converged on their parents, pleading. "I'll look after him, Dad," Billy said. "I won't let him get into any trouble or bother anybody. Honest, I won't. Please, please?"

The adult Bensons exchanged looks. Then Norma Benson nodded. "Well, just for a little while. Until lunch."

Jill had been thinking of games that might involve a mystery. She needed something that would keep the children occupied and use up some of their bottled-up energy. "How about a scavenger hunt?"

The Coles had been listening, amusement on their faces. Now Rita Cole tilted her head to one side, smoothing back her ponytail. "A scavenger hunt? What's that?"

"It's a game," her husband said. "Used to play that when I was little. Got a list of things to find or things to do, and the first person—or team—that finds all the stuff on the list wins. Am I right, Miss McLeod?"

"Yes, you are." Jill moved to the writing desk and pulled out a pen and a sheet of stationery. She wrote a list of things that would be easy for the children to find on the train, starting with the items on the desk—pen, stationery, envelope, postcard. She added magazine and newspaper, as there were plenty of those discarded after folks had read them. Coaster and menu—the children could find those in the lounge. There were lots of promotional items in the cars, such the *California Zephyr* pamphlet called "Vista-Dome Views." At this time of year, there were *CZ* Christmas cards as well. And timetables, she added. One from the Western Pacific and one from the Denver & Rio Grande Western, just to make it interesting. She looked over the list and quickly wrote out another copy.

"All of these things are on the *California Zephyr*," Jill said. "The mystery is where you find them. We're due into Denver at seven o'clock, so let's see how many of these things you can find and bring back here to the Silver Solarium by five o'clock. I've made two lists, for two teams, with each team finding all the things on the list. Team one will be Nan, Cathy, and Emily. Team two will be George, Tina, Billy, and Chip."

"That's great." Nan took one list and George took the other.

"Remember, girls," Mrs. Finch said. "Don't take any personal items. At least not without asking for permission."

"And don't go into other people's rooms," Mrs. Benson added, directing a stern look at her sons. "You should be able to find those things without bothering the other passengers. Understood?"

"We'll be good," Billy assured his mother. "I'll watch Chip."

The other children chorused their replies, promising to behave themselves, and surged forward, heading toward the sleeper cars.

Mr. Finch smiled at Jill. "They'll find all those things by lunch, Miss McLeod. Then we'll have to figure out another way to keep them busy."

"By then it will be time for the Christmas party," Mrs. Tatum said.

"I hope they won't make a nuisance of themselves," Norma Benson said.

"I'll go check on them in a half an hour or so," her husband said. "In the meantime, let's enjoy some peace and quiet."

"Miss McLeod, how much longer until we reach Grand Junction?" Mrs. Tatum asked.

Jill looked at her watch. "It's just after ten. We're due into Grand Junction at eleven forty-three. I'd say an hour and forty minutes."

"Thank you, dear. I'll stay here a while longer, then I'll go back to my bedroom and get my things ready. I'm really looking forward to seeing my daughter and her family."

Mrs. Finch closed her book and turned to Mrs. Constanza. "Like the children, I'm tired of reading. How about another rubber of bridge?"

———

The *California Zephyr* crossed the Utah–Colorado state boundary, at a place called Westwater. It had once been a railroad and farming town, but now it was a ghost town. It was here that the train joined the Colorado River, flowing out of the Rockies in the distance. The Silver Lady would follow the silvery upstream course of the river for the next 238 miles.

Jill went up to the Vista-Dome over the Silver Hostel and looked out at the river. It was covered with ice on both banks, with the swift current running in the middle. She spotted a bald eagle perched at the top of a snag, a dead tree that was still standing, and then another one, skimming the water. "Bald eagles are fish eaters," she told the passengers. "That's why you see them near rivers and lakes. Look, there's another one. In just a few minutes we'll be entering Ruby Canyon."

The canyon, twenty-five miles long, got its name from the red sandstone, vivid even in the thin winter sunshine. Erosion over thousands of years had carved steep cliffs, spires, and arches. The train slowed as it wound alongside the canyon walls, in places just a few feet from the tracks. To the south was the Colorado River, white water in the middle between sheaths of ice. In places the canyon walls receded into side canyons, with trees poking from slopes covered with snow.

It began to snow as the train neared the end of Ruby Canyon, lazy flakes swirling from a gray sky. The terrain leveled out into farming country. The train whistle blew a crossing warning as it went past a country road. Jill left the Vista-Dome and walked back to the sleeper cars to help Mrs. Tatum get ready to leave the train when they reached Grand Junction, the next stop.

When Jill entered the Silver Palisade, she heard raised voices and saw several people in the corridor outside the bedrooms. One was Frank Nathan, the porter, standing back from the group as Mrs. Clive shook her finger at him. The other passengers in that section, Mrs. Loomis, Mrs. Tatum, and Mrs. Benson stood in the doorways of their bedrooms.

"I'm glad you're here," Norma Benson said, her boys crowding in behind her. "Ed went to find the conductor."

"What's happened? Is something wrong?"

Mrs. Clive turned to Jill, her face red with indignation. "My gold cigarette case is gone. I left it here when I went to the observation car. When I got back it was gone."

"Perhaps you've misplaced it," Jill said.

"No, I haven't," Mrs. Clive snapped. "Someone stole it. I want this car searched, and you can start with that colored man."

Frank Nathan shook his head. "I didn't take your cigarette case, ma'am. I've never even seen it."

Mrs. Tatum spoke up, her voice placating. "It may have fallen on the floor and slipped under the seat."

"Don't be ridiculous. It's been stolen, I tell you." Mrs. Clive glared at the porter. "That colored man is the thief. He's the only one that's in and out of these rooms."

The conductor, Mr. Wilson, rounded the corner from the roomette section of the car, followed by Mr. Alford, the Pullman conductor. Ed Benson brought up the rear.

"What seems to be the problem?" Mr. Wilson asked.

"My cigarette case has been stolen." Mrs. Clive glared at Frank Nathan. "That colored man must have taken it."

"We will certainly look into the matter," Mr. Wilson said. "What does the cigarette case look like?"

"It's gold, about three inches by five." Mrs. Clive sketched a shape in the air. "It looks like an envelope, with a triangular flap on one side. On the other side it's engraved, to look like an address and a stamp. It has great sentimental value, besides being quite valuable. I really must have my case back."

Jill remembered seeing the cigarette case when Mrs. Clive checked in at the Oakland Mole. Shaped like an envelope. Oh, dear, she thought. The children, the scavenger hunt. Surely they wouldn't...

"I do think we should look through your bedroom, just to be sure," the conductor told Mrs. Clive. "Miss McLeod, will you help us?"

Jill and the conductor quickly searched Mrs. Clive's bedroom, but the cigarette case was nowhere to be found. Before they went out to the passageway, she told him about the scavenger hunt. "I hope one of the children hasn't mistaken the cigarette case for a real envelope."

Mr. Wilson frowned and shook his head. "Yes, I saw some children earlier, taking postcards from the lounge. They told me about the scavenger hunt. They don't seem like they'd take something from one of the bedrooms. But the cigarette case is definitely missing. And so is that gold pen you told me about this morning. We have a thief aboard."

They stepped out into the passageway. "The case isn't in the bedroom," Mr. Wilson said.

"I told you it was gone. It's been stolen." Mrs. Clive glared at Frank Nathan, who was standing with the Pullman conductor, then she turned an equally poisonous look on Billy and Chip Benson, who clustered around their parents. "This is just the limit. It's bad enough to have to deal with these grubby, noisy children running wild all over the train."

Norma Benson put her hands on her hips and scowled at Mrs. Clive. "Now just a minute. What is that supposed to mean?"

"You know perfectly well what I mean," Mrs. Clive said. "Those boys of yours are loud and out of control. Yesterday your brats were prowling around in other people's rooms. For all I know they've been in my bedroom, pawing through my things with their sticky fingers."

Now Mrs. Benson took a step toward Mrs. Clive. "My boys—"

"Slow down." Mr. Benson reached for his wife. "Let's go inside."

"I assure you, we'll make every effort to locate the cigarette case," the conductor said.

Mrs. Clive's face reddened with indignation. "The president of the Denver and Rio Grande will certainly hear from me." She turned and went into her bedroom, shutting the door with a thump that reflected her pique.

The conductor gestured at Frank Nathan and Mr. Alford. "I'll have a word with you, Mr. Nathan."

Jill followed them forward past the roomettes to the small porter's compartment next to the vestibule. "I didn't steal that lady's cigarette case, sir," Frank said.

"I don't believe you did," Jill said.

"I will vouch for Mr. Nathan," Mr. Alford said. "He's been with the Pullman Company going on five years, with never a complaint. In fact, I know he's found wallets and returned them to their owners with nary a bill missing."

"We have to investigate." Mr. Wilson took out his watch. "We're due into Grand Junction soon, and that's where I leave the train. I'll brief the new conductor. Mr. Alford, you're the Pullman conductor and the porters are your responsibility. You'll have to search through the public areas of the sleeper cars and see if you can find that cigarette case. Miss McLeod, please talk with the waiters and stewards, just on the off chance Mrs. Clive left that case in the diner or the lounge."

"I'll do that as soon as I help Mrs. Tatum," Jill said. "She's blind and she'll need some assistance leaving the train."

Grand Junction was the largest town on the Western Slope of the Rockies. The *Zephyr* would be on the ground for ten minutes here, changing both crew and equipment. The whistle blew more crossing warnings as it moved through the outskirts of Grand Junction. Then it slowed as it approached the yellow brick station.

Mr. Webb was waiting in the vestibule when Frank Nathan carried Mrs. Tatum's suitcase past the roomettes, followed by Jill and Mrs. Tatum herself, holding her white cane.

"I don't for a minute believe you took that case," Mrs. Tatum said.

"Thank you, ma'am," the porter said.

Mrs. Tatum slipped a rolled bill into Frank's hand. "And I appreciate all the help you've given me on this trip."

"It's been a pleasure having you aboard, Mrs. Tatum." He pocketed the tip.

"Yes, it has," Jill said. "I hope you have a wonderful Christmas with your daughter."

"Same goes for me," Alvah Webb said. "I surely enjoyed getting to know you."

"I plan on having a lovely Christmas, my dear." Mrs. Tatum squeezed Jill's hand. Then she turned to the tall cowboy. "And you, Mr. Webb. I know you'll have a fine Christmas, too, with your daughter and her husband and those grandkids. It will be all right, you'll see."

"Thank you, ma'am. I'll hold that thought. Good-bye, Mrs. Tatum," Mr. Webb said. Then he headed forward, to his own car.

As soon as the train stopped, Frank Nathan opened the vestibule door, lowered the steps, and put his step box on the platform. Then he held out his arm. "I'm right here on your left, ma'am, if you'll just take my arm." He carefully guided Mrs. Tatum down to the platform, then reached for her suitcase. "Is your family here to meet you? Never mind, I see them."

Two children, a boy and a girl, left the shelter of the station and raced down the platform, calling, "Grandma, Grandma." Just behind them were a man and a woman. The man took the suitcase from Frank as the woman and the children embraced Mrs. Tatum.

"Oh, Mama, it's so good to see you," the woman said. "Did you have a nice trip?"

Mrs. Tatum hugged her daughter. "It was lovely. These people took good care of me. Is that snow I feel?"

"Sure is," her son-in-law said as the fat flakes swirled around them. "Been snowing off and on all morning. Supposed to have more of it today and tomorrow. We'll have a white Christmas for sure."

A white-haired man carrying a small suitcase approached Frank and held out his ticket. "That's the Silver Gull, sir, next car up."

Jill left the vestibule and walked back to the Silver Solarium, where earlier she had seen Mrs. Clive climbing the stairs to the Vista-Dome. She wanted to take a look, to see if the cigarette case was up there.

It wasn't. Jill sighed. Maybe Mrs. Clive was right, and there was a thief aboard the train. But she didn't believe it was Frank Nathan.

She walked down the stairs and headed forward. As she entered the Silver Palisade, Mrs. Benson hailed her.

"I just want to slap that woman, after what she said about my boys," Norma Benson said. "That's not why I waved you down, though. I know when you wrote out that list for the kids' scavenger hunt, you put 'envelope' on it. I saw Mrs. Clive's cigarette case last night in the lounge, and it does look like an envelope. Ed and I talked with the boys. They didn't take it. Billy and Chip may be rambunctious, and I know they were poking around in the empty rooms yesterday. But I know they wouldn't take something that doesn't belong to them."

"Of course they didn't take it," Jill said.

"But the thought occurred to you," Mrs. Benson said.

Jill nodded. "Yes, it did. I thought that one of the children might have taken the cigarette case, because it looks like an envelope. But I dismissed that. She says she left the case in her bedroom. I just don't think one of the children would go into the bedroom and take the case."

"So that leaves us with what?

Jill shook her head. "I'm not sure. Either Mrs. Clive misplaced the cigarette case. Or someone took it. But we just don't have an answer yet."

Outside Jill heard the new conductor's call of "All aboard."

Chapter Thirteen

THE TRAIN PICKED up speed as it left the outskirts of Grand Junction, heading east through snow-covered fields toward the agricultural community of Palisade. Jill walked forward to the Silver Palace. In the office below the Vista-Dome, she introduced herself to the new Denver and Rio Grande Western conductor, a tall, rangy man in his forties.

"I'm Jim Gaskill," he said, shaking her hand. "Before he left the train, Mr. Wilson told me about the missing items. I've also talked with the Pullman conductor, and the porter on the Silver Palisade. They've looked through the common areas of the sleepers, the linen lockers, washrooms, and so forth. But they didn't find the cigarette case or the pen. Any thoughts?"

"I know Frank Nathan," Jill said. "I've been on several runs with him. I'm sure he wouldn't steal anything. I think Mrs. Clive must have misplaced the case. She was up in the observation car Vista-Dome this morning. I went up there to look, in between and under the seats. Nothing there except a couple of candy wrappers."

"Let's keep an eye out. And talk with the crew, to see if anyone saw anything." Mr. Gaskill frowned. "I hate to think we've got a thief aboard, and I certainly wouldn't want it to be a member of the crew. The railroad takes a dim view of such things. Between you and me, whoever took that case may be a passenger, in my experience. I've seen similar incidents in my years on the trains. We do get our share of miscreants—drunks, cardsharps, thieves and the like. Anything else to report?"

"Until now, it's been an uneventful run. There are a lot of

children on board. Some of them are pretty lively. Mrs. Clive has complained about the Benson boys. The Bensons have two double bedrooms, right next to her. Billy and Chip are rather high-spirited. I got some of the children involved in a scavenger hunt, to keep them busy."

The conductor nodded. "Mr. Wilson told me about that, too. Is it possible one of the children took the case?"

Jill shook her head. "I considered it, but no, I don't think so. The children are supposed to find an envelope. They're all old enough to know the difference between that and a cigarette case, even if it does look like an envelope."

"Keep looking," Mr. Gaskill said.

"I will. Anything in the train orders about the weather up ahead?" Jill asked.

"Wet weather," the conductor said. "Be on the lookout for loose and falling rocks. That's always a problem this time of year, when the rocks freeze and thaw over and over. We've had a lot of snow in this area over the past few days. And there's snow in the forecast as we move over the mountains. Let's hope the weather doesn't make this run even more interesting. December in the Rockies, that's always a possibility."

Jill started to leave the office, then turned back to the conductor. "By the way, I'm having a Christmas party for the children in the diner, as soon as it closes after lunch, about two-thirty. Please join us and have some cake."

Mr. Gaskill smiled. "I may do that."

———

Jill walked back to the Silver Hostel. In the coffee shop, passengers filled the tables, ordering sandwiches from the steward. When he had a moment she asked him if he'd seen the cigarette case. He shook his head. Jill left the coffee shop. When she rounded the corner to the passageway that ran alongside the lounge, she saw Mr. Paynter walking toward her, coming from the direction of the diner. He climbed the stairs up to the upper level Vista-Dome. Jill paused in the doorway leading to the lounge. Mrs. Tidsdale sat alone at the table near the bar. She waved at Jill. "Have you seen Emily?"

"Not lately," Jill said. "The last time I saw her, she was in the observation car."

"Collecting things for this scavenger hunt you started," Mrs. Tidsdale said. "I guess she'll turn up when she's hungry. Speak of the devil...er, the little angel," she added as Emily appeared.

"I'm hungry," Emily said. "Let's go to the diner."

Mrs. Tidsdale stubbed out her cigarette in the ashtray. "Care to join us, Miss McLeod?"

"Yes, I will." An early lunch was a good idea. As soon as she finished, Jill could start preparing for the children's party.

She followed as Mrs. Tidsdale and Emily left the lounge. Just ahead of them, Mr. and Mrs. Cole came down from the Vista-Dome. They, too, walked toward the dining car. It was filling up now that it was past noon, and they joined the queue of passengers waiting in the passageway next to the kitchen and pantry. When they reached the counter in the middle of the car, the steward seated the Coles at a nearby table for four and beckoned to Dr. Kovacs, who was walking toward the counter from the sleeper cars.

The professor glanced at his ex-wife and her husband. Then he shook his head, refusing the seat. "Thank you, no. I'll wait for another table. I should like to sit with Miss McLeod and Mrs. Tidsdale."

"Certainly, sir," the steward said. He seated another couple with the Coles. The Finches were walking this way, and Emily darted around Jill, running to meet Nan and Cathy.

Mrs. Tidsdale winced and put one hand to her head. "Oh, damn. All of a sudden I have a headache."

"There's aspirin in my first-aid kit," Jill said. "Would you like some?"

"I have aspirin back in the bedroom. I'll take some and lie down. But I don't feel like having lunch. You and Emily go ahead."

Mrs. Tidsdale stepped past the steward and the Finches and walked through the diner, heading for the sleeper cars.

"Why don't you join us?" Mrs. Finch said. "The girls can sit together."

They took a table near the middle of the dining car, with Jill

and Dr. Kovacs facing the steward's counter and the Finches opposite them. On the other side of the aisle, the three girls, Nan,
Cathy, and Emily, had a table to themselves. Jill introduced the
professor. "This is Dr. Laszlo Kovacs. He teaches at my alma mater,
Cal Berkeley."

"We went to Berkeley as well," Mr. Finch said, reaching for a
menu. "That's where we met, back in the 'thirties. I majored in
engineering, and Margaret's major was public health."

"What department are you in?" Margaret Finch asked.

"Physics," Dr. Kovacs said. "I have been on the faculty since
nineteen forty-seven."

"That's LeConte Hall, over by the Campanile," Mr. Finch said.
"I had a few classes there in my undergraduate days. Do you work
up at the radiation lab with Dr. Lawrence?"

Yes, he did, Jill knew, recalling the talk he'd given on campus,
and what the Bensons had told her about Dr. Kovacs working on
the Manhattan Project during the war. But the professor seemed
to sidestep Mr. Finch's question. "I have some research projects
up at the lab. But mostly I teach." He plucked a menu from the
stand and perused it.

Across the aisle, Nan Finch took one of the lunch menus
from the stand, folded it and put it in her pocket. With the pencil
used to mark the meal check, she drew a line through one of the
items on the scavenger hunt list Jill had created earlier. "That's
the menu. Cathy, you got a coaster?" Her sister nodded. "Emily,
did you get the envelope and stationery?"

"I got a piece of stationery," Emily said. "But all the envelopes
were gone from the writing desk. I'll find another one."

"Are you young ladies ready to order?" the waiter asked,
looming over the girls' table. The girls reached for menus and
meal checks, and marked their selections. "Let's see, that's one bacon, lettuce, and tomato; one chicken salad; one toasted cheese;
and three milks."

As the waiter turned to the adults' table, Dr. Kovacs marked
his meal check. "This braised beef with a potato pancake sounds
good."

"Yes, it does," Jill said. "That's what I'm going to have."

"Stewed chicken with buttered noodles, that's for me." Mr. Finch turned to his wife. "What about you, dear?"

"I'll have the navy bean soup and cornbread, with the combination salad." She put her menu back in the holder. Both the Finches marked their checks and handed them to the waiter. As he headed for the kitchen, Mrs. Finch gestured at the landscape outside the train window. "Goodness, look at it snow. I wonder if it will be like this all the way to Denver."

What had been a flurry of snow when the *Zephyr* left Grand Junction was now a curtain of swiftly falling flakes obscuring the scenery. "Snow in the forecast, but that's to be expected in December," Jill said.

"Quite a change from the weather we get in the Bay Area," Dr. Kovacs said.

They chatted about the weather until the waiter brought their lunches. The professor picked up his fork and cut into his entrée. Then he stopped and looked up. Jill followed the direction of his gaze. Was he looking at Mrs. Cole? The sight of his ex-wife, and the fact that she was on the train with her new husband, certainly seemed to bother Dr. Kovacs. But no, that wasn't what the professor was looking at. Mrs. Cole had left her husband and their dining companions at the table, and was now walking back toward the sleeping cars. As Mrs. Cole passed the table, Dr. Kovacs still stared, frowning, at the steward's counter, where Mr. Paynter stood, waiting to be seated. Did the professor know Mr. Paynter?

The moment passed as quickly as it had come. Dr. Kovacs took a bite of his braised beef and pronounced it delicious.

At the girls' table, Nan picked up her sandwich. "Emily, if you want something to read, you can borrow one of my Nancy Drew books. I brought a bunch but I've read them all. I read really fast."

Emily was using a table knife to cut the crusts from her sandwich. "I've never heard of those books."

"You haven't?" Nan sounded scandalized. "Oh, Nancy Drew is the best. You have to start with *The Secret of the Old Clock*. That's the first one. You just have to read about Nancy. She's a girl detective. She has her own car and she solves crimes, with her friends Bess and George. She has a boyfriend, too. Ned Nickerson."

Emily wrinkled her nose. "Boyfriend? Ick."

"When girls get older they have boyfriends," Nan said. She lowered her voice. "I have one, but don't tell Mom."

"Is it that guy Fletcher?" Cathy demanded. "I saw him kiss you after the school play."

Nan shushed her younger sister, then all three of the girls burst out in giggles. Jill smiled. It was good to see Emily having fun, since she'd been such a shy little mouse when she'd boarded the train.

The snow stopped as the *California Zephyr* passed the Roller Dam, with its red-roofed outbuildings, which diverted water from the Colorado River to the Highline Canal, feeding the area's vineyards and orchards. Then everything outside the window darkened. The train had entered the Beaver Tail Tunnel. When it came out the other end, they were near DeBeque Canyon. The river was close to the tracks here, and the canyon was prone to rock slides.

When they'd finished lunch the waiter cleared their plates and asked if they'd like dessert. Dr. Kovacs declined and excused himself, heading back to his roomette in the Silver Palisade. The Finches decided to share a piece of pie.

Jill glanced at her watch. It was 12:42 P.M. The train was due into the small town of Rifle in twenty minutes. They would reach Glenwood Springs, the next station stop, at 1:35 P.M. After that she'd need to get ready for the party.

"No dessert for me," she said. "But I'll have coffee."

Chapter Fourteen

THE MIDDLE-AGED COUPLE, Mr. and Mrs. Kelsey, had boarded the train in Green River, Utah, traveling to Ottumwa, Iowa, for the holidays. Now Mr. Kelsey stood outside the doorway to compartment H, a distressed look on his face as he spoke to the conductor.

"We went back to the observation car, up to the Vista-Dome," Mr. Kelsey said. "After that, we had lunch in the dining car. Then we came back here to our compartment. Once we were inside, my wife noticed that her overnight case had been moved. She looked inside, and well, something is missing. It's a brooch, belonged to her grandmother. She's pretty upset about it."

"I am sorry, Mr. Kelsey," the conductor said. "We will do everything possible to locate your wife's brooch."

That lets out the children, Jill thought, watching the exchange. Even if the kids were collecting items for the scavenger hunt, jewelry is most definitely not on the list.

Mr. Kelsey was giving a description of the brooch to the conductor. "It's gold, and it's shaped like a basket, about two inches across, with flowers. The petals are rubies and sapphires. I told Edith to put it in her purse, but she had it wrapped in a hankie, stuck down in that case with her makeup. We've traveled on the *Zephyr* before, y'know, and this is the first time anything has turned up missing. I sure hope you can find it. It's got some monetary value, of course, but since it was her grandmother's, it's got more sentimental value to my wife."

"If you'll allow us to search the compartment," Mr. Gaskill said, "just to be sure the brooch hasn't fallen and rolled into some sort of hiding place."

Jill and the conductor searched the Kelseys' compartment, but there was no sign of the brooch. They left the unhappy Mrs. Kelsey sitting on the bench seat inside, her makeup case beside her, as she twisted the lace handkerchief in which the brooch had been concealed.

Outside in the corridor, Mr. Gaskill sighed. "People will get careless and leave their valuables in their rooms. It's human nature, I guess, trusting that things won't get taken."

"For the most part, they don't," Jill said.

Passengers felt safe while traveling in the enclosed atmosphere on the train. As the conductor said, human nature made them let their guard down, relax the vigilance that they might ordinarily use. People were inclined to be careless about their personal belongings. But the sleeping accommodations—roomettes, bedrooms, and compartments—locked only from the inside. So passengers were well-advised to keep valuables with them. But not everyone took such precautions.

Over his shoulder, Jill saw the worried look on Mr. Lovell's face. He quickly masked it, hiding his feelings. But she knew the porter was afraid he would be blamed for the theft, as Frank Nathan had been blamed earlier, when Mrs. Clive's cigarette case disappeared. It was unfortunate, but when things went missing on the train, suspicion often fell on members of the crew, particularly the Pullman porters, who were in and out of the passengers' compartments. And some passengers were quick to blame the Negro members of the crew. At least Mr. Kelsey hadn't directly accused Mr. Lovell, the way Mrs. Clive had Frank Nathan.

Things happened, she knew. In the two years Jill had been a Zephyrette, she knew that a waiter had been dismissed for pilfering food from the train's stores. And another member of the crew, a brakeman, had been fired for excessive drinking. But the porters she had worked with seemed to be hardworking and honest.

"It wasn't Mr. Lovell," the Pullman conductor said now. "I'll vouch for him, just like I vouch for Mr. Nathan. Never a hint of trouble from either man."

Mr. Gaskill looked perturbed. "I am aware of your concerns and I will take that into consideration. Now, one instance of theft, I might consider a member of the crew. But three—that gold pen yesterday and the case and brooch today? We definitely have a thief on board. A thief who waits until passengers leave their compartments to go to the diner, or up to the Domes or the lounges."

Mike Scolari had been listening to the exchange from the doorway of his compartment. "My grandfather may have seen something important," he said now.

"Then I'd like to speak with your grandfather," the conductor said.

Mike opened the door wider. Jill followed the conductor into the Scolaris' compartment. Jill had spoken to old Mr. Scolari several times during the journey. He was nearly bald, and what remained of his hair was snowy white. Lines and wrinkles furrowed his face. He sat on the bench seat, a small plaid blanket thrown over his legs. "Gramps, this is the conductor, Mr. Gaskill. And you've met Miss McLeod, the Zephyrette."

His brown eyes twinkled like those of a younger man. "Yes, I have met her. Just like you said, she's very pretty."

"Gramps," Mike said, a warning in his voice. "None of that now. This is serious. Tell the conductor what you told me, about that fellow coming into the compartment."

Mr. Scolari turned his gaze from Jill to Mr. Gaskill. "Mike and I had lunch here. I'm crippled up with this arthritis of mine, so I have trouble walking. Makes it hard to go to the diner. After we ate lunch and the porter collected our trays, Mike went back to the observation car to look at the scenery. I don't expect him to stay here with me all the time. If I need help I ring for the porter. And he's a good fellow, that porter."

Mr. Scolari stopped and cleared his throat. Then he continued. "Anyway, a few minutes after Mike left, a man opened the door and took a step in, like he was coming inside. Then he saw me, and backed out in a hurry. Mumbled something, saying he'd gotten the wrong compartment. After he shut the door, I heard him—or someone—open the door of the next room. I didn't think anything of it at the time. Guess anyone could open the door by mistake. Bet it happens all the time. But now, Mike tells me something's missing. That makes me wonder about that fellow I saw."

"It makes me wonder, too," the conductor said. "Can you describe the man?"

"Not very well," Mr. Scolari said with a shrug. "I was dozing. I get sleepy after I eat. And I saw him for just a few seconds. Let's see." He thought for a moment. "Younger than me, that's for sure. He was middle-aged, forties or fifties, maybe. Ordinary-looking clothes. A face you wouldn't pick out of a crowd, that's for sure. Oh, and he was losing his hair. Sorry I can't be more specific."

"Thank you, Mr. Scolari," Mr. Gaskill said. "If you think of anything else that might be helpful, please let us know."

Jill followed the conductor out of the compartment. "Is there anyone traveling in compartment G?" he asked.

Both Jill and Si Lovell shook their heads. Compartment G had been the Gunthers' compartment. They had left the train early that morning.

"That compartment's been empty since the passengers got off in Salt Lake City," the porter said. "It'll be empty till we get to Denver."

"So our thief went down the line of compartments, looking for one that was occupied—and empty," Mr. Gaskill said. "Once inside, he searched for something valuable. In this case, he found it. I wish the old man had given us a better description. Middle-aged, ordinary, losing his hair. That description could fit half the men on this train."

Mr. Gaskill looked at Mr. Alford, the Pullman conductor. "We'll have to keep a sharp eye out for anyone who looks like he's prowling around the compartments. Alert the other Pullman porters about the thefts. I'll speak with the dining car steward and the waiter in charge. All of us need to be on the lookout for anything suspicious."

As the conductor headed forward and the Pullman conductor went back to the other sleepers, Jill looked at her watch. They were due into Glenwood Springs soon. It was time for her next announcement. She went to the public address system in the diner and lifted the mike.

"We are now approaching Glenwood Springs, railroad gateway to the world-famed Glenwood Springs–Aspen winter and summer recreational area.

"Leaving Glenwood Springs, we will enter the western end of Glenwood Canyon of the Colorado River, the great beauty of which inspired the Vista-Dome car. It was here that Mr. C. H. Osborn, vice president of General Motors Corporation, first conceived the Vista-Dome idea. In commemoration of that event, a stone monument has been constructed across the river near the highway about midway through the canyon. The monument supports a stainless steel scale model of a *California Zephyr* Vista-Dome car. If you watch carefully, you may see the monument as we pass the station of Grizzly."

After she replaced the microphone, Jill walked back to the Silver Solarium. The observation car's lounge was full of passengers. She went up to the Vista-Dome, and found all four of the Finches in the front seats, Mr. and Mrs. Finch on one side, their two daughters, and Emily, on the other. Just behind the girls, the Bensons crowded into two seats with Billy and Chip sitting on their parents' laps.

"I'm really looking forward to the view as we go through Glenwood Canyon," Mr. Finch said. "The scenery is spectacular. Now that the snow has let up we should be able to see everything."

Ed Benson pointed as the train approached a bridge. The tracks crossed the river several times on this stretch. "Here we go, crossing the river again. Lots of ice on the banks, but that water in the middle is flowing fast."

"I'll bet it's cold," Billy said.

"Sure is, sport," his father said.

They were coming up on another snag, a dead tree. At the very top Jill saw a bald eagle. "Look, another eagle. We should see more in Glenwood Canyon and the canyons after that, Gore and Byers." As they went through the tiny community of New Castle, Jill pointed at a slope to the south of the tracks. "You see that mountain over there, that patch with no snow?"

"All the other mountains have snow," Nan said. "Why is that one bare?"

"It's called Burning Mountain," Jill said. "There's a coal seam fire that's been burning for over fifty years, under the surface. The soil is too hot for plants to grow, and in the winter, it's so hot it melts the snow."

In another ten minutes the *Zephyr* reached the outskirts of Glenwood Springs. Outside, the Colorado River roiled along on the north side of the tracks, making a channel between the ice that extended from the shoreline. Jill pointed to the south side of the tracks, where another river flowed swiftly from the slopes, rushing toward its confluence with the Colorado River. "That's the Roaring Fork River. It flows into the Colorado. We're coming up on the bridge now." The familiar *clickety-clack* of wheels on rails changed timbre as the observation car rumbled over the bridge. "Upstream, other rivers flow into the Roaring Fork. One is called the Crystal River and the other is the Fryingpan River."

"Fryingpan?" Nan laughed. "That's a funny name for a river."

"Good fishing in the Fryingpan, so I've heard," Mr. Finch said.

The *California Zephyr* slowed, then came to a stop at the Glenwood Springs station, on the south side of the river. Jill glanced at her watch. The train was right on schedule. On the platform, people were bundled against the winter cold. Beyond the station snow that had fallen earlier had been cleared and shoveled into piles.

The stately old Hotel Colorado was on the north side of the river. Built of brick and sandstone in the 1890s, the hotel's bulk stood out amid the smaller buildings surrounding it. Clouds of steam rose from the large hot springs pool in front of the hotel.

"The springs look inviting." Mrs. Finch smiled. "Let's come back and stay there."

"That's a splendid idea," her husband said. "Perhaps in the spring, when the girls are on a break from school."

"President Theodore Roosevelt stayed at that hotel," Jill told Emily. "Your teddy bear is named for Teddy Roosevelt."

Emily looked dubious. "My bear is called Benny."

"I know. But teddy bears are named that because of Teddy Roosevelt."

"Was he the same family as the other President Roosevelt?" Cathy asked.

"Franklin? Yes, they were cousins, several times removed," Jill said. "Mrs. Eleanor Roosevelt was Teddy Roosevelt's niece. Her father was his brother. What other presidents were related?"

"John Adams," Emily said, "and John Quincy Adams."

"That's right." Jill looked out the Vista-Dome and saw the conductor walking along the platform. She couldn't hear him call, "All aboard," but the station stop at Glenwood Springs was brief and the train would be on its way soon. A moment later the *Zephyr* began to move, picking up speed as it headed east. She pointed at the north side of the river. "Those are the Yampah Caves. They were used by the Ute Indians. I'm told that *yampah* means 'big medicine.'"

All around her the passengers were exclaiming over the canyon's beauty. Glenwood Canyon wound for fifteen miles, carved by the Colorado River through layers of Paleozoic limestones, sandstones, and shales, then Precambrian granites of coarse pink. Layers of limestone near the town of Glenwood Springs held lots of caves, many with hot springs. Here and there water seeped from the canyon walls, creating waterfalls that froze in the winter.

"The railroad was built through here in eighteen eighty-seven," Jill said. "It was narrow-gauge, and then it was converted to standard gauge. Here comes Jackson Tunnel. It's the longest of the tunnels here in Glenwood Canyon, just over thirteen hundred feet."

Jill stayed in the Vista-Dome until the eastbound *Zephyr* passed the westbound *Zephyr*, at a place called Grizzly Creek. The passengers waved at their counterparts in the Vista-Domes on the other train. In another five minutes they would reach the Shoshone Dam, which had been built in 1905.

Jill checked her watch. "They'll be done serving lunch in the dining car at two. As soon as everything is cleared away, the crew and I can get ready for the Christmas party. Excuse me, I have some things to get from my compartment."

As the train passed the dam and entered the Shoshone tunnel, Jill went down the stairs to the lower level of the Silver Solarium, then headed forward through the Silver Rapids and the

Silver Pine. When she reached the Silver Palisade, she stopped at bedroom A, tapping lightly on the closed door. No answer. Mrs. Tidsdale must be asleep. Best not to disturb her.

Jill continued forward past the roomettes, heading toward the vestibule. As she reached roomette two, Dr. Kovacs called to her. "Miss McLeod, I wonder if you would do me a favor?"

"Of course, I'd be happy to."

He rose from his seat and held out a sealed white business-sized envelope, addressed to himself at the physics department in LeConte Hall on the Berkeley campus. "Would you keep this for me, please? Just until we get to Denver. Then I will relieve you of it. I would be most grateful for the favor."

Jill hesitated. Then she took the envelope. "All right. I'll put it in my quarters right now."

"Thank you," the professor said. "I do appreciate it. I'm concerned about someone...well, I will explain later."

"It's something to do with Mrs. Cole, isn't it? Your ex-wife."

"Her name was Rivka Mehler when I met her." The professor's mouth quirked, as though the words tasted sour. "So now she's married again, to this man Cole. I take it they are traveling in one of the sleeper cars. Is it this one?"

Jill shook her head. "They're in the Silver Gull. That's the sleeper car between this one and the diner."

"We are both Jews who came to the United States in nineteen thirty-nine, before the war started in Europe," Dr. Kovacs said. "I'm Hungarian, from Budapest. She is from Czechoslovakia, a town called Cheb, near the German border, in an area known as the Sudetenland. You were a history major, so I think you must know about the Sudetenland."

"I do," Jill said. "Annexed to Nazi Germany in October of nineteen thirty-eight. Neville Chamberlain and 'peace in our time.'"

He nodded. "*Kristallnacht*—the Night of Broken Glass—happened just a few weeks later. The Nazis burned synagogues and destroyed Jewish businesses all over Germany. Rivka's father was a Socialist, she said. Socialists were targets of the Nazis, as well as Jews and Communists. She left Czechoslovakia, went to Poland

and Sweden, then to the United States. We met in New York City in 'forty-two, and married a short time later. A hasty marriage. It didn't last. She went with me to..." He stopped.

"Los Alamos," Jill finished. "Where you worked on the Manhattan Project."

"Yes. I reported to the Hill in 'forty-three. She arrived a few months later. She hated New Mexico, hated the isolation, the primitive conditions we lived in up there. She left late in 'forty-four and divorced me the following year. I have not seen her since she left Los Alamos, and that was eight years ago." He sighed. "Our relationship is long over. I was just surprised to see her on the train, with her new husband. And something else, another man."

"Mr. Paynter," Jill said. "You've seen him before. I could tell from the way you looked at him in the dining car. And I think you also know Mrs. Tidsdale."

"You don't miss much," the professor said.

"It comes with being a Zephyrette for nearly two years. It's taught me to read people and situations."

"This situation is complicated," Dr. Kovacs said. "I have written about it. That's what's in the envelope, that and some other things. If you will keep the envelope safe until we reach Denver, I will explain it all to you."

"You don't have to. It's your business." Jill tucked the envelope under her arm. She continued forward, with a brief nod to Frank Nathan, who was taking a few minutes' rest in his porter's seat. She went through the Silver Gull, then into the diner, now closed for lunch service. There was a flurry of activity as the waiters cleared tables. "I'm getting my things for the Christmas party," she told them. "I'll be right back, to help set up."

"Wait till you see the cake I baked, Miss McLeod," the chef said as she headed past the kitchen prep area. "It's almost too pretty to eat."

"Nothing's too pretty to eat," one of the waiters chimed in.

Jill laughed. "I'll be back in a minute."

She reached the Silver Hostel. Once inside her compartment, she set the professor's envelope down next to the Agatha Christie novel. She reached for the blue carpetbag she'd brought with her when she boarded the train in Oakland.

Emily darted into the compartment. "Is this where you sleep? It's awfully little."

"Yes, it is." Jill looked at the tiny space, which seemed crowded now, with herself and the nine-year-old girl.

Emily sat down on the bench seat and gave it an experimental bounce. "I want to help you get ready for the Christmas party."

Jill hefted the blue bag. "Okay, you can help me. We have lots of stockings to stuff." She opened the compartment door and stepped out to the passageway, stopping abruptly as she came face-to-face with Mike Scolari. "Hello. We're heading for the diner to get ready for the children's Christmas party. Come on, Emily."

The little girl stepped into the passageway, smoothing the sweater she wore over her plaid skirt.

"Let me help with that." Mike Scolari took the bag and peered inside.

"It's just a few things I picked up at Woolworth's," she said. "Christmas stockings and candy for the children's party."

"On your own dime? That's really nice of you." He rooted around in the bag. "Candy canes. Bit-O-Honey. Sky Bars. Necco Wafers. Hey, Hershey's Kisses. My favorite. Did you know there was a shortage of Hershey's Kisses during the war?"

"Yes, and I really missed them." Jill loved Hershey's Kisses, and the little chocolate candies had been in short supply during and just after the war. Rationing of raw materials during that time meant no aluminum foil for the wrappers. "If you'll help us stuff these stockings, I'll see that you get some Kisses."

He grinned. "Chocolate, or the other kind?"

Jill put on her best no-nonsense face. "Chocolate, Mr. Scolari."

"Well, I'll take whatever kisses I can get, Miss McLeod."

Emily tugged on Jill's sleeve. "Come on, let's go. We gotta get ready for the party."

Mike Scolari laughed. "Lead the way."

"I like Necco Wafers," Emily said as they walked to the diner. "So did my dad."

"My father loves them," Jill said. "He likes the lime green ones. What flavors do you like?"

"The yellow ones, lemon," Emily said. "I don't like the black ones, 'cause I don't like licorice."

"Brown for me, the chocolate," Mike Scolari said. "I'm a chocolate kind of a guy."

"I gathered that," Jill said.

In the diner, the waiters had the tables set for the party. On a table in the center of the diner was a two-layer cake frosted in snowy white, its top decorated with a Christmas tree drawn in green icing, with colored candy balls as ornaments and red frosting piped around the rim.

"It's beautiful," she told the chef. "You've outdone yourself."

"Vanilla," he said, "with a chocolate custard between the layers."

"Good." Jill smiled as Mike Scolari set the bag on the steward's counter. "We were just having a conversation about chocolate."

Jill wasn't sure how many children would be on the train this Christmas Eve. During her foray to Woolworth's, she bought fifty Christmas stockings. Whatever was left over could be used another time. Once on the train, she'd kept track of the children. Some had gotten off the train at earlier stops. Right now there were twenty-seven children on board, ranging in ages from infants to teenagers.

She pulled the stockings from the bag. Each stocking, made of red or green felt, was six inches deep, had a white cuff and was decorated with a Santa Claus, a Christmas tree, a snowman, or a wreath. Jill handed Emily a fistful of candy canes and directed the little girl to place one candy cane at each place setting.

"This canyon is beautiful," Mike said as he tucked a Bit-O-Honey bar into a stocking.

"I never tire of it." Jill glanced out the window of the dining car, as she picked up a handful of Hershey's Kisses.

"Have you ever stayed at the Hotel Colorado?" he asked.

"Once." Jill smiled at the memory. Her family took the train, one of the *Zephyr*'s precursors, to Glenwood Springs and they'd spent several days at the old resort hotel, soaking in the hot springs and exploring the town. "That was the summer of nineteen forty-one. We were living in Denver then. My father's a doctor, he was at St. Joseph Hospital. Then came Pearl Harbor. Dad joined the Navy. We stayed in Denver and lived with my grandmother."

"Where did your father serve during the war?"

"The South Pacific. He was on a carrier, the *Essex*."

"Then he saw action at Wake Island and Tarawa," Mike said. "I was on the *Intrepid*, at Leyte Gulf."

"Were you a flier?" Jill asked. He nodded. "I thought so, when I saw that leather jacket you were wearing. Did you go to Korea?"

He nodded again. Jill was just about to ask him more questions when Emily appeared, scowling at her. "You're supposed to put candy in stockings, not talk. The other kids will be here soon."

Jill looked at her watch. "Goodness, she's right. It's twenty minutes past two, and the party starts at half past."

The train had left Glenwood Canyon by now. It was nearing the little town of Dotsero, where the Eagle River flowed into the Colorado. The old mining town was also the southern end of the cutoff that had joined the Denver and Rio Grande Western line with the Moffat Route—so named because of its founder, David Moffat, the man for whom the tunnel under the Continental Divide had also been named.

Outside the window, snow blurred the landscape as the train followed the curve of the Colorado River. Jill, Emily, and Mike finished stuffing candy into the stockings, just as Billy and Chip Benson ran into the dining car, followed by their mother.

"They're so excited about the party I couldn't keep them still," Norma Benson said. "Here, give me a bunch of those stockings. I'll put them on the tables."

As the train emerged from the Sweetwater tunnel, more children streamed into the dining car. George Neeley was at the head of the group from the sleeper cars, while Tina Moreno came from the other direction, with a contingent of children from the chair cars. Soon the dining car rang with voices as the children and adults sang "Rudolph, the Red-Nosed Reindeer." Jill led a chorus of "Deck the Halls." Then four waiters harmonized like a barber-shop quartet as they sang of chestnuts and an open fire.

When Mr. Gaskill, the conductor, arrived, he boomed a question in his "All aboard" voice. "Does everyone know the words to 'Jingle Bells'? Good. Let's see if we can sing loud enough for the engineer to hear us."

The children obliged and the familiar Christmas song reverberated through the dining car. Then, with great ceremony, the chef cut the cake. The waiters distributed plates and glasses of milk. In between bites of cake, Mr. Gaskill let the children try on his conductor's hat.

"This is a lot of fun," Mike Scolari said. "It's really nice of you to put on a party for the kids, especially on your own hook."

Jill smiled. "I enjoy it, too. Since I'll be away from my family at Christmas, this helps me bring Christmas to the train. Look, it's snowing even harder." Jill gestured at the white flakes, spinning and dancing above the icy river.

Mike Scolari stood beside her and smiled. Then he sang in a light tenor, "I'm dreaming of a white Christmas."

Chapter Fifteen

THE LAST OF THE CAROLS had been sung, and the lovely Christmas cake had been reduced to a pile of crumbs on the big platter. Children and parents straggled out of the dining car, the youngsters carrying their stockings and candy. The waiters laughed and talked as they cleared up, carrying dishes and cutlery to the kitchen.

Jill and Mike Scolari gathered the remaining stockings and candy, tucking them into the carpetbag they'd set atop the steward's counter.

"The train's stopping," he said as the *Zephyr* slowed.

Jill looked at her watch. "Three-twelve, on schedule. This is Bond. We have an engine crew change here, getting a new engineer and fireman. We won't be here very long."

As Jill predicted, the train halted briefly, then got underway again. As the *Zephyr* picked up speed, three children appeared from the rear of the car, Tina Moreno, followed by Billy and Chip. They ran through the diner, sidestepping the waiters, and darted into the passageway alongside the kitchen and pantry, heading forward to the Silver Hostel and the chair cars.

Jill smiled. "Goodness. Wonder what that's all about?"

"I bet it's the scavenger hunt you told me about," he said. "They're going to find all the things on that list and beat the other team."

"Something tells me I shouldn't have proposed that scavenger hunt." Jill put the last of the candy into the bag. "I really appreciate your helping me with the party, Mr. Scolari."

"Call me Mike."

"Not on duty," Jill said. Though she wouldn't mind calling him Mike off duty.

"Ah, strictly business." He inclined his head. "All right, Miss McLeod. Is there a chance I can see you off duty? Say, after the holidays, when I get back to San Francisco?"

She nodded. "I think that's possible. I'm just across the bay, in Alameda."

"You know, *Oklahoma!* just opened at the Geary Theatre. I really want to see that. How about you?"

"I love musicals," Jill said. "And I would very much like to see *Oklahoma!*"

"Great. I'll get your phone number before I get off the train in Denver." He grinned as he picked up the bag. "So, we take these Christmas goodies back to your compartment?"

"Yes. Then I need to start making dinner reservations. It's quarter past three already."

Now other children boiled into the diner, coming from the rear of the train. Emily headed the group, flanked by Nan and Cathy, with George bringing up the rear. Emily stopped in front of Jill and looked up. "I can't find Tidsy. She's not on the train."

"Of course she's on the train. She must be in your bedroom. Or in the lounge." Then Jill paused, considering. If Mrs. Tidsdale had left her bedroom and gone to the lounge in the Silver Hostel, she would have to come through the dining car. Surely Jill would have seen her, even with all the children here for the party. Mrs. Tidsdale stood out in a crowd.

Emily shook her head. "She's not. We've looked in every car between here and the Silver Solarium."

Jill frowned. "What about the chair cars?"

"Tina and Billy and Chip are looking at the chair cars," George said.

So that was why the three children had rushed through the diner just moments ago. Now they were back. "No Tidsy, no Tidsy," Chip called.

"I climbed up to all the Vista-Domes," Billy said.

"I even looked in all the ladies' restrooms," Tina reported. "I didn't see her."

Emily put her hands on her hips. "We can't find her any-where."

"It's a mystery, like Sherlock Holmes," George added.

Little Chip Benson repeated his chant. "No Tidsy, no Tidsy."

"Hush up, Chip." Billy put a hand over his younger brother's mouth. All the children looked expectantly at Jill.

"Uh-oh," Mike Scolari said.

"Uh-oh, indeed." Jill's mind whirled. Mrs. Tidsdale had to be on the train. Before lunch she'd been in her usual spot in the lounge on the Silver Hostel, at that table near the bar, with her cigarettes and ashtray in front of her, a tumbler of Scotch close at hand. Then she and Emily had gone to the dining car with Jill. But suddenly Mrs. Tidsdale complained of a headache. She was going to take an aspirin and have a nap, she'd said as she left the dining car.

An unwelcome thought crept into Jill's mind. Mrs. Tidsdale had been flirting with Mr. Paynter, ever since they'd met the day before. What if the two of them were in his bedroom on the Silver Gull? It wouldn't be first time people had used the Pullman cars for assignations.

Jill drew a quick breath as another unwelcome thought occurred to her. What if the children were right and Mrs. Tidsdale wasn't aboard? What if the woman had stepped off the train during the brief stop at the Glenwood Springs station? What if she hadn't boarded again? It was tempting for passengers to walk over to the Hotel Denver, just beyond the station. It wouldn't be the first time a passenger left the platform during a short stop and got left behind. Jill had seen it happen before, at the longer Grand Junction stop and the crew change in Oroville.

"I'll look for her," Jill told the children. "I'm sure the conductor, the porters, and I can find her. We can look in places that you can't go. You kids go back to the Silver Solarium. And please don't tell anyone about Mrs. Tidsdale, not just yet."

"But we want to help look for her," George said.

"You've already done your part," Mike said. "I think we should do what Miss McLeod says. After all, she's the Zephyrette. She's a member of the train crew, and we passengers have to do what the train crew says. Let's all go back to the Silver Solarium and keep out of Miss McLeod's way. " The children grumbled, but they turned and headed for the sleepers.

"Thanks," Jill said. "I'd rather they didn't spread the news that Mrs. Tidsdale seems to be missing. After all, she may turn up."

"Right." Mike set down the bag. "I'll check on Gramps. Then I'll go back to the observation car and keep those kids occupied."

Jill put her hands to her temples. She was getting a headache herself. She'd like nothing better than to take some aspirin and spend fifteen minutes stretched out on the berth in her compartment. But she had to find Mrs. Tidsdale.

Jill looked at the dining car steward, Mr. Gridley, who'd been listening. "She didn't come through the diner during the party," he said. "She'd have passed right by the counter, and I've been here most of the time."

The waiter nearby, putting fresh white cloths on the tables, shook his head. "I haven't seen her, Miss McLeod, not since she left the diner during lunch. I'll ask the kitchen crew and the other waiters, but I agree with Mr. Gridley. She didn't come through the diner."

Jill left the bag behind the steward's counter and walked back to the sleeper section. In the Silver Palisade, she passed the roomettes and rounded the corner to the passageway outside the bedrooms. She knocked on the door of bedroom A. No answer. She looked up and saw Frank Nathan, walking toward her from the rear of the car.

"How was the Christmas party?" he asked.

"It went very well. The children enjoyed themselves. Mr. Nathan, when was the last time you saw Mrs. Tidsdale?"

He thought a moment. "Before we got to Glenwood. There were several folks heading up to the diner for lunch. Mrs. Tidsdale was coming from that direction. She stepped aside to let the other people pass, right near the door to my compartment. I said hello to her. She told me she had a headache and she was going to lie down."

"She's not answering the door." Jill rapped again. "Mrs. Tidsdale?" She turned the handle. The door wasn't locked. She opened it. Bedroom A was empty.

The porter shook his head. "She's not there. I didn't see her leave. Is there a problem?"

"I'm not sure." Jill retraced her steps forward. As she reached roomette 2, she saw the door was ajar. Professor Kovacs was inside, papers piled around him. He looked up, then he set his papers aside and stood, opening the roomette door wider.

"Hello, Miss McLeod. A lot of coming and going this afternoon. I gather there was a party for the children. I overheard some of them talking."

"Yes, there was. Professor, about Mrs. Tidsdale... You do know her."

He nodded. "Grace Tidsdale and I met in nineteen forty-one, before Pearl Harbor. I was at Georgetown University and she worked in a government office. She was a widow. Grace and I had a relationship. There was a time I thought of marrying her. But... it didn't happen. Then I met Rivka and married her. I went to Oak Ridge and then to Los Alamos."

There was more to the story, Jill was sure. Someday she hoped to hear it. But now the problem was more immediate. "Professor Kovacs, have you seen Mrs. Tidsdale this afternoon? In the past hour or so?"

The professor frowned. "Not since we were in the dining car, when she complained of a headache and left. She said she was going to lie down. She's not in her bedroom?"

"No, she isn't. Thank you, Dr. Kovacs."

Jill headed forward. In the diner, she grabbed the bag of Christmas stockings and candy she'd left behind the counter. The steward had polled the kitchen and dining car crew. None of the waiters or chefs had seen Mrs. Tidsdale come through the car. In the Silver Hostel, she stashed the bag in her compartment, then headed for the lounge to talk with the steward behind the bar, who was polishing glasses with a cloth. He hadn't seen Mrs. Tidsdale since she left the lounge right before lunch. Jill thanked him and continued forward, to the Silver Palace.

Jim Gaskill was in the conductor's office at the rear of the car, a cup of coffee on his desk, talking with the brakeman. Jill stood in the doorway. The office wasn't much bigger than her own compartment, and three people inside would make it very crowded indeed.

"Hello, Miss McLeod," Mr. Gaskill said. "Mr. Bradshaw and I were discussing the train orders we got in Bond. Same as before— wet weather, and watch for loose and falling rocks."

"Yes, sir, I imagine so, with all the snow we've had," Jill said.

"The Christmas party was a lot of fun," the conductor added. "I appreciate your putting that together, and I'm sure the children and their parents do, too."

"Yes, sir. I'm glad you enjoyed yourself. Mr. Gaskill, we may have a missing passenger."

The conductor frowned, the lines in his face deepening as Jill explained the situation. "Is it possible she left the train at Glenwood?"

"I don't know," Jill said. "We weren't on the ground long in Glenwood, we never are. I can't imagine why she'd get off the train during such a short stop. Mrs. Tidsdale has spent a great deal of time in the lounge, drinking. She was... Last night when she was leaving the lounge, about ten o'clock, she got turned around and headed forward, instead of back to the sleeper cars. She was singing. And weaving. She seemed to be quite intoxicated."

"Sounds like she's got a hollow leg," the brakeman said.

Jill nodded. "She does seem to drink constantly. She's also been flirting with one of the male passengers, Mr. Paynter. He's traveling on the Silver Gull, in bedroom A. I've seen them together several times in the lounge, most recently this morning after breakfast. And I believe she had a drink with another male passenger, a Mr. Washburn, in his bedroom. That's also the Silver Gull, bedroom J. There may be nothing to it, but I'm considering every possibility. If Mrs. Tidsdale didn't get off the train and she's not in her bedroom or in any of the common areas of the train, she may be in someone else's compartment."

"She drinks a lot and she has an eye for the gents? Not a good combination," Mr. Gaskill said. "I agree with your conclusions. She may be holed up in a compartment with one of those men.

Happens all the time on these trains, even if the man and the woman are married to someone else. If that's the case, I'll bet the porters have spotted something. We'll have to search the train. Please find the Pullman conductor, and have him meet us in the diner."

"Yes, sir." Jill walked back to the sleeper cars. She found Mr. Alford in the Silver Pine, and relayed Mr. Gaskill's message. Together they headed for the diner. Mr. Gaskill and the brakeman were already there. They stood at the counter with the dining car steward.

"We search the train," the conductor said, after briefing the others on the problem. He turned to the brakeman. "Mr. Bradshaw, head forward and relay that to the attendants in each of the chair cars. Check the baggage car, see if she might have gone up there, though I don't know why she would. But anything's possible."

The brakeman nodded and headed toward the front of the train. Mr. Gaskill turned to the Pullman conductor. "Mr. Alford, you're in charge of the sleeping cars. I understand Miss McLeod has already spoken with the porter in Mrs. Tidsdale's car. Please speak with the other porters. See if there's any chance Mrs. Tidsdale is...spending some time in another compartment or bedroom with another passenger. Miss McLeod, please come with me. We're going to do a walk-through of our own."

Jill followed the conductor and the chief porter to the sleeper section. In the Silver Gull, Si Lovell was at the open door of one of the linen lockers. He looked at the delegation and frowned, shutting the locker. Mr. Alford took him aside and the two men conferred.

"I did see Mrs. Tidsdale. I was delivering lunch to the Scolaris in compartment F." He indicated the door in the middle of the sleeper car. "Young Mr. Scolari asked for lunch to be delivered at a quarter past twelve. I fetched the tray from the kitchen and carried it back here. Stepped into the compartment with the tray and helped the young man get everything set up so he and his grandfather could eat. Anyway, it was when I was carrying that tray that I saw Mrs. Tidsdale come into the car."

"Coming from the diner?" the conductor asked.

Si Lovell shook his head and gestured to the door at the rear of the Silver Gull. "No, sir. She was coming forward from the sleeper cars."

Jill considered the timing. She, Mrs. Tidsdale, and Emily had gone to the diner. That was shortly after noon. It wasn't long after they'd arrived in the diner that Tidsy had begged off, saying she had a headache. She must have returned to the Silver Palisade, which was the next sleeper car to the rear of this one. Then she'd walked forward again, to this car, the Silver Gull. Why? To visit Mr. Paynter in bedroom A?

But Mr. Paynter had gone up to the Vista-Dome in the Silver Hostel. She'd seen him climb the stairs as she, Emily, and Mrs. Tidsdale had left the lounge, heading for the diner. Then Mr. Paynter had arrived in the diner as well. She'd seen him at the steward's counter, after she, Dr. Kovacs, and the Finches had been seated.

"Did you see her go into any of these compartments?" the conductor asked Mr. Lovell.

"Not then. I stepped into compartment F about the time I saw her enter the car. So I'm not sure if she walked on through or went into a compartment."

Mr. Gaskill mulled this over, then asked the question that Jill had on her lips. "You said 'not then.' Had you seen her go into a compartment on this car at another time?"

The porter sighed. "Yes, sir. Twice. Both times yesterday. I saw her go into that Mr. Washburn's bedroom, that's bedroom J. It was last night, before dinner. He's a fellow that brought a lot of liquor with him. He'd been bothering Miss McLeod a time or two."

"Is that true, Miss McLeod?" Mr. Gaskill scowled.

"Just a wolf, sir. I can handle that," Jill said. "Go on, Mr. Lovell. You saw Mrs. Tidsdale go into bedroom J."

"Yes, I did. Guess she had a drink with him, but she didn't stay. Short time later I saw her come out. And the other time I saw her go into bedroom A. That's where Mr. Paynter is staying."

"Thank you, Mr. Lovell," Mr. Gaskill said. "Well, nothing for it but to ask."

Bedroom J was near the end of the row of accommodations. Now the conductor led the way to the door. He rapped sharply.

Mr. Washburn had a bottle of bourbon in his hand when he opened the door. He looked past the conductor at Jill and grinned. "Hey, there, little lady, c'mon in. Bring your friends. We'll have a party."

"No, we will not have a party," Mr. Gaskill said.

"What? Why not? Got some really good bourbon here." Mr. Washburn raised the bottle, weaving back and forth in the doorway.

"Are you alone, Mr. Washburn?" The conductor's question was a formality. Even Jill, peering past Mr. Washburn, could see that there was no one else in the bedroom.

"Was until now." Mr. Washburn reeled as the train headed into a curve. He grabbed the door jamb to steady himself. "Nobody here but us chickens."

"I understand a passenger named Mrs. Tidsdale came to your compartment last night before dinner and had a drink with you."

"Oh, yeah." Mr. Washburn leered. "That little blonde is a hot number, I can tell you that. Had a couple belts of bourbon. Then she left. Said somethin' about had to look after some kid. But I got my suspicions. She's spreadin' it around, with some other guy."

Mr. Gaskill was looking at Mr. Washburn as though the man had three heads. Jill tightened her lips at Mr. Washburn's implication. But wasn't that what she'd been thinking? That Mrs. Tidsdale was in a man's compartment? Now that she thought about it, maybe Mr. Washburn had seen something.

"What makes you say that?" she asked.

"Trying to get into that other bedroom, wasn't she?" Mr. Washburn took another swig from his bourbon. "Saw her. She was trying the door handle."

"Which compartment?" the conductor asked.

"The one at the end."

"Which end?" There was a hint of exasperation in Mr. Gaskill's voice.

Mr. Washburn stuck his head through the doorway and looked down the corridor, first to the left, then to the right. "Was it that one, or that one? Not sure. Maybe it wasn't even the end. Maybe it was the one next to it. What the hell does it matter? Say, are we done with the questions now? Gonna rest my eyes a little bit before dinner." Mr. Washburn didn't wait for a reply. He backed into his bedroom and shut the door.

The conductor shook his head. "Not a very reliable witness. The man is three sheets to the wind." He looked at the bedroom next to Mr. Washburn's quarters, at the very end of the row. "Is there anyone traveling in bedroom K?"

"That bedroom is empty, sir," the porter said. "The passenger got off in Helper."

"That leaves bedroom A at the other end of the corridor. And we know Mr. Paynter is in bedroom A. Who's traveling in compartment B, next to Mr. Paynter?"

"A married couple, Mr. and Mrs. Cole," the porter said. "And bedroom C was a Mrs. Casey, but she got off in Green River, Utah. Can't think why Mrs. Tidsdale would try to open either one of those doors, if she did. She must have reached out to steady herself."

"You're probably right. That leaves Mr. Paynter." Jill followed the conductor as Mr. Gaskill walked to the other end of the corridor. The conductor knocked on the door of bedroom A. Jill heard Mr. Paynter's voice. "Who is it?"

"The conductor. Open the door, please."

The door opened and Mr. Paynter stared out at Jill and Mr. Gaskill. "Yes?"

"Mr. Paynter, we're looking for a passenger named Mrs. Tidsdale," the conductor said. "It's come to my attention that you and she have spent some time together during the trip. I understand she came to your quarters for a drink last night. And the two of you were together in the lounge this morning."

Mr. Paynter looked over Gaskill's shoulder, straight at Jill, but she couldn't read the expression in his dark eyes. "Yes. Mrs. Tidsdale and I have had several drinks together since the train left Oakland."

"When was the last time you saw her?"

Mr. Paynter shrugged. "This morning, in the lounge. It was after breakfast. I didn't note the time. Why do you ask?"

"We're tracing Mrs. Tidsdale's movements," Mr. Gaskill said. "She seems to be missing. It's been suggested—"

"I know what you're suggesting." Mr. Paynter addressed his words to the conductor, but he was looking at Jill. "Just because I've had a few drinks with the woman doesn't mean she's here in my bedroom. She did come here last night for a nightcap, but she didn't stay. The woman's attractive, and I wouldn't mind getting to know her better. But it didn't work out that way. That kid she's traveling with puts a damper on that sort of thing. But if it will make you and Miss McLeod feel better, go ahead, have a look."

Mr. Paynter stepped back and beckoned for the conductor to enter the bedroom. Mr. Gaskill looked inside. "Thank you, Mr. Paynter. Sorry to disturb you."

Mr. Paynter smiled, barely moving his lips. Then he shut the door.

"Now what?" The Pullman conductor asked as they moved toward the rear of the car. "We can't search every bedroom and compartment."

"We look through the other cars," Mr. Gaskill said. "Check all the common areas. Talk to the train crew and the porters."

The conductor led the way into the vestibule of the Silver Palisade, where they spoke with Frank Nathan in his compartment at the end of the aisle of roomettes. They looked at bedroom A, which was usually occupied by Mrs. Tidsdale and Emily.

The conductor had just stepped out of bedroom A when the door to bedroom D opened and Mrs. Clive came out. "You're not the same conductor."

"No, ma'am, that was Mr. Wilson. I'm Mr. Gaskill. I boarded in Grand Junction."

"I'm Mrs. Clive. My gold cigarette case has been stolen." She glared at Frank Nathan. "I'm sure this porter took it. What are you going to do about it?"

Mr. Gaskill inclined his head. "I'm aware of the situation, Mrs. Clive. Mr. Wilson, the conductor you spoke with earlier, gave me a full report before he left the train. Rest assured that we're doing everything we can to locate your property."

Mrs. Clive sniffed. "Well, it's not enough. I want my cigarette case. I expect the matter to be dealt with fully before we get to

Denver." She swept past them and walked forward, in the direction of the lounge.

"Sir, I didn't take that case," Frank Nathan said.

"Let's deal with one crisis at a time." Mr. Gaskill gestured toward the rear of the train. "I want to check the other sleepers, and the Silver Solarium."

The porters in the Silver Pine and Silver Rapids hadn't seen Mrs. Tidsdale. They entered the Silver Solarium. As they passed the bedrooms, Jill heard the typewriter behind the closed door of bedroom C, Miss Stafford working on her book. In the buffet, the Finches and Constanzas were playing bridge. Mr. Finch hailed the conductor, asking questions about their location. Mr. Alford moved to the bar and took the porter aside.

Jill continued back to the lounge. All the seats were full of passengers. She climbed up to the Vista-Dome, following the sound of Mike Scolari's voice. He was at the front of the car, with the children.

"Look at those deer tracks on the river bank." He pointed, then he glanced up and saw Jill, an inquiring look on his face. She shook her head. Then she walked down the stairs, speaking briefly to the adults in the observation car, trying not to let on that there was a problem.

When they returned to the diner, the brakeman was standing with the steward at the counter. "No sign of her," he told the conductor. "If she's on this train, it's not in the baggage car or any of the chair cars."

"She doesn't seem to be in any of the Pullmans either," the conductor said.

"What do we do now?" Jill asked.

"We—" Mr. Gaskill broke off as Alvah Webb entered the diner, coming from the passageway alongside the kitchen and pantry.

"Is something wrong, Miss McLeod? I seen the porter in my car and that brakeman looking like they was searching for someone."

"We're looking for Mrs. Tidsdale," Jill said. "The woman you saw last night in the Silver Hostel. Have you seen her?"

"I saw her in that lounge car this morning, but not since."

Jill made the introductions. "This is Mr. Webb. He's the passenger I told you about, the one who helped me get Mrs. Tidsdale turned around last night when she was…"

"Drunk," the conductor finished.

"Beg your pardon," Alvah Webb said, "but there's something I need to say about Mrs. Tidsdale. She was play-acting."

"What do you mean?" Mr. Gaskill asked.

"I mean she was play-acting at being drunk."

The crew members stared at Mr. Webb.

"She smelled of liquor when she got on the train in Oakland," Jill said. "For most of the trip she's been in the lounge, drinking. The steward can back me up on that."

"I'm an alcoholic," Mr. Webb said. "Recovering, as we say. I know drinkers, because I am one. And that Mrs. Tidsdale, she's not a drinker. Last night she was play-acting."

"But why would she do that?" Jill asked. Now she doubted her own eyes. Mrs. Tidsdale had certainly spent most of the trip in the lounge with a glass of Scotch in front of her. But had she really consumed that much?

Mr. Webb shook his head. "I don't know. But she must have a reason for wanting people to think she's a drinker."

The conductor frowned. "Whether she's a drinker or not, the woman is missing. She doesn't seem to be aboard the train. I can only conclude that she got off in Glenwood Springs and didn't get back on. There's nothing else we can do except send a wire back to the station in Glenwood Springs, to see if Mrs. Tidsdale has turned up at the station there."

He consulted his pocket watch, then leaned over and looked out the window, where the Colorado River ran swift and cold between icy banks. They were coming up on a milepost, one of the markers that was placed every mile along the tracks.

"We're almost to State Bridge," Mr. Gaskill said. "Then we'll be heading into Gore Canyon, and Byers Canyon after that. Once we get out of the canyons, we can stop at Granby and send a message."

Chapter Sixteen

STATE BRIDGE CONSISTED of a lodge with a few rental cabins on the north side of the tracks. Mount Yarmony loomed in the distance. The bridge that gave the place its name crossed the Colorado River, the road heading south. This had been a stagecoach stop in the 1890s, before the railroad came through here in 1905. The lodge attracted hunters, now as well as then. Among them was Theodore Roosevelt, who'd stayed in cabin number three back in the days before he was president. During Prohibition the lodge lured other sorts of patrons, those in search of illegal liquor. Its remote location was far from the reach of law enforcement, making it easy for the liquor trade and other vices to flourish.

Now the place looked deserted, frozen in time on this late December afternoon. Then Jill spotted smoke coming from the lodge's chimney.

"What is this place?" Ed Benson asked as the *Zephyr* passed the lodge. He and his wife were seated on one of the rear-facing settees at the back of the Silver Solarium. Billy was standing at the curved fish-tail end of the car, looking out at the snowy landscape, while Chip dozed on his mother's lap.

"It's called State Bridge," Jill said. "It used to be a speakeasy."

Mr. Benson smiled. "A long way for a fellow to come for a drink."

"It was a long way out for the sheriff, too," Jill said. "I guess that's why it was a successful speakeasy."

Jill opened the dinner reservation binder. If nothing else, she could take refuge in her daily routine. The Christmas party and the search for Mrs. Tidsdale had put her behind, and it was less than an hour until the first seating for the Chef's Early Dinner. She'd have to speed through the cars to make sure the reservations were completed by then. She asked the Bensons about their dinner plans.

Mrs. Benson smoothed Chip's dark hair as the little boy stirred on her lap and woke. "We get into Denver at seven. The boys will be too hungry if we wait until then. We'd better have the early dinner at five like we did last night."

Jill filled out the reservation card and handed it to the Bensons. "Come on, sport," Mr. Benson said. "Time to go back to our room." He stood and took Chip's hand.

"Daddy, I found a treasure," Chip said.

"Sure you did, sport," his father said.

"But I didn't take anything," Chip said. "I'm a good boy."

"Yes, you are a good boy. Especially when you're asleep." He grinned at his wife and walked forward through the lounge, heading for the sleeper cars.

"He must mean the scavenger hunt," Mrs. Benson said, her arm around Billy's shoulder.

"He's been calling it a treasure hunt," Billy said. "Say, Miss McLeod, when are we gonna find out who wins the scavenger hunt?"

"We'll do that after I finish making dinner reservations," Jill said.

The Bensons left, and Jill made reservations for the other passengers in the lounge. The Finches and the Constanzas were still playing bridge. "I think we'd better have an early dinner, too," Mrs. Finch said, "since we're getting off in Denver. Five o'clock?" She looked at her husband and he nodded. Jill filled out a reservation card and gave it to Mrs. Finch.

"I shall miss our bridge games," Mr. Constanza said. "It's been a pleasure traveling with you."

"Where are we now?" Mrs. Constanza asked Jill after she'd made an eight o'clock reservation for the opera singer and his wife. "It's so beautiful, with all the snow and the ice on the river."

"We just passed State Bridge and Yarmony." Jill looked at her watch. "In about twenty minutes we should be near a place called

Radium, and then we go into Gore Canyon, which is very beautiful. I recommend that you go up to the Vista-Dome. You should be able to see most of the canyon before the sun goes down. This late in December, that will be about a quarter to five."

Mike Scolari greeted her at the top of the stairs leading to the Vista-Dome. "No sign of Mrs. Tidsdale?"

"No. In the meantime, I'm making dinner reservations. You're getting off in Denver. Did you want something earlier, for you and your grandfather?"

"I'll have the porter bring some food around five-thirty. I'm heading back to our compartment. I seem to have reached my limits for entertaining kids. George left a while back and the girls are looking at the scenery."

He headed down the stairs. Jill went to the front of the Vista-Dome, where Emily was crowded into the front seat with Nan and Cathy.

"Did you find Tidsy?" Emily asked, jumping to her feet. When Jill shook her head, Emily's eyes filled with tears. "What if something awful happened to her, like what happened to my daddy? I thought she was kind of strange at first, but I got used to her. And I like her. What are we going to do? About me? Tidsy was supposed to make sure I get to Denver all right."

Jill set down the binder, knelt, and put her arms around Emily. She hugged the little girl close, then leaned back and looked at Emily's tear-stained face. "I don't know what's happened to Mrs. Tidsdale, but we'll find out. And I'll make sure you get to Denver all right. We get into Union Station at seven o'clock. That's just a few hours. I'll bet your grandma and your Uncle Robert will be there to meet you. In the meantime, I'm really behind my schedule. Will you help me make dinner reservations? Let's do that, and then we'll have dinner in the diner."

Emily brushed the tears from her eyes. "Okay. It's those cards, right? Different colors for different times?"

"That's right." Jill picked up the binder. "On the second day out the colors are different for the Chef's Early Dinner, light blue for four-fifteen and yellow for five. For the other times, the colors are the same, red for six o'clock, white for seven o'clock, and blue for eight o'clock."

A man sitting nearby smiled and said, "We'll take a white card, then, for seven o'clock."

"Certainly, sir." Jill filled out the card. Then she and Emily went down the stairs. They left the observation car, walking forward through the Silver Rapids and Silver Pine. Emily insisted on holding the binder as they made their way along the aisles of the sleeper cars, while Jill talked with passengers and distributed the cards. There were fewer reservations for this second night on the train, because so many of the passengers were getting off in Denver.

When they reached the Silver Palisade, Frank Nathan was near the vestibule, at the door of the clean linen locker. He smiled as he shut the door. "Have you got an assistant?"

"Yes, Emily's helping me."

Jill and Emily rounded the corner. Mike Scolari was at the doorway of bedroom F, talking with Ed Benson, who was showing off his camera. "I got this Nikon earlier this year and I really like it."

"I was admiring the camera when you were back in the observation car," Mike said, hefting the camera. "Thanks for letting me take a look at it. My camera is a Leica but it's pretty old." He smiled at Jill and Emily. "Dinner reservation time."

"That's right." Jill glanced down at Emily. "I've already made a reservation for the Bensons. The next bedroom is D. That's Mrs. Clive."

Emily shifted the binder from one arm to the other. "Is she that crabby lady who's been fussing at Billy and Chip?"

Crabby, indeed, Jill thought, agreeing with Emily's characterization.

"Crabby lady is right," Ed Benson said with a sigh. "She's been complaining about my boys since she got on the train. I think she went to the lounge. Haven't seen her come back."

Jill tapped on the door, but there was no answer. Mrs. Clive had not returned from the lounge. Bedroom C was vacant for now, since Mrs. Tatum left the train in Grand Junction. It was likely another passenger would be traveling in that room once the train left Denver. Jill knocked on the door of bedroom B.

"Oh, sure, I'll take a six o'clock reservation," Mrs. Loomis said when she opened the door. Jill let Emily fill out the red card.

Frank walked past them, heading for the front of the car, then he stopped as Norma Benson called to him. "I'm afraid Billy spilled something. We need some clean towels."

"Yes, ma'am, I'll get those for you." Frank retraced his steps to the clean linen locker at the rear of the car.

Jill and Emily rounded the corner at bedroom A, heading into the aisle between the roomettes. Jill tapped on the door of number 10, dreading the response from the unpleasant Mr. Smith. "Did you want a dinner reservation, sir?" she asked when he opened the door.

"God damn it..." he began.

"You shouldn't say bad words like that," Emily said. She crowded closer and looked past Mr. Smith into his roomette. "You're messy, too. You have a lot of stuff in there."

"Mind your own business, you little brat." He glared down at her and shut the door with a bang, before Jill could see the mess that Emily was talking about.

Mrs. Barlow appeared in the doorway of roomette 9. "That nasty man. Doesn't have a pleasant word to say to anyone, just swears or calls the porter names. I just can't abide rude people. And he's so odd, holed up in that roomette, or skulking around the corridors. Are you making dinner reservations, dear? Good, I'm famished. You wouldn't think so, with the lunch I had. But traveling on trains makes me hungry. I think I'll take an early reservation tonight, at six o'clock. I'm getting off the train later this evening, you know, in Akron, Colorado."

"Yes, Mrs. Barlow, I remember. You're spending Christmas with your son and his family. So let's make a six o'clock reservation, Emily." The little girl pulled a red card from the binder and Jill filled it out, handing it to Mrs. Barlow.

"Thank you, dear." Mrs. Barlow smiled. "You'll make a fine Zephyrette some day."

"Maybe I will be a Zephyrette," Emily said. "I like riding on trains."

They moved on to the next roomette, which was occupied by a middle-aged man who'd boarded the train in Helper, Utah. While Emily asked him if he'd like to make a dinner reservation, Jill thought back to what Mrs. Barlow had said about Mr. Smith.

Ever since he'd boarded the train in Sacramento, he'd stayed mostly in his roomette. But not always. He'd moved around the train as well.

Jill had seen Mr. Smith on the Silver Gull that morning, after breakfast, when Si Lovell had bumped into the man and Mr. Smith had turned on him, swearing and calling him names. At the time Jill assumed that Mr. Smith was returning from breakfast. And Mr. Smith could fit the description of the man who'd supposedly entered the Scolaris' compartment by mistake.

There had been three thefts aboard the train—three that they knew of—all on different sleeper cars, items taken while people were in the diner, lounge, or observation car. What if Mr. Smith...?

Emily tugged on Jill's sleeve, interrupting her speculation about the thief. "Miss McLeod, we need a red card, for a six o'clock reservation."

Jill filled out the card and gave it to the man. Then they continued down the aisle. They worked their way to the end of the aisle. Roomette 1 was empty, the passenger having left the train in Glenwood Springs. Jill knocked on the door of number 2, Dr. Kovacs's roomette. There was no answer. She tapped again.

"I guess he's not there," Emily said.

"Maybe he's gone forward to the lounge," Jill said. "We didn't run into him walking back to the observation car."

The train suddenly swayed as it moved into a curve and the pocket door to roomette 2 slid open. It hadn't been closed all the way. Jill reached for the handle so she could shut the door. Then she saw Dr. Kovacs slumped in the seat, his head tilted toward the window. The papers that were usually on the seat next to the professor were strewn on the floor. His glasses were on top of them.

"The professor's here after all. He's napping." Jill reached for his glasses, picking them up by one of the earpieces. "I'll just leave these glasses on the seat. We wouldn't want the professor to step on them when he wakes up."

The train came out of the curve as Jill set the glasses on the seat. Then she stared. The professor's head had shifted with the movement of the train. His eyes were open. He wasn't asleep. He was... No, that couldn't be.

Chapter Seventeen

JILL STEPPED INTO THE roomette and reached for Laszlo Kovacs's hand. It was cold and she could not find a pulse. The professor was dead.

She fought down shock and tried to be calm and professional. The professor could have had a heart attack. Or could it be something else? She moved closer, looking for any signs of injury. Then, on the front of his shirt, she saw blood staining the area around a small tear. Blood, and right above the heart.

He's been stabbed, she thought. She tried and failed to banish the image of a knife plunging into his chest. Dr. Kovacs had been murdered.

Emily stood in the doorway. "Is something wrong with the professor? Let me see."

Jill straightened and blocked the door, taking the binder from Emily. "No! Go find Frank. He's back in Billy's bedroom. Go as fast you can."

Emily darted down the passageway. Jill took a deep breath, trying to slow the rapid beating of her heart. She discarded the dinner reservation binder on the seat in the empty roomette. Then Frank Nathan rounded the corner, followed by Ed Benson and Mike Scolari. They hurried toward her.

"Where's Emily?"

"With Norma and the boys," Ed Benson said.

"Emily says something's wrong with Dr. Kovacs," Frank said.

"He's dead," Jill said, keeping her voice low.

"Heart attack?" Mike asked.

Jill shook her head. "I think he's been murdered. There's blood on his shirt. Go find the conductor."

"Good Lord." Frank stared inside the roomette, then he spun around and headed forward.

Ed Benson stepped into the compartment, knelt, and peered over for a close look at the professor's body. "You're right. He's been stabbed in the heart. We've got to secure the scene and take pictures. I'll get my camera." He backed out into the passageway and Jill shut the door of roomette 2.

"It's secured for now. As for anything else, we wait for the conductor. He's like the captain of the ship. He gives the orders. But yes, get your camera. I'm sure he'll want pictures."

"Are you okay?" Mike asked as Ed Benson headed back to his quarters.

Jill nodded. She had succeeded in slowing her breathing. "It's just such a shock. But I'll be all right. Oh, Mike, he was such a nice man."

He reached for her hand and squeezed it. She squeezed his, glad he was there. They stood there for a moment. Then Ed Benson returned with his camera, followed soon after by Mr. Gaskill and Frank Nathan.

The conductor opened the door to roomette 2 and stood looking down at the professor's body. "Well, it never rains but it pours. First a thief. Then a missing passenger. Now a murder. And I thought this was going to be a nice, quiet holiday run."

Mr. Gaskill backed out of the roomette and turned to Ed Benson, who was standing nearby with his camera. "You, sir, with the camera, I'm sure we will need some pictures for evidence. Though I don't know a damn thing about investigating a crime."

Mr. Benson took the cap off the camera lens. "I do. I'm an investigator. I work in insurance now, checking out claims. During the war I was an MP, military police. I did a lot of investigative work then."

"Ever investigate any murders?"

"No, sir. Some unexplained deaths, but not murders. I know we should leave the body where it is and photograph it to preserve visual evidence."

"Sounds like you're the closest thing we have to a detective," the conductor said. "Go ahead and photograph the body and the roomette. Once you're finished with your picture-taking, we'll shut the door and leave it until we get to the next town."

Jill had moved out of the way into the vacant roomette, number 1, across the hall. The conductor joined her as Mr. Benson went into roomette 2 and began taking photographs, the camera flashing rapidly as he moved in close for shots.

"I'd better check on Gramps," Mike said. "I'll talk with you later." He headed forward, toward the Silver Gull. Just then a family from the Silver Pine came through the car and stopped, curious. The conductor stepped into the passageway and shut the door to roomette 2. He spoke with the passengers and they continued forward. Jill saw a light blue card in the man's hand and realized the family was heading for the diner.

Jill looked at her watch. It was ten past four. The *California Zephyr* had entered Gore Canyon, with its beautiful rugged scenery, remote and forbidding, too, in its winter isolation. The train moved slowly along the sinuous curve of the Colorado River, which had narrowed as they traveled farther upstream. Right now they were close to the river, white water rushing between ice-clad boulders, pines marching up the steep slopes on the other side, a landscape of white, gray, and dark green.

"When was the last time you saw Dr. Kovacs alive?" the conductor asked as he returned to roomette 1.

Jill turned from the window. "It was when we were looking for Mrs. Tidsdale. He knew her, you see, during the war. I gather from what he told me that they had a romantic relationship. He was very concerned to hear that she's missing. There's something else you should know. Mrs. Cole, traveling in compartment B on the Silver Gull, she's Dr. Kovacs's ex-wife."

"Well, that's certainly interesting. Did Dr. Kovacs tell you anything about Mrs. Cole that might be important?"

"We talked right after lunch, when I was heading for my compartment to get the bag of stockings and candy for the Christmas party. Dr. Kovacs told me about his marriage to Mrs. Cole. They were both refugees who came to the United States just before the war. They divorced toward the end of the war."

"And this professor, where did he teach?" the conductor asked.

"At the University of California in Berkeley," Jill said. "That's where I met him, at a talk he gave when I was an undergraduate. Dr. Kovacs was a physicist. During the war he worked on the Manhattan Project, at Oak Ridge, Tennessee, and then Los Alamos, New Mexico."

"The atomic bomb." Mr. Gaskill considered this. "Interesting, but I'm not sure how it relates to this murder. It may just be a coincidence that the Coles are on the train at the same time as Dr. Kovacs."

The door to roomette 2 opened and Mr. Benson came out. "I'm finished with the pictures."

"Good." The conductor turned to Frank Nathan, who had moved out of the way, to his small porter's compartment next to roomette 2. "Stay here and keep an eye on that roomette. Don't let anyone go inside."

"Yes, sir," the porter said.

"I was telling Mr. Gaskill about Los Alamos," Jill said. "The Bensons were there, too."

"That's where I was in the MPs," Ed Benson said. "My wife was a WAC, driving in the motor pool. We both remember the professor but he didn't remember us. I'd seen his wife, too, that redhead who's Mrs. Cole now. My wife is sure she's seen Mr. Cole before, at Los Alamos. But Miss McLeod here says she overheard him say he'd never been to New Mexico. Maybe Norma can jog her memory, figure out where she's seen that guy before."

"New Mexico keeps cropping up," Mr. Gaskill said. "Can you recall anything else that might be important?"

Jill thought for a moment as the train entered one of the many tunnels in Gore Canyon. After a few seconds of darkness, the *Zephyr* emerged into the waning light. Dusk came quickly in the canyon.

"Dr. Kovacs knew Mr. Paynter, the man traveling in bedroom A on the Silver Gull," Jill said. "Or at least he'd seen him before. When Mr. Paynter came into the diner during lunch, the professor seemed troubled at the sight of him. When I talked with the professor after lunch, he admitted that he'd seen Mr. Paynter somewhere before. And he..." She stopped, remembering the rest of the conversation. "Dr. Kovacs gave me an envelope. He asked me to keep it until we got to Denver. He didn't say what was in it, just that he'd written down some things and he'd explain when we got to Denver."

"Where's the envelope now?" the conductor said.

"In my compartment. I left it there when I got the bag of things for the party."

"I want to take a look at it." Mr. Gaskill turned to Mr. Benson. "Please ask your wife to think hard about Mr. Cole and where she's seen him."

Ed Benson nodded and turned, heading back toward the Bensons' bedrooms at the rear of the car. The conductor and Jill walked forward, through the Silver Gull and the dining car, where the first seating was underway. A family from the chair cars was there, talking with Mr. Gridley, the steward.

"The Zephyrette didn't come around and make reservations," the man said.

"I'm so sorry," Jill said. "We've had a delay and I didn't get to the chair cars."

"Just seat people as they come in, whether they have a reservation or not," the conductor told the steward. He led the way down the passage that ran alongside the kitchen and they went through the vestibule to the Silver Hostel.

Jill opened the door to her compartment and stepped inside the narrow space. Where had she put the envelope? She'd tossed it onto the bench seat, next to the Agatha Christie novel, and turned away, intent on getting the bag of candy and stockings for the Christmas party. The book was there, on the orange upholstery, just below the window. But she didn't see the envelope. Jill picked up the book. Had she tucked the envelope inside the book? No, it wasn't there. She stuck her hand down in the spaces at the back and sides of the seat.

The she straightened, and turned to face the conductor, who stood in the doorway. "It's not here."

"Step outside and let me take a look," Mr. Gaskill said. Jill complied. The compartment wasn't big enough for both of them. She watched as the conductor knelt, then leaned over, running his hands under the seat. Then he got to his feet, brushing off his trousers. "Nothing under there except lint. Are you sure you brought the envelope to your compartment?"

"Yes, I did. I put it on the seat and—"

She stopped as a man and a woman with a little boy came down the corridor, heading for the dining car. "We don't have a reservation for dinner," the man said. "I thought you would come through the cars and give us a reservation card."

"I'm sorry, I was delayed," Jill said. "The dining car steward is aware of the situation. He'll seat you."

After the passengers departed, the conductor stepped out of Jill's compartment. "Let's go to my office. We can continue this conversation in private."

Jill followed the conductor to the Silver Palace. Mr. Gaskill opened the door to the conductor's office at the rear of the car. Once they were inside, he shut the door. "Now tell me again what happened when Dr. Kovacs gave you the envelope."

Jill played the scene over in her mind. "I set the envelope on the seat, near the book. Then I took the bag down and... Emily Charlton came in. She's the little girl Mrs. Tidsdale is escorting to Denver. She said she wanted to help me get ready for the Christmas party. So I took the bag and carried it..."

She stopped and thought for a moment. "Emily sat down on the seat. She was bouncing up and down. Then just as I left, I ran into Mr. Scolari, the man who's traveling with his grandfather on the Silver Gull. He offered to help with the party. Then Emily came out of the compartment and the three of us went to the dining car."

Now Jill frowned and looked at the conductor. "Emily could have taken the envelope. I wasn't looking at her while I talked with Mr. Scolari. My back was to the compartment. She could have, because of the scavenger hunt."

"Where is she?" he asked.

"She was with me when I found the professor, helping me make dinner reservations. She's with the Bensons now."

"Let's talk with her." The conductor opened the office door as the train moved into a curve. Then the *Zephyr*'s whistle blew, a succession of short, repeated bursts. That was the warning signal for an emergency, or to alert people or livestock on the tracks. The engineer was stopping the train. Jill felt the *bump, bump, bump* as the air brakes began to engage in each car ahead of them.

"What the hell?" the conductor said, leaning toward the small window of his office.

Something heavy hit the roof of the train. The loud bang was followed by more thumps, some louder than the others. Jill heard someone screaming in the passenger car as the train slowed and finally came to a stop.

"Rock slide," the conductor said.

Chapter Eighteen ————————

THE BOULDER was about the size of a grand piano. It had been pushed along the rails by the impact of the lead locomotive. Now the huge rock lay in the middle of the tracks, inches from the front of the engine. Jill shivered in the open door of the vestibule. She was in the first chair car, the Silver Pony, looking out at the boulder, which was visible from here because of the curve of the tracks. Other rocks, smaller in size, lay around the boulder, and beside the train, all the way back to the Silver Solarium at the end. The Colorado River was below, its water looking black as it rushed along between snow-covered banks and icy rocks.

Mr. Gaskill and the brakeman had climbed down to the snowy verge of the track, but they couldn't walk forward more than a few feet, because of the rocks and the cliff overhanging the river. Now they returned to the vestibule and climbed aboard.

"They'll have to blast that son-of-a-bitch," Mr. Gaskill said. "Those smaller rocks we can push out of the way. But that big one will have to be blown up."

The attendant on the Silver Pony shut and locked the vestibule door. "We got people hurt, sir. One of those rocks broke the glass on one of the panes up in the Vista-Dome."

"Go through your car and find out how many people are injured," the conductor said. Then he headed forward, through the baggage car. Jill hurried to catch up with him. The baggage man was busy righting sacks and packages that had fallen. One of the coffins that had been loaded on the train in Oakland was still aboard, the other three having been taken off the train at their earlier destinations. Fortunately it was strapped down.

At the front of the car a connecting door opened onto the rear locomotive. After the winter cold of the open vestibule, Jill felt heat emanating from the 1500-horsepower engines and the boiler that provided steam and hot water for the passenger cars. She followed the conductor and the brakeman into the back end of the locomotive, the smell of diesel fuel filling her nostrils. The space behind the engines was dark and grimy, with a toilet in one corner for use by the engine crew. A passageway to the right of the huge engine led up to the front, where another door led to the next engine.

The engineer, walking back from the lead engine, met them here. Jill stood in the doorway, straining to hear over the sound of the engines, loud even on idle. The engineer removed his blue-and-white-striped cap and wiped sweat from his forehead.

"Saw that boulder coming down in front of me," he said. "I throttled down and braked, but I knew I was gonna hit it. Not enough time to stop. It's big. This time of year, with the freezing and thawing, I expect rock slides. But I haven't seen a boulder this big in a while. And the damn rocks are still coming down."

As if to punctuate his words, more rocks rained down on the *Zephyr*, banging as they hit the roof and sides of the train.

"Can we push the boulder out of the way?" the conductor asked.

The engineer shrugged. "Maybe. We've got the power to move it. I've done it before, with smaller rocks. This one's mighty big, though."

"Give it a try. It's nearly sundown. We're losing the light. But first..." Mr. Gaskill beckoned to the brakeman. "Tommy, shinny up that telegraph pole. Send a message back to Glenwood and ahead to Kremmling. Tell them what happened. They'll send a track crew. And tell them one of the passengers is dead, a Dr. Kovacs. It looks like murder."

At the surprised looks from the crew, he added, "I'll fill you in later. Don't say anything to the passengers about this suspicious death. In the meantime, we have injuries. There's a broken window in the first Vista-Dome, and who knows what else. Miss McLeod, get your kit and set up a first-aid station in the Silver

Hostel. Get on the PA system and let people know. Tell the on-board crew to make note of injuries and damage. While you're at it, see if we've got any doctors or nurses aboard, anyone with medical training."

Jill nodded. She left the warmth of the locomotive and walked back through the baggage car to the Silver Pony, the first chair car. At the stairs leading up to the Vista-Dome, a male passenger was holding a handkerchief to a woman's bleeding forehead. Above him, the porter was helping a woman and a child down the stairs. "We got nine people with cuts, Miss McLeod," he called. "Some bruises and scrapes, too."

"We're setting up a first-aid station in the Silver Hostel," Jill said. "Have the injured people make their way back there. With that window broken in the Vista-Dome it will get cold in this car. See if the baggage man has something to patch it with, a big piece of cardboard and some tarps, some canvas. Do the best you can."

She headed back through the Silver Palace, where the porter was tending to an elderly man who had fallen and twisted his ankle when the train stopped. Mr. Webb hailed her as she went by. "What can I do to help?" he asked.

"We're turning the Silver Hostel into a treatment station." She indicated the old man. "If you'd help that gentleman back to the car, we'll put some ice on that ankle."

Mr. Webb nodded and moved toward the injured man. "Let me help you there. If you'll just put your arm around my shoul-der..."

Jill continued through the Silver Saddle, relaying the same message. In the Silver Hostel, she told the steward to get ready for injured passengers. When she reached the Silver Plate, she raced past the kitchen and pantry to the steward's counter. There two of the waiters were supporting one of the chefs, who was groaning with pain.

"Boiling water splashed all over his hands when the train stopped," the steward said. "We put ice on it right away, but he's hurting bad."

"Take him to the lounge." Jill keyed the mike on the PA

system. "This is Miss McLeod, the Zephyrette. The train has been hit by a rock slide. There is a large boulder on the tracks ahead of us. Porters, stewards, and other crew members, please check with all the passengers on your cars and determine if anyone is hurt and whether there is any damage to report to the conductor. All injured passengers and crew members, please come to the Silver Hostel, where we're setting up a first-aid station. If there are any doctors, nurses, or people with medical skills on board, please come to the lounge as well. We need your help."

She hung the mike back on the board and turned to the passengers and waiters who'd been in the dining room. "Is anyone hurt?"

"Thank the Lord, no," one of the waiters said. "Just a few bumps and bruises."

The sandy-haired man at the table nearest Jill was traveling in one of the chair cars with his wife and two small daughters. Jill had seen the family board in Green River. "Pete Carlisle," he said. "I was a Navy hospital corpsman during the war. You got a kit?"

"In my compartment," Jill said.

Mr. Carlisle nodded and turned back to his wife. "Take the girls back to the car, Ella. I'm gonna help out."

"The glass in the Vista-Dome on the Silver Pony broke," Jill told the steward and the waiters. "We have some people with cuts. We'll need bandages. Please bring some clean napkins."

One of the waiters spun off toward the linen locker. Jill led the way back to the lounge car, stopping at her compartment for the first-aid kit. She and Mr. Carlisle headed for the lounge. The steward had cleared the tables, setting glasses and ashtrays on the counter separating the lounge from the kitchen.

Most of the passengers had left, except for one, Mrs. Clive, who was arguing with the steward. Now she rounded on Jill, an angry expression on her face. "This is so annoying. First my cigarette case gets stolen by that porter and you're not doing anything about it. Then the train stops and my drink spills all over my dress. Now we're going to be late getting into Denver. How late will we be?"

"I have no way of knowing that, ma'am," Jill said. "We've

sent messages back to Glenwood Springs and ahead to Kremmling. A track crew is on its way, but it will take some time for them
to clear that boulder from the tracks."

The woman sniffed. "Well, honestly. I'll have to have this
dress cleaned and I want the railroad to pay for it."

Jill sighed and resisted the urge to smack Mrs. Clive. "We'll
deal with that later, ma'am. Please return to your car. We have
injured people and we need to treat them."

Mrs. Clive huffed and puffed, muttering imprecations and
threatening to call the head of the railroad. But she left.

Then the tall, white-haired man who'd boarded the train in
Grand Junction entered the lounge, carrying a small leather bag.
"I'm Dr. Parker. Retired, but I still know how. And I have my own
kit. I always carry it when I'm traveling."

"Thank you, Doctor," Jill said. "This is Mr. Carlisle. He was
a Navy hospital corpsman. Here's the train's first-aid kit. There's
not much in here besides Merthiolate and aspirin, and some soda
mints. We have people with cuts from broken glass in the first
chair car. One of chefs in the diner was injured when boiling water spilled on his hands."

"We'll manage." Dr. Parker set his bag on the counter and
opened it.

The chef who'd been burned came into the lounge, groaning
in pain as he held out his burned hands and forearms. "It hurts
bad."

"Ice, and plenty of it," Dr. Parker said, examining the burns
on the chef's hands. The lounge steward sped toward the kitchen
and filled a bowl with ice, passing it over the counter to the doctor.

The woman with the cut forehead arrived on the arm of the
male passenger who'd been with her earlier, holding the blood-
stained handkerchief to her head.

"Let me take a look at that," Mrs. Constanza said from the
doorway. She smiled at Jill. "I was a nurse in Italy before I married
my husband."

Mrs. Finch was there, too, a step behind Mrs. Constanza. Her
smile had a grim touch. "I was a Red Cross volunteer during the

war. Give me something to do, even if it's dispensing aspirin. This is turning out to be an eventful trip."

"If you'll get some water, Margaret," Mrs. Constanza said, "we'll clean this cut and see how serious it is."

"I'm way ahead of you, ma'am," the steward said, passing a bowl of water and a white napkin over the counter. Mrs. Finch took it and she and Mrs. Constanza took the injured woman's arm and steered her to the seat nearest the bar.

More injured passengers from the chair cars began straggling in, with cuts from the broken glass. Others came from the sleeper cars, some with bruises and bumps. Mr. Carlisle worked in the coffee shop area, while Dr. Parker examined people in the lounge. Jill moved from place to place, helping where she could. In the passageway she saw Mike Scolari, holding a bloody handkerchief to his chin.

"How did you get that?" She drew him into the lounge and pulled away the handkerchief. He winced as she dabbed a napkin in warm water and cleaned the blood from the inch-long cut.

"I was helping Gramps back from using the toilet. The train braked, and Gramps lost his balance. So I threw myself between him and the bulkhead, to break his fall. He's okay, just a little shaken up. But I banged my chin on something, not even sure what it was. Hurts like hell. Pardon my French. Am I going to have a scar on my noble visage?"

Jill smiled. "Probably not. It bled a lot but it's not too deep. A scar would just give you character."

"I'm enough of a character as it is. Or so my family tells me." He winced as Jill applied Merthiolate to his cut. "Ouch. That stuff stings. What about that other matter?"

He was referring to the murder. "The brakeman telegraphed the stations in Glenwood and Kremmling," Jill said. "So they've been notified about the rock slide, and the other matter. Not much we can do now, except wait for a track crew to clear the rocks."

"Can I help with anything?"

Jill put a bandage on his cut. "We've got plenty of help here. It would be best for you to go back to your compartment. It will take a while for a track crew to reach us and get that boulder out of the way. Oh, would you check on Emily, please? She's in the Bensons' bedroom on the Silver Palisade."

"Will do," he said, departing with a wave. He returned a short time later, reporting that Norma Benson had fallen when the train stopped. "She's okay. Just strained her back. She took some aspirin and she's lying down. Emily, Billy, and Chip went back to the Silver Solarium so their mom can rest."

"Thanks. I'll go back and check on her later."

For now, Jill had plenty to do. Passengers kept coming to the lounge, complaining of cuts, bruises, and sprains. Jill turned to a new arrival. "Sit down and put your feet up, ma'am. Yes, it's bruised. I'm sure it hurts. We'll put some ice on that."

Chapter Nineteen

JILL FELT AS though she'd spent the whole evening here in the Silver Hostel, seeing to injured passengers and answering questions. But when she checked her watch, it had been less than an hour since the train hit the boulder. Most of the people who'd been injured had been treated in the lounge and coffee shop and had returned to their seats and sleeping accommodations.

Darkness enveloped the train. The conductor came into the lounge and reported that track crews were on their way to clear the rock slide. There was no estimate of when they'd arrive. Dinner was being served in the dining car, retaining some semblance of normality.

"Thanks for all your help," Jill told the passengers who had helped their injured compatriots.

"Glad to be of service," the doctor said, shutting his bag. "I believe I'll check on that chef who burned his hands before I head back to my bedroom."

"He's lying down in the dormitory," the lounge steward said. "If you'll follow me."

Mr. Carlisle closed Jill's first-aid kit and headed back to the chair cars. Mrs. Constanza washed and dried her hands, while Mrs. Finch stretched and yawned. "Goodness, it's time for dinner. I'd rather stretch out on my bed and take a nap."

As she and Mrs. Constanza left, heading back to the sleeper cars, Jill wished she could lie down as well. But she'd have to settle for washing her face in the basin in her compartment. Then she'd get some dinner. Her stomach felt empty.

She picked up the first-aid kit and carried it out of the lounge.

As she went up the steps just outside, heading back toward her compartment, Jill was surprised to see Clifford Cole at the end of the car. It looked as though he was closing her door. But surely that was her imagination.

"Are you looking for me, Mr. Cole?" She set the first-aid kit on the floor. "May I help you with something?"

"Yes, my wife's been hurt," he said. "It happened when the train stopped. She banged up her ankle. She's got a really bad cut and it hurts when she tries to walk. Please come back to our compartment."

"Let me get the doctor. He's just here in the dormitory, seeing to an injured crew member." Jill turned and took a step.

Mr. Cole clamped his hand on her arm. "The doctor's busy. If you'll just come and take a look." Jill looked at his hand, frowning. He released her, his brow furrowed underneath his blond crew cut. "I'm sorry, I really am. I'm just worried about my wife. Please." He reached down and picked up the first-aid kit.

"All right," Jill said. She led the way to the vestibule of the dining car, walking down the passageway next to the kitchen, with Mr. Cole at her heels, then along the aisle between the tables, where many of the passengers were eating dinner. They might as well, Jill thought. With the rock slide, it would be a while before they got to Denver.

They entered the Silver Gull, passing the porter's seat, but Jill didn't see Si Lovell. When they reached compartment B, Mr. Cole opened the door and held out his hand, ushering Jill inside. She entered the compartment. The upper berth was still down, a tangle of blankets on top. That was odd. The porter should have made it up, unless the Coles wanted it down so they could nap. They certainly couldn't have lowered it themselves without the porter's key.

Rita Cole was in the seat below, her legs stretched out in front of her. Mr. Cole entered the compartment and shut the door, setting the first-aid kit on the floor. Mrs. Cole turned to face Jill. Her forehead was scratched, an angry red mark, and she had a large bruise on her cheek.

"Oh, Mrs. Cole, your husband didn't tell me your face—"

Suddenly Mr. Cole grabbed Jill's right arm and twisted it behind her. Jill cried out in pain. Why? What on earth was going on?

Mrs. Cole rose from the seat, moving toward Jill. She had something in her hand. Something made of dull gray metal. A gun.

"I know Laszlo gave you an envelope," Rita Cole said. "Where is it?"

"What are you talking about?" Jill gasped again as Mr. Cole twisted her arm.

"It's not in her compartment," he said.

So he had been coming out of her quarters. What was in that envelope? What was so important?

"You killed him," Jill said.

Rita Cole didn't answer. Instead she slapped Jill, hard.

"Where's the envelope?" Clifford Cole hissed in her ear. Then she felt something cold, something metal, pressing against her throat. It was a knife.

"I don't know," Jill said, finding her voice. "The envelope's gone. I looked for it after I found the body. It must have fallen on the floor, or slipped between the seat and the wall."

"Bullshit," he said. "I searched your compartment from top to bottom. It's not there. You gave it to someone. Who? The conductor?"

"I didn't give it to anyone. I tossed it onto the seat in my compartment after the professor gave it to me. When I came back after I found the body, the envelope was gone. I'm telling you the truth. I don't know where it is."

"You're lying," Cole said. He pressed the knife harder. "Maybe a little cut would make you tell the truth."

Jill heard the sound of a latch being released. The wall that separated the Coles' compartment from bedroom A moved, folding in on itself. She stared. Neal Paynter stood just the other side of the wall, his face impassive, tossing a porter's key in his hand.

"No, I think she is telling the truth," Paynter said.

"Then where the hell is it?" Cole demanded.

Rita Cole examined Jill, a speculative look on her face. "I have an idea. It's that game. That scavenger hunt you started, with those kids roaming around looking for things. I saw you write out the list of things for the children to find. Things like an envelope."

Jill didn't say anything. She'd already come to the same conclusion herself. But she wasn't going to tell them anything.

Paynter nodded and tucked the porter's key in his pocket. "Yeah, that would explain it. But which kid? Damn brats are roaming all over the train collecting things."

"I'm betting on Emily," Mrs. Cole said. "The one who is our Zephyrette's little shadow. Cliff, you go forward. Neal, go back through the sleeper cars. You find Emily, and I'll bet that we will find that envelope."

"I don't like leaving you alone with her," Cole said.

"I'm fine. I have this." Rita Cole pointed the barrel of the gun at Jill.

The pain in Jill's arm lessened and Clifford Cole took the knife away from her throat. He circled around in front of her, a cold look in his eyes as he folded the knife and stuck it in his pocket. Then he opened the door and left the compartment. Neal Paynter left bedroom A. Now Jill was alone with Rita Cole.

Where was Emily? Now she remembered. After the murder, the little girl had been with Mr. and Mrs. Benson in their quarters on the Silver Palisade. But after the rock slide, Mike Scolari told her that Norma Benson had been injured when the train stopped. So all three children—Emily, Billy, and Chip—had gone back to the Silver Solarium. Were they still there?

Jill didn't know much about guns. They always looked as though they could do a lot of damage at close range. Particularly this one, pointed at her, just a few feet from her. Jill glanced down at the first-aid kit, near her feet. Could she grab it and hit Mrs. Cole? Maybe, if she could distract the woman.

"The professor recognized Mr. Paynter," Jill said. "He told me that, when he gave me the envelope."

"What else did he tell you?" Mrs. Cole asked.

"He told me about your marriage. You were a refugee, like

him. When you married him, he was working at Oak Ridge. Then you went with him to Los Alamos, but you didn't like it there in New Mexico, so you left."

Jill looked at Mrs. Cole's scratched face. She didn't think the woman had gotten that wound when the train stopped. It looked as though she'd been in a fight. With whom? Now she recalled what Norma Benson had said, about having seen Clifford Cole before, at Los Alamos.

"Was it Los Alamos where you met Mr. Cole?" Jill asked. Mrs. Cole frowned, as though Jill's words had hit home. "I know your husband says he's never been to New Mexico. But I think he has. I'll bet that's where you met him, while Dr. Kovacs was working on the Manhattan Project. I get the feeling this is all tied up with New Mexico. There's someone else on the train who worked at Los Alamos during the war. Someone who has seen Mr. Cole before."

That got a rise out of Rita Cole. Her mouth tightened, and so did her hand, on the grip of the gun. "What do you mean by that?"

Jill shrugged. "Just what I said. Someone recognizes your husband."

"Who?" Rita Cole leaned toward her. "Tell me, or I'll knock it out of you."

Jill backed away. Her right leg brushed the first-aid kit. If she could lean down and...

The door to bedroom A opened and Neal Paynter stepped inside. He held Emily by her left arm. Clifford Cole, his hand on Emily's right arm, shut the door behind them.

"See, we told you Miss McLeod wants you," Paynter said.

Emily wrenched herself free and sped through the door that separated bedroom A and compartment B. She threw herself at Jill, wrapping her arms around the Zephyrette.

"Now, Emily," Mrs. Cole said. "I think you took something that doesn't belong to you. An envelope. I want you to tell us where it is."

Emily's voice was muffled, her face buried in Jill's jacket. "I don't know anything about an envelope."

"Don't lie, you little brat," Cole said, stepping into the compartment, his right hand raised. "Your pal Billy said you had an envelope. Now where is it?"

"Stop it. Let me handle this." Rita handed the gun to Neal Paynter. Then she moved to Emily and pulled the little girl's arms away from Jill. "Emily, you wouldn't want us to hurt Miss McLeod, would you?"

Emily looked from Rita to Jill and back again. Then she shook her head.

"You took the envelope before the party, when I was talking with Mr. Scolari," Jill said, recalling how Emily had smoothed the front of her sweater when she left Jill's compartment. Before the party. That seemed like such a long time ago. "I was distracted, and the envelope was lying there next to my book. So you took it, for the scavenger hunt. It's all right. You can tell me."

Slowly Emily nodded. "It was just a game. I was going to give it back."

"It's not a game anymore. Tell them where it is, and they'll let us go." Even as she said the words, Jill didn't believe them.

Emily considered this. "I hid it. So I could bring it out when it was time to see if we won the game. You said we had to find everything on the list by five o'clock and bring it to the Silver Solarium. Then we found the professor and I had to stay with Mr. and Mrs. Benson. And then we had the rock slide—"

"Never mind about the damn rock slide," Clifford Cole said, leaning forward. Emily shrank back. "Where's that envelope?"

"I hid it," Emily said.

"Where? The observation lounge? That's where you kids have been playing. Where is it? Up in the Dome, or downstairs?"

"You're scaring her," Jill said as the frightened child leaned into her.

"I mean to scare her." Cole reached for Emily.

"No, wait." Paynter held up his hand. "She'll tell us. Won't you, Emily? So Miss McLeod doesn't get hurt."

"I hid it." Emily drew out the words, as though she was stalling for time.

Where could the little girl have hidden the envelope? Jill

wondered. Was it somewhere in the bedroom Emily was sharing with Mrs. Tidsdale? If not in the bedroom, there were a number of possibilities. The soiled linen locker was in the middle of the sleeper car, next to bedroom A. The clean linen locker was at the rear end of the car. And there was another locker just off the vestibule, across from the porter's compartment. Perhaps she'd hidden it in an empty roomette.

Cole snarled at Emily. "Come on, tell us where."

"I hid it in..." Emily stopped. "In the car where Mrs. Tidsdale and I stay. But not in our room. It's in another room on the sleeper car."

"In the porter's compartment?" Rita Cole asked. "One of the roomettes? Or another bedroom?"

Emily shook her head. "No. It's not any of those. I found a special hidey-hole. I have to show you."

"Then take us there," Paynter said. "And everything will be fine. We'll leave Miss McLeod here, just for safekeeping."

He handed the gun to Rita. Then he opened the door to bedroom A and looked out into the corridor. "Good evening, Porter."

Jill heard Si Lovell's voice, just outside. "Evening, sir. Everything all right?"

Jill opened her mouth, but Rita Cole anticipated her, laying the barrel of the gun alongside Jill's cheek.

"Yes, everything's fine, Porter. Any idea on when the train will start moving again?"

"No, sir, just that the track crew is coming. They're gonna have to blow up that boulder that's in front of the train. I'm afraid we're going to be a few hours late getting into Denver."

"Nothing for it but to have dinner in the diner," Paynter said, his voice jovial.

"Yes, sir, you do that. They are serving dinner now."

"Yes, I'll head down to the diner soon. Thank you, Porter." Paynter waited a moment. "He's gone, into another compartment. Come on."

Cole took Emily out of the compartment. Now Jill was alone with Rita Cole, wondering if Emily really had secreted the envelope in the Silver Palisade in a special hiding place. Perhaps she'd put it in another car, instead of the Silver Palisade. Maybe Emily was trying to misdirect their captors.

Jill erased this new thought from her mind. She didn't want to reveal anything on her face. She certainly didn't want Rita Cole to guess what she was thinking.

She looked around the compartment, her gaze coming to rest on the open upper berth. She frowned. The sight of the open berth had bothered her earlier, and it bothered her now. Even if the Coles had been taking naps, surely they would have had the porter put the berth back up into the wall. Or they could have done it themselves, since Paynter had somehow acquired a porter's key. With the berth put up in the wall, the Coles would have more space and wouldn't have to look at that untidy, rumpled blanket.

The blanket moved.

Chapter Twenty

JILL STARED, AND THEN she quickly masked her expression. Someone was in that upper berth, concealed under the blanket.

The blanket moved again. A hand snaked out. A woman's hand, wearing a ring. Jill recognized the square-cut ruby. That was Mrs. Tidsdale's ring.

Jill moved to one side and Rita moved as well. "There's no need to wave that gun at me. I'm not going anywhere. It's just that I've been standing so long. My feet hurt."

She moved farther to the side and again Rita moved so that she was facing Jill. Now Rita's back was to the open upper berth.

The blanket moved again, the hand and an upper arm visible. Jill saw a slim cord wrapped around the woman's wrist. Then a face, shadowed by the blanket. Tidsy's face.

Jill pretended to stumble over the first-aid kit at her feet, moving forward, toward Rita Cole. The other woman moved backward. She was out of Jill's range, but well within the reach of that hand moving out from under the blanket.

Grace Tidsdale grabbed Rita Cole's ponytail and yanked it upward. Rita screamed in pain, her left hand clawing at her hair as she tried to free herself. Jill picked up the first-aid kit and swung it at Rita. Then Tidsy came down out of the upper berth, landing on Rita. Both women sprawled on the floor of the compartment. Mrs. Cole lost her grip on the gun and it skittered away, coming to rest at Jill's feet. Jill reached down and picked up the gun, holding it carefully as Tidsy struggled with the taller woman. Then Tidsy straddled Rita Cole and slapped her, once, twice. Mrs. Cole's head fell back and she moaned.

Tidsy got to her feet. Blood streaked her blond hair and there was a lump on her forehead. A handkerchief, used as a gag, had been tied around her jaw. There were red marks on her wrists where the cord had bound them together. Now she took the gun from Jill, fury blazing in her blue eyes as she glared down at Rita Cole. "You bitch. You killed Laszlo, you and your friends. I'll see all three of you get what's coming to you."

"You're hurt," Jill said. "Where were you?"

"I've been here all along," Tidsy said, freeing her other wrist from the cord as Rita struggled to rise. "Don't even think about it. Come on, help me tie this one up, before she gets ideas."

Tidsy shoved Rita Cole back onto the floor, rolled her onto her stomach, and with Jill's help, tied the woman's hands behind her back. Jill opened the first-aid kit and pulled out a roll of tape. She tied it around Mrs. Cole's legs and looped another length around the leg of the chair for good measure. Then she straightened.

"That ought to hold her. So what happened?"

"I faked the headache at lunch," Tidsy said. "Then I came back here to search this compartment. Never mind why, I'll tell you later. But I got caught. Rita came back from the dining car early. She hit me over the head. Then she and Cole and Paynter tied me up and stashed me in the upper berth. I was out for a while. Don't know how long. Then I came to and started working on getting my hands free. Took a hell of a long time. The train stopped. Rock slide, they said. Then I heard them talking about Laszlo. They killed him, looking for something."

"That envelope he gave me, the one Emily took," Jill said.

Tidsy hefted the gun and made for the door. "Right. Now we've got to get Emily."

They stepped outside. A few doors to the left, Si Lovell was talking with Mike Scolari in front of the doorway of his compartment.

"I tell you, I thought I heard someone scream," Mike said. Then he looked past the porter and gasped. "Jill! Mrs. Tidsdale! What the hell?"

Mrs. Tidsdale didn't answer. She stalked past Mike and the porter, gun in hand, heading back to the Silver Palisade.

"Mr. Lovell," Jill said as she hurried to catch up. "Please go find the conductor. There's a criminal in compartment B."

Jill followed Tidsy past the rest of the Silver Gull compartments, through to the Silver Palisade vestibule. They stopped. Tidsy opened the door, slowly. Jill heard someone coming up behind them and glanced back to see Mike. She put her finger to her lips. Then she looked ahead and saw Clifford Cole walking along the corridor between the roomettes, behind the much taller Neal Paynter. She didn't see Emily. The little girl must be between the two men.

"Porter's compartment is empty," Jill whispered. "So's roomette one."

Tidsy nodded. They slipped through the door, Tidsy into the tiny porter's compartment, Jill and Mike into the slightly larger roomette 1. Jill looked out into the passageway. Paynter and Cole reached the soiled linen locker in the middle of the car, turning to their right. Now she saw Emily. Cole had hold of the girl's arm.

Now Paynter and Cole stepped aside as the Benson boys ran into view, Chip in front and Billy following his younger brother.

"Hey, Emily," Chip said. "I found a treasure but Billy doesn't believe me. I'll show both of you." Chip stopped, pushed open the door of the nearest roomette, and took a step inside. Then he froze and looked up.

"Uh-oh," Chip said.

"God damn it to hell, you little..." Mr. Smith came out of roomette 10. The burly man loomed over Chip, grabbing the little boy's arm.

"You leave my brother alone." Billy began flailing at Mr. Smith with his fists, then he kicked the man in the shins.

Smith bellowed and released Chip, who ran back the way he and Billy had come. Now the little boy barreled into Cole and Paynter. Cole let go of Emily's arm. The little girl darted around the corner, heading back toward the bedrooms.

"Son of a bitch," Paynter said. He and Cole followed Emily, disappearing from view.

"What in the world is going on out here?" Mrs. Barlow stepped out of roomette 9. She shook her finger at Mr. Smith. "I am really annoyed by your language and your loudness. I'm going to complain to the conductor."

Smith growled something and backed into his roomette. Mrs. Barlow harrumphed and went back into hers.

Tidsy came out of the porter's compartment and moved quickly down the passageway. Jill and Mike followed her to the place in front of the soiled linen locker, where the corridor jogged to the right. Now they heard loud voices.

"She's locked herself in the damn bedroom," Paynter said.

"What seems to be the problem, sir?" That was Frank Nathan's voice, coming from the other end of the car.

"That little girl stole my watch," Paynter said. "I want it back. Can't you unlock this door?"

"I don't believe you, sir," Frank said. "Emily wouldn't do anything like that. Besides, she looked like she was scared of you."

"Of course she was scared of me," Paynter said, "after I caught her stealing."

Now Jill heard Cole's voice. "Are you doubting my friend's word? I saw her take his watch. He just wants it back."

"I don't think Emily would do that, sir," Frank said. "All I'm saying is you are mistaken. I am not going to let you into that bedroom. That little girl is my responsibility."

"Now listen..." Paynter said.

There was a flurry of movement. They were coming back this way. Jill saw Frank Nathan being propelled forward as she motioned the others into the nearest refuge, Mrs. Barlow's roomette.

"Good heavens." Mrs. Barlow looked aghast as three extra people crowded into her roomette. Her eyes widened when she saw the gun in Tidsy's hand. "What do you need me to do?"

"Get out there and distract those men," Tidsy said, "and make sure one of 'em has his back to me."

Through the partly closed door of the roomette, Jill saw Neal Paynter. He had Frank Nathan backed up against the door to the soiled linen locker in the middle of the car. Clifford Cole was in the aisle.

Mrs. Barlow compressed her lips and she stepped out into the corridor. "You let that porter go, young man."

"Mind your own business, you old biddy," Cole said.

"And you mind your manners," Mrs. Barlow said.

Now other passengers were coming into the aisle, curious about the commotion. Ed Benson rounded the corner from the bedroom section. "Let's all calm down now," he said, his voice reasonable. "Obviously there's been some kind of misunderstanding. Why don't we all take a step back and talk about it."

"Here comes the conductor," Mrs. Barlow said, pointing in Ed Benson's direction. Clifford Cole took a step back and turned to look. Tidsy came out of roomette 9. She brought the butt of the gun down on Cole's head and he crumpled, falling into the door of roomette 10. The door opened and the grumpy Mr. Smith leapt to his feet as Mr. Cole fell headfirst into the roomette, knocking over the open valise on the floor. The contents spilled out, wallets, jewelry, a gold pen, a cigarette case that looked familiar.

Mike and Jill came out of the roomette, watching as Ed Benson advanced on Neal Paynter. Tidsy leveled the gun at Paynter. "This game is over."

Another gun appeared, in Paynter's right hand as he shoved Frank Nathan to one side. "Looks like a standoff to me. Now get out of my way. I'm getting out of here."

"Where will you go?" Jill stood in the middle of the aisle, her hands on her hips. "We're in the middle of Gore Canyon. There are no roads here. There's no way out, except on the train or on the river. It's miles either way to the next town. It's dark and cold outside. Go ahead. Get off the train. Try it! You'll die of hypothermia before the hour is out."

Chapter Twenty-One

EMILY HAD LOCKED herself inside bedroom A, and the toilet, for good measure. At first the little girl refused to come out, despite the efforts of Jill and Mrs.Tidsdale to convince her that she was safe. Finally Jill heard the faint click of a latch and a creak as the toilet door opened. Then Emily spoke from the other side of the bedroom door.

"Tidsy, is that really you?"

"You bet it's me, sweetie. Come on out and see for yourself."

"Are those bad people really gone?"

Jill leaned close to the door. "Yes, they are. The brakeman and the fireman took those bad people to the baggage car. They're going to lock them up and make sure they can't hurt you, or anyone else."

Finally they heard the latch click and Emily opened the door. Jill knelt and put her arms around the little girl. Emily took Mrs. Tidsdale's hand, questions tumbling from her mouth.

"Tidsy, you have blood on your head. How come? Does it hurt? Where did you go? I was worried about you. Me and Billy and Chip and the other kids looked everywhere for you."

Tidsy managed a wan smile. "You were worried about me? Thanks, sweetie. Mrs. Cole whacked me on the head, because I was snooping in her room. I'll say more about that later. Yes, hurt a lot, still does, though not as much as it did. I was out for a while. They tied me up and kept me in the Coles' compartment. That's why you couldn't find me."

"I'd like to get the full story on that," Mr. Gaskill said. "But it will keep till later."

The conductor, the brakeman, and the fireman had arrived in the Silver Palisade right after Jill had told Paynter to get off the train and take his chances in the cold and the dark. Outnumbered and outfoxed, Paynter had been relieved of his gun by Ed Benson, while Mike Scolari hauled Cole to his feet and took his knife. Now the two men and Mrs. Cole had been incarcerated in the baggage car, their hands tied, and guarded by the baggage man, until the authorities arrived.

"Which authorities?" Mr. Gaskill wondered aloud. "Glenwood Springs is in Garfield County, Dotsero and Bond are in Eagle County, and Gore Canyon's in Grand County. I have no idea when or where the murder occurred, or who has jurisdiction. The county sheriffs will have to sort that out. I would appreciate all of you passengers writing out statements of what you saw. That will help us with the investigation."

Now the conductor turned and scowled at Mr. Smith. The occupant of roomette 10, in the custody of Mike Scolari, was soon on his way to join the others in the baggage car. In his hand the conductor held Mrs. Clive's gold cigarette case, which had been among the treasures that spilled to the floor of Smith's roomette. The objects had been scooped up and returned to Smith's leather valise. "It looks like you've been pilfering things from compartments since you got on the train in Sacramento. That means you've broken laws in California, Nevada, Utah, and Colorado. However, since we caught you in Colorado, they can damn well prosecute you in Colorado."

"I just knew it," Mrs. Barlow said, crowding closer for a better look. "That nasty man, stealing things from passengers."

"I want my cigarette case back," Mrs. Clive demanded.

Mrs. Loomis, watching from her doorway, rolled her eyes, while Mrs. Barlow said, "Well, I'm sure you'll just have to wait. They'll need it for evidence."

The conductor fixed Mrs. Clive with an annoyed look. "The cigarette case that you accused the porter of stealing? It appears you were wrong about that. As the lady said, the case and the other items are evidence. I'm holding onto them for the time being, while I make a list and write my report. I'll give you a receipt. When we get to Denver, these things will be returned to their owners. In the meantime, we have more immediate concerns. The track crew just arrived. We've got to get that boulder off the tracks and the train rolling again."

He nodded at the brakeman and they headed forward, toward the baggage car, with Mr. Smith between them.

"Well, of all the impertinence," Mrs. Clive complained. "I want my—"

Tidsy, her white face streaked with blood, silenced the other woman with a glare. "Put a lid on it, sister. Or I'll put a lid on you. I've had enough for one day. And I've sure as hell had enough of you."

Mrs. Clive squeaked with alarm and retreated to her bedroom. "I ought to deck her just for good measure," Tidsy added. "She's getting on my last nerve."

Mrs. Loomis and Mrs. Barlow laughed. Norma Benson, standing outside her bedroom with her hands restraining her curious sons, said, "Mine, too, the minute she boarded the train."

"I told you I found a treasure," Chip said. "I know I wasn't supposed to go in other people's rooms, but the door came open and I looked inside. That man wasn't there but that bag was. And it was full of all those pretty things."

"Next time I'll believe you." His mother tousled his dark curls. "You sure did find a treasure. And a lot of trouble to go with it."

Billy was of a more practical bent. He tugged on his mother's sleeve. "We haven't had our dinner."

"I know. We'll go to the dining car now." Norma shepherded her two sons forward.

"I'll come with you, dear," Mrs. Barlow said, stepping up to join them. "My goodness, all this excitement has left me with an appetite."

"You did good, Mrs. B," Tidsy said.

"So did you, my dear," Mrs. Barlow said. "Now here comes the porter with the doctor. You'd better get that head of yours seen to."

Frank Nathan had gone to the Silver Gull to fetch Dr. Parker. The doctor frowned. "There's a lot of blood. But it may look worse than it actually is. Let's go inside so you can sit down and I can get a closer look."

Mrs. Tidsdale went into her bedroom and sat down, leaning back with a sigh. Emily sat next to her, holding her hand. Jill opened the toilet door and pulled down the sink over the commode. She dampened a washcloth in the basin and then leaned over Tidsy, wiping the blood from the woman's forehead and hair. Dr. Parker examined the wound. "You were struck on the head and unconscious for a time. Any idea how long?"

"Long enough for those goons to truss me up. They stashed me in the adjoining compartment. I think I fell asleep at some point, then woke up again."

The doctor's frown deepened. "I don't like it that you were unconscious twice, whether it was due to the blow on the head or something else. The possibility of a concussion worries me. But you don't seem confused now. That's a good sign. Any headache, double vision, dizziness, or nausea?"

"No, I'll be okay."

"All the same, I recommend that you go to a hospital as soon as we get to Denver. You'll need a couple of stitches on this cut. For now I'll sterilize the area and apply a bandage." The doctor cleaned the cut and dabbed it with Merthiolate from Jill's first-aid kit, then he covered it with gauze and tape.

Dr. Parker left. Then a loud blast reverberated through the canyon. Emily jumped up, looking frightened. "What was that?"

"The track crew got here, with dynamite," Jill said. "They're blowing up that big rock that's in front of the engine. Once it's in smaller pieces, they can push them off the tracks. Then the train will start moving and we'll be on our way to Denver. We'll be late, but I'm sure your grandmother will be there to meet you. I'm so glad you got away from those men and locked yourself in the bedroom."

"I was back in the Silver Solarium when those men came after me," Emily said. "They said you wanted me, that they were going to take me to you. I was with Billy and Chip. I didn't like to leave them alone. You know, Chip gets into mischief."

Mrs. Tidsdale laughed at this, and Jill nodded. "Yes, I know he does. So those men persuaded you to come with them to the Silver Gull."

Emily nodded. "And then I told them I'd show them where I

hid the envelope. So we came back here, and you saw what happened. When that man let go of my arm, I ran around the corner and locked myself in this bedroom, and inside the toilet, too. I heard yelling outside. Then I heard you and Tidsy calling to me."

Emily snuggled closer to Mrs. Tidsdale. "I'm so glad you're okay, Tidsy. I wasn't sure I liked you when I first saw you. But you grew on me."

Tidsy smiled and stroked Emily's hair. "That was all an act, sweetie. Me pretending to be drunk. You grew on me, too. You're a pretty good poker player for a nine-year-old. You know how to bluff. So where did you really hide that envelope?"

"It's in the Silver Solarium," Emily said. "It's really important?"

Mrs. Tidsdale got to her feet and straightened her red silk dress over her hips. "Yes, it is. Let's go get it." She glanced at Jill. "I must look like the wrath of God."

"You look fine."

They walked back through the Silver Palisade into the Silver Pine, then through to the Silver Rapids. The Perlmans stopped Jill, worried about the delay and fretting about making their connections in Chicago. She assured them that the train would make up time.

They continued to the Silver Solarium, walking alongside the car's four sleeping compartments, down the steps and past the buffet and the bar, where the Finches and the Constanzas were at the booth in the corner, playing bridge again to pass the time. Miss Stafford had left her typewriter and was having a drink at one of the smaller tables, talking with another passenger. "What an adventure this has been. I may have to write a train book."

As Emily led the way up the steps to the observation lounge, Jill glanced at the waist-high water dispenser tucked into the corner just below the stairs leading up to the Vista-Dome. That door opened, she recalled, noting the hinges on the left and the small handle on the right. Had Emily hidden the envelope there?

No, Emily walked back through the observation lounge, where two small sofas faced the car's fish-tail back. The Finch girls and George Neeley sat cross-legged on the floor in the space between the sofas and the rear door, bouncing a ball back and forth between them. As Emily approached, all three children scrambled to their feet.

"Hey, you found Mrs. Tidsdale," George said. "We looked everywhere, even in the bathrooms. Well, the girls looked in the bathrooms. Where were you? Hey, you got a bandage. Did you bump your head?"

"It's a long story," Mrs. Tidsdale said. "And yes, I do have a bump on my head."

On either side of the Solarium's rear door were two small tables built into the sides of the car. The one on the right held the silver tinsel Christmas tree. The table on the left held an empty glass. Emily moved the glass out of the way, setting it on the nearby windowsill.

"Are we going to do the scavenger hunt now?" Nan asked. "We were supposed to do it at five, but Miss McLeod's been busy since the train hit the rock. But Billy and Chip aren't here."

"We'll do the scavenger hunt later," Jill said.

Emily reached for a pointed end of the triangular-shaped table and lifted it. Both the tables were hinged, with spaces inside. The one on the right contained an emergency brake valve, but the one on the left was an empty space. Now Emily pulled out a pillowcase and reached inside, removing the envelope Dr. Kovacs had given Jill, the envelope that the Coles and Paynter had killed him for.

Emily handed the envelope to Jill. "I'm sorry I took it from your compartment. I shouldn't have done that."

Jill took the envelope, feeling a pang as she looked at the professor's handwriting. Then she held it out to Mrs. Tidsdale. "Will you tell me what's inside?"

"Won't know that until I open it. But I'm not going to do that here in the lounge where everyone can see." Mrs. Tidsdale turned to leave.

George tugged at her sleeve. "Hey, Mrs. Tidsdale, can we play another game of poker before we get to Denver?"

Tidsy grinned. "Feeling lucky? Sure. After Emily and I get some dinner. Then I'll meet all you kids in the lounge. Remember, the name of the game is seven-card stud."

Chapter Twenty-Two

THEY GOT BACK to the Silver Palisade just as the Bensons returned from the dining car. Norma Benson hailed them. "Miss McLeod, Mrs. Tidsdale, I remember now where I saw that guy Clifford Cole. Remember, I was sure I'd seen him. It came to me at dinner."

"Was it Los Alamos?" Tidsy asked, pausing at her door.

Norma looked surprised. "Yes, it was. How did you know?"

"A lucky guess."

"I'd really like to hear more," Ed said. "Can you give us the lowdown?"

Tidsy considered this. "You and your wife might be able to fill in some gaps."

Ed beckoned them to bedroom E. "Let's talk in here. We've got the wall open between our rooms."

The Bensons sat on the bench seat in bedroom F, with Billy and Chip, both boys drowsy after dinner. Mrs. Tidsdale and Jill took the seats in E, Emily crowding in with Tidsy on the larger of the two.

"Are you going to open the envelope?" Emily asked.

Mrs. Tidsdale nodded. She inserted one red fingernail at the end of the flap and tore open the envelope. She pulled out several sheets of paper, unfolded them, and read, frowning. Then she folded the papers and put them back in the envelope.

"Can you tell us what it says?" Jill asked.

Mrs. Tidsdale shook her head. "Not really."

"What did you do during the war, Mrs. Tidsdale?" Ed Benson asked.

She smiled at him. "I worked for a man named Donovan."

"Wild Bill? You were O.S.S.?"

"Yeah. I probably shouldn't talk too much about that. Let's just say I was a government girl. I grew up in San Francisco, in the Mission District, like you did, Mr. Benson. Got married in nineteen forty-one, November, a month before Pearl Harbor. My husband was in the Army Air Forces and he went with Doolittle on the Tokyo raid, in April of 'forty-two. He was one of the guys who didn't make it back. We'd been married all of six months." She looked at Jill. "So when you told me about losing your fiancé in Korea, well, I do know what that's like, sweetie."

"You were going to get married?" Emily asked Jill. "But he went to Korea and died, like my daddy? I'm sorry."

"I am, too," Jill said. "I still miss him. It was two years ago, and it does get a little better as time passes. And if you keep busy. That's why I became a Zephyrette."

"I decided to keep busy, too," Mrs. Tidsdale said. "And do my bit for the war effort. I went back east and got a job in Washington, working as a secretary for this organization that we won't talk about. At first all I did was type and file and answer the phone. Then I got involved in the more interesting stuff. Went through a training course, learned how to use a gun and handle myself in a scrap."

"Is that where you met Dr. Kovacs?" Jill asked. "In Washington?"

Tidsy nodded. "Yeah. He was working on something top secret. Now we know what that was. We had a fling, I guess you'd call it."

"What's a fling?" Billy asked.

"Never mind about that," his mother told him. Billy shrugged and snuggled closer to his mother. Chip was already asleep, his head burrowed against his father.

Tidsy shrugged. "Things happened, we both moved on. But we were still friends, so we kept in touch. We'd see each other from time to time. Then he met that redhead, Rivka, or Rita as she calls herself now. I knew she was bad news the first time I laid eyes on her. Turns out I was right. Now, Mrs. Benson, it's your turn. What do you remember about Clifford Cole, and Los Alamos?"

"I went on a double date one night with another gal that worked in the motor pool," Norma said. "My date was a supply clerk, the less said about him the better. My friend's date was Clifford Cole. That was the first time I saw him. Later I saw him with Mrs. Kovacs. I was down in Santa Fe, on a pass. I saw Mrs. Kovacs and Cole having drinks in the bar in the lobby of La Fonda. It looked to me like *they* were having a fling. Anyway, Cole was a machinist. He worked in Theta Shop, Special Engineer Detachment, along with a guy named David Greenglass."

"Ethel Rosenberg's brother," Jill said, surprised. "I remember reading about him, in all the news coverage about the Rosenberg case."

"That's right," Tidsy said. "In the early 'forties Greenglass joined the Young Communist League. That happened a lot in those days, after the Depression, and with the Soviets being our allies during the war. But Greenglass lied about that to get his security clearances. He was a machinist, too. He worked at Oak Ridge, then he got transferred to Los Alamos in the summer of 'forty-four."

"I remember Greenglass, and Special Engineer Detachment." Ed Benson shook his head. "Those guys in the detachment were screw-ups, not regular army at all. They gave us MPs the royal fits. We were always having to go into the Tech Area and sort them out. A bunch of techs, grad students and scientists. Their barracks was like a college dorm. Those guys were shooting craps in the latrine. They'd line up beer bottles in the hallway and use them for bowling pins. And Greenglass, I saw him a few times. Just got the impression he was a loudmouth jerk, all the time spouting off about how great the Russians were. I pegged him as a left-winger, just didn't realize then that he was passing information. To tell you the truth, I didn't think he was that smart."

"He didn't have to be smart," Tidsy said. "He just had to be there. People like those scientists at Los Alamos talked about their work. And people like Greenglass and Cole listened. They heard a lot of stuff that was classified. All they had to do was memorize it and walk out the gate on a pass."

"You're right," Ed said. "When I look back on it, though, it's a wonder we didn't have more security breaches on the Hill. The mail was censored, but people were working in shops where they were designing and making components of the bomb. That's what those guys saw and heard."

"And they passed on the information," Tidsy said. "About the bomb components, the buildings, how many people were working there, even the names of scientists who were working on the project. Just by having the names and knowing those scientists' work, the Soviets could get an idea of where the project was headed."

"How did they get the information out?" Jill asked.

"Greenglass's wife was living in Albuquerque," Tidsy said. "He would visit her and pass the information to a guy named Harry Gold, who was in contact with a scientist named Klaus Fuchs, who was a Communist passing secrets to the Soviets. The FBI arrested Gold in nineteen-fifty, and he gave them Greenglass and the Rosenbergs. Evidently Cole was better at covering his tracks, until now."

"But how does Paynter figure into all of this?" Norma asked. "Cole I remember from Los Alamos, but Paynter I've never seen before."

"Paynter was in New Mexico," Tidsy said. "Not at Los Alamos. He was in Santa Fe and Albuquerque. He was probably one of Klaus Fuchs's contacts, like Harry Gold. Greenglass and Fuchs were the only ones who were prosecuted for taking information out of Los Alamos. We've never been able to pin anything on Cole or Paynter, till now."

"So what happened to trigger all of this?"

Tidsy sighed. "Something went missing at the University of California, some notes and papers for a project Laszlo was working on. He notified the authorities, but he didn't have any idea who might be responsible for the breach. At some point Laszlo saw Paynter in LeConte Hall, where the physics department is located. He knew Paynter wasn't a professor or grad student or on the staff. A few weeks after that, Laszlo saw Paynter at a restaurant in downtown Berkeley, with a secretary who works in the physics department. He recognized Paynter as the man he'd seen before. Laszlo didn't want to think the secretary had anything to do with the missing notes. But he couldn't ignore the possibility. He asked around and discovered the secretary had a new man in her life."

"A guy named Neal Paynter," Norma said.

Tidsy smiled. "That's right. Laszlo saw Paynter coming out of an office in LeConte, late in the day, an office where he shouldn't have been. Laszlo reported this to the UC authorities, and he told me. I'd moved back to San Francisco after the war. Laszlo and I saw each other from time to time, going to the theater or the opera. He loved opera." She paused, remembering.

"Well, I still have some contacts in Washington, even if I am no longer a member of a certain organization. I checked around and found out Paynter had been investigated during the war, as a possible associate of Harry Gold, David Greenglass's contact. And a possible associate of one Clifford Cole, who knew Greenglass at Los Alamos. But there wasn't enough to pin on either Paynter or Cole. I knew Laszlo was going to a conference at Fermi Institute in Chicago, planning to stop over in Colorado and spend the holidays with another scientist at the university who'd also worked at Los Alamos."

Now Tidsy held up the envelope. "He was taking some documents with him, to the conference, documents about his research. He shouldn't have brought this stuff with him, but academics, scientists... Laszlo was focused on his research. He didn't think he was vulnerable, but I did. I offered to come with him. He said no, he didn't need a minder. Then I got a call from one of my old Washington buddies, Robert Charlton."

"Emily's Uncle Robert," Jill said. Emily was asleep now, her head leaning on Tidsy's shoulder.

Tidsy nodded. "The very same. Robert explained the situation, that his mother had broken her ankle and couldn't come get Emily and take her back to Denver. He had an important meeting in Washington and he couldn't do it. Was there any chance I could chaperone Emily? I looked at the dates and realized it was the same train Laszlo was taking. It even turned out to be the same car, the Silver Palisade. So I said yes. I didn't tell Laszlo, that's why he looked surprised when he saw me on the train."

"Did you know the Coles were going to be on the train?" Ed asked.

Tidsy shook her head. "No. Laszlo and I were both surprised to see Rita and her new husband, none other than Clifford Cole. All three of them on the train, Paynter and the Coles in adjoining compartments, and the same train as Laszlo, well, that couldn't be a coincidence. I figured Paynter, through his contact with the secretary, knew about Laszlo's trip to Chicago, that he might be carrying some documents with him. Cole and Paynter didn't know me, though I'd seen their photographs. I'd met Rita once, early in the war, and I was hoping like hell she didn't remember me. As it turned out, she didn't. My hair was brown then. I figured if I played the role of the flirty drunk, they wouldn't see me as a threat."

There was a knock on the door. "Come in," Ed Benson called.

The door opened and Frank Nathan stepped inside. "Mr. Benson, sir, have you seen Miss McLeod? The conductor's looking for her."

"I'm here," Jill said, standing up. "Is something wrong? Where's Mr. Gaskill."

"No, Miss McLeod. Everything's fine. They got that rock off the tracks and we're ready to start rolling again. Mr. Gaskill is up in the diner. He wants you to make an announcement on the PA system."

"That's good news," Jill said, looking at her watch. "I wonder how late we'll be into Denver."

Emily stirred next to Mrs. Tidsdale, then she woke up and yawned. "I'm hungry. Are we going to eat dinner?"

"I'm ravenous." Tidsy got to her feet, holding the envelope. "Let's go to our compartment, sweetie. Then we'll go to the dining car. I want the biggest steak they've got. Then it seems to me we have a date to play poker in the lounge."

Billy woke up in the adjoining bedroom, rubbing his hands against his eyes. "I want to play poker."

"Not tonight, sport," Ed Benson said. "We've got to get our things all packed up so we can get off the train in Denver. You're going to see your aunt and uncle and cousins."

Jill left the Bensons' compartment and hurried forward to the dining car. "There you are, Miss McLeod," the conductor said, looking up from the steward's counter. "The crew just moved the last of that boulder off the tracks. Looks like we'll be a few hours late into Denver. We'll have an unscheduled stop in Kremmling to turn over our criminals to the authorities. I've written out a short announcement for you to make."

Jill took the sheet of paper from the conductor and moved to the public address system. Just then, the *California Zephyr*'s whistle blew twice. As the train began to move, the passengers in the dining car cheered.

Chapter Twenty-Three

THE LIGHTS OF DENVER—the Mile High City—glittered in the distance as the *California Zephyr* left the Front Range of the Rocky Mountains and began its slow descent down the S-curve known as the Big Ten. The wind blew hard along the foothills and gusted out onto the high plains, kicking up snow from the drifts piled on either side of the tracks.

Jill gazed out the window of the coffee shop on the Silver Hostel, where she sat with Mike Scolari and Alvah Webb. "That's a beautiful sight, those city lights below. It always is, but especially tonight, after everything we've gone through. We're almost there. Once we get down the Big Ten, it's half an hour to Union Station."

"What's the Big Ten?" Mike forked his last bite of apple pie and lifted it to his mouth. "And why do they call it that?"

"We're in it right now," Jill said. "The tracks loop around in a big S, with a tight ten-degree radius of curve. We've just come out of the Front Range, where the mountains rise from the foothills. So we're at the top of the S. From here, it's quite a drop in elevation all the way down to Denver on the high plains. You'll see it better in daylight, on the return trip."

The waiter appeared, carrying a carafe of coffee. "Want me to freshen your cups?"

Jill shook her head. "I've had enough."

"No more for me," Mike said. "That was some fine apple pie, by the way."

"Yes, it was. Just a splash more coffee, thank you." Alvah Webb pushed away his plate.

The waiter poured coffee into his cup. Then he set the pot on a nearby table and removed the plates. "Glad to know you liked the pie. I'm partial to it myself."

"Now I'm curious, Mr. Webb," Jill said. "You told the conductor you knew Mr. Smith, the man who was stealing from the sleeper cars. Was it...?"

"Yes, ma'am, it was." Alvah Webb took a sip of his coffee, cradling the cup in his hands. He looked at Mike. "Miss McLeod knows, but you don't, Mr. Scolari. I did some time at Folsom Prison. And this Mr. Smith, I can't say I knew him, except by sight. He was there same time I was, doing a stretch for grand theft. As soon as I seen the conductor walking him through the car, I recognized him. I guess now he'll be doing a stretch in Cañon City."

They sat and talked as the *California Zephyr* wound around the top of the big S-curve, then entered the lower half of the bend. At the bottom of the Big Ten, the CZ straightened and picked up speed, moving toward the beckoning lights. The whistle blew a warning as they approached a crossing. Now they could see more houses, more cars on the road.

"This town we're coming to is Arvada," Jill said to Alvah. "That's where your daughter lives."

"It sure is. She'll be at Union Station in Denver to meet me. That's what she said in her letter. I'm looking forward to seeing her after all these years." Alvah stood, towering over Jill and Mike. "It's a real pleasure riding on this train, Miss McLeod. And getting to know you was real special. I hope you have a nice holiday. You, too, Mr. Scolari."

"Thanks, Mr. Webb," Jill said. "Have a wonderful Christmas with your family."

Alvah Webb nodded, then he left the coffee shop. Mike reached for Jill's hand. "Now, you were going to give me your phone number."

She smiled. "Yes, I am."

He took a small leather book from his jacket and wrote down the number. "So we've got a date to see *Oklahoma!*"

"I'll have to check my work schedule, of course, when I get back home. What about you? You know, I never did ask you what you do for a living."

"I'm about to go to school at Berkeley," Mike said. "I just got out of the Air Force, so I figure on using my G.I. benefits."

"Were you in Korea?" Jill asked.

"Yeah. I was a navigator. I got discharged. I was injured in a plane crash, not too bad, but enough to get me a ticket home."

"At least you came home."

"And he didn't," Mike said. "That other guy you're thinking about."

She shook her head. "No, he didn't."

Mike took her hand. "That must have been rough."

"It was. But I'm all right now." And she was. For the first time since Steve's death, Jill felt the pain of his loss lessen. She sighed. "I would like to sit and talk, Mike, but I have lots to do before we arrive at the station."

Mike smiled and released her hand. "So do I. Got to get Gramps ready to go. Come on, I'll walk with you."

They left the Silver Hostel and walked back through the dining car to the Silver Gull. Mike opened the door to the compartment. "We're almost to Denver, Gramps."

Mr. Scolari beckoned to Jill. She stepped into the compartment and leaned over the old gentleman. With age-spotted hands, he took hers. "Now Miss McLeod, you're a nice girl. I think you should know. My grandson, he's sweet on you."

Jill felt her cheeks redden. Behind her, Mike said, "Gramps!"

"He's a good catch," Mr. Scolari said. "You keep that in mind."

"I will, Mr. Scolari." Jill straightened and left the compartment. She walked back through the sleeper cars, where she could feel the energy coming from passengers who were departing the train in Denver, their voices buzzing as they gathered their belongings. As she walked through the transcontinental sleeper, the Perlmans hailed her. "Oh, Miss McLeod, how late is the train?" Mr. Perlman asked. "I'm still concerned about making our connection in Chicago."

"We were due into Denver at seven o'clock this evening," Jill said. "It's almost ten-thirty now. So we're three-and-a-half hours behind schedule. But we'll make up time during the night, as we go through eastern Colorado and Nebraska."

He shook his head. "Over three hours. That's a lot of time to make up. Maybe we should fly next time."

"Not me," Mrs. Perlman said. "Flying is boring. I'd much rather take the train and see the scenery. Relax, Irving. We'll get to Chicago when we get there."

Jill left the Silver Rapids and went back to the Silver Solarium. As she passed the closed doors of bedrooms A and B, the door to bedroom C opened and Miss Stafford stepped out.

"We'll be at Union Station soon," Jill said.

"How long will we be there?" Miss Stafford asked.

"Usually fifteen minutes," Jill said. "We have some crew changes and we switch the engines. But I think it may be longer tonight, because of the accident. There are broken windows in the first Dome car. They'll switch out that car as well."

"That will put us farther behind schedule. But we'll make up time, I should think, heading across the Midwest. Doesn't really matter to me." Miss Stafford shrugged and waved a hand at her portable typewriter and the stack of paper. "That's a few more hours for me to wrestle with this book."

In the lounge section at the end of the Solarium, the Finches were saying good-bye to the Constanzas. "I have really enjoyed the trip, playing bridge and talking," Mrs. Finch said. She sat at the writing desk, moving pen across paper. "Now, this is our address and phone number. The next time you come to San Francisco, call us. We'll come over to the City and have dinner." She handed the paper to Mrs. Constanza.

Mr. Finch took out his wallet and removed several bills, handing them to the porter, who was picking up glasses from the nearby tables and setting them on a tray. "Thank you for all your help on this trip. I hope you have a nice Christmas when you get to Chicago tomorrow."

"Thank you, sir. Merry Christmas to you and your family." Mr. Parsons pocketed the tip. Then he carried the tray back to the bar section of the car.

Mr. Finch turned to his wife. "Where are the girls? We're almost to Denver."

"They went back to say good-bye to Emily and Mrs. Tidsdale,"

Mrs. Finch said, just as Nan and Cathy hurried into the lounge. "Here they are now. Are you girls all ready to go? We're just about to the station."

Jill excused herself and left the Silver Solarium, walking forward through the Silver Rapids. In the Silver Pine, she stopped and said good-bye to George Neeley and his family. The Benson boys boiled out of bedroom F as Jill entered the Silver Palisade.

"Hey, you boys settle down. Don't bump into Miss McLeod." Ed Benson followed his sons out of the bedroom and grabbed one with each hand. "Come look out the window. In a few minutes we're going to cross the South Platte River."

"Where does it go?" Billy asked.

"Goes all the way to Nebraska, just like this train. Then it comes together with another river called the North Platte. After that, they just call it the Platte."

Norma Benson stepped into the corridor and smiled at Jill. "They are way past their bedtime. Almost there."

"Yes, we are. It's been fun having you and the boys aboard."

"Keeping things lively, that's for sure." Mrs. Benson glanced back. "Chip, your shoe's untied. Sit still and let me tie that."

A few steps down, Jill stopped and tapped on the door to bedroom A. Mrs. Tidsdale opened the door. Just beyond, Emily sat on the single chair, with Benny the Bear beside her, as she leaned over to close her pink overnight case.

"All ready to go?" Jill asked.

"Believe me, sweetie, I'm more than ready to get off this train," Mrs. Tidsdale said.

"How's your head? I do hope you'll see a doctor as soon as possible."

"I will. I have to deliver this envelope first." Tidsy patted her hip.

Jill glanced down and saw, under the folds of Mrs. Tidsdale's red silk dress, the outline of the envelope that was the cause of Dr. Kovacs's death. "Who will you give it to?"

Tidsy crossed the bedroom and sat down on the bench seat, crossing her legs. She took her compact and lipstick from her red leather purse. "Robert Charlton. He was due to arrive from Washington today. He is, shall we say, a high-level government official. I've known him since my Washington days. Anyway, he'll know what to do with the information. And prosecute those three... well, never mind. Emily doesn't need to hear what I think of them."

Jill turned to Emily. "Are you ready to see your grandma?"

Emily nodded, holding her bear. "I hope I like living in Denver."

"I did, when I lived here during the war. I have lots of aunts, uncles, and cousins here. I come to visit them. So maybe next time I'm here, I can visit you."

"That would be nice," Emily said, hugging her teddy bear to her. "I just have my grandma, and Uncle Robert. I don't think he's married yet, so I don't have any cousins."

"You'll be fine, sweetie." Tidsy freshened her lipstick. She closed her compact with a snap. "You can build a snowman in your grandma's yard. You can go ice skating and sledding in the mountains. And learn how to ski. Skiing is a lot of fun. I do that up in the Sierra Nevada, and I've even done it here, in Colorado."

"What about you, Mrs. Tidsdale?" Jill asked. "Where are you staying in Denver?"

"Robert Charlton made a reservation for me at the Brown Palace. And I have an invitation to Christmas dinner with his family. Then on the twenty-seventh I'll head back to San Francisco on the *Zephyr*."

Jill laughed. "Then I'll see you after Christmas. I'll be on that westbound train."

————

The *California Zephyr* rumbled over the bridge across the South Platte River. The train slowed, moving through the Denver & Rio Grande Western yards. From the vestibule of the Silver Palace, Jill stood and looked out at Union Station, the tall Beaux-Arts building constructed of Colorado Yule marble that fronted Wynkoop Street at Seventeenth. Then the train turned to the north and pulled away from the station. It stopped, the whistle blew three times, and the Silver Lady backed slowly into place along the platform, positioning itself for its departure. Jill looked out the window and saw people crowding the platform, some there to greet the arriving passengers and others there to board the train.

"The crew is swapping out the engines, and that chair car with the broken Vista-Dome window." Mr. Gaskill, the conductor, had joined her in the vestibule. "Well, Miss McLeod, it's been an eventful trip. Here's where I leave the train. I hope the run to Chicago is downright boring."

She smiled. "So do I. Merry Christmas, Mr. Gaskill."

As soon as the train stopped, the car porter opened the vestibule doors. Jill stepped down and took a deep breath, filling her lungs with cold air. The platform exploded with activity and noise as passengers left the train, hailing Red Caps and waving at family members.

She moved away from the vestibule as passengers exited the car. One of them was Alvah Webb. Under the cowboy hat, his face held a mixture of emotions, hope mingled with trepidation. He looked around, shifting his valise from one hand to another. Then he stopped. A young woman with a cloud of curly dark hair, bundled into a red wool coat, waved at him, calling, "Daddy? Daddy!" Alvah took a step. Then his daughter covered the rest of the distance and flung her arms around him. He dropped his valise and wrapped both arms around her. Then she stepped back and beckoned to the rangy young man who stood nearby, a sleeping infant on his shoulder and a little boy who stumbled drowsily near his father's leg.

It will be all right, then, Jill thought.

Alvah's daughter took her baby from her husband, who picked up the little boy and draped the child over his shoulder. Alvah reached for his valise and put his other arm around his daughter. Then he walked toward the station with his newly found family.

Jill turned and looked at the front of the train. The Denver & Rio Grande Western locomotives that had pulled the Silver Lady over the Rocky Mountains had been uncoupled from the train, and now they moved forward. Once they were out of the way, and the damaged chair car switched out, three Chicago, Burlington & Quincy engines would back into place. Once coupled, the new locomotives would pull the *Zephyr* on the rest of her run, through the high plains of eastern Colorado, across the rich Midwestern farmlands of Nebraska, Iowa, and Illinois, to the train's final destination in Chicago.

Jill shivered. It was cold out here on the platform. She walked briskly past the diner where one of the cooks leaned out a window, having a smoke. She reached the Silver Gull just as Mike Scolari, wearing his battered leather jacket, carried his grandfather down the vestibule steps and settled him into the wheelchair. A group of people rushed over to greet them, hugging Mike and the old man.

Farther down the platform, Jill saw another wheelchair, this one with an elderly woman in a gray coat, hugging Emily. Grace Tidsdale stood nearby, pulling her mink jacket close against the evening chill, as she talked with a tall man who must be Robert Charlton, Emily's uncle.

"Bye, Miss McLeod, bye! Merry Christmas." Jill turned. Billy and Chip Benson were waving at her. Jill waved back. Then the Bensons, surrounded by members of their family, moved away from the train, heading down the platform to Union Station's cavernous high-ceilinged central waiting room, where checked baggage was collected.

"Gramps is right," a voice said behind her. "I am a good catch."

She turned and smiled at Mike. "We'll see about that."

"Hey, it's cold out here on this platform. You'd better get aboard and get tucked into bed in your compartment."

"No bed for me, not just yet," Jill said. "I have to work on my trip report before I get to sleep. It's going to be quite a long report, given everything that's happened today."

"When you do get to sleep, sweet dreams." Mike leaned down and kissed her.

Jill shivered, and not just because of the cold. "Mr. Scolari, you shouldn't do that. The conductor might see you. I'm not supposed to get familiar with the passengers."

"When we get back to San Francisco, I won't be a passenger, and you'll be my girl. Until then, Merry Christmas, Miss McLeod."

She watched him walk back along the platform to where his grandfather sat in his wheelchair, surrounded by members of the Scolari clan. Then she climbed the steps to the vestibule of the Silver Palisade, where Frank Nathan waited, ready to shut the door.

The conductor walked by, a big man with his pocket watch in his hand, a Chicago, Burlington & Quincy insignia on his billed cap. His voice echoed along the platform.

"Now boarding, the *California Zephyr*. Destination Chicago, with stops in Akron, McCook, Hastings, Lincoln, Omaha, Ottumwa, Burlington, Galesburg..."

AUTHOR'S NOTE AND ACKNOWLEDGMENTS

Death Rides the Zephyr required a great deal of research—train trips, interviews, and lots of time spent climbing around on old railroad cars. I even took a locomotive for a spin.

When writing about a historical period or a particular subject, I strive to be accurate in conveying information. I worked hard to make this book as accurate as possible, though I may have tweaked facts from time to time for the sake of plot, characters, and a good story. Any errors are my own.

Many thanks to Camille Minichino for explaining theoretical physics to this layperson.

My heartfelt thanks go to two of the Zephyrettes who worked aboard the historical streamliner known as the *California Zephyr*. Cathy Moran Von Ibsch was a Zephyrette in the late 1960s and rode the Silver Lady on her last run. Rodna Walls Taylor rode the rails as a Zephyrette in the early 1950s, the time period of the book. I greatly appreciate their generosity in answering my many questions. I couldn't have written this book without them.

In 2010 I was a passenger on a special excursion train to and from Portola, California, via the Feather River Canyon. My thanks to Fred Isaac for helping me make this journey. The famed and scenic Feather River Route was part of the Western Pacific Railroad portion of the *California Zephyr*. I took advantage of this wonderful opportunity to see what the passengers of the original *CZ* saw on their journey through the Sierra Nevada. This route has been primarily traversed by freight traffic since the old *CZ* ceased operations, so traveling the canyon on a passenger car was a treat. My accommodations for that trip were aboard the Pacific Sands, a 1950 Budd 10/6 Pullman sleeper built for the Union Pacific, a car very much like those that traveled on the *CZ*.

Several of my fellow Pacific Sands passengers and I have

since referred to ourselves as the Pullman Pals and we've taken another trip aboard the car. So here's to the Pullman Pals: Roger Morris, Glenn Stocki, Leland House, and Nancy Struck. Particular thanks go to Roger Morris and Glenn Stocki, both railfans, who have been quick to answer my many train-related questions, and thanks again to Roger for the wonderful cover art.

I would also like to thank Doug Spinn, owner of the Pacific Sands, for those wonderful trips aboard this vintage Pullman sleeper. Learning firsthand the layout of a Pullman car was important in writing this book. The car is part of the LA Rail consortium of private rail cars. Read more about it at the LA Rail website: http://www.larail.com/cars/pacificsands.html.

Thanks to Roy J. Wullich II, owner of the Silver Solarium, for tours of this vintage dome observation car from the original *California Zephyr*; the dome chair car, the Silver Lariat; and the transcontinental sleeper, the Silver Rapids. Find out more at the Rail Journeys West website: http://www.railjourneyswest.com/silversolarium.html.

We are fortunate to have railroad museums to preserve the remaining artifacts of this country's rail era, particularly the streamliners like the *California Zephyr*. Both the California State Railroad Museum, Sacramento, California, and the Colorado Railroad Museum, Golden, Colorado, have excellent research libraries as well as rail cars and locomotives. The Western Pacific Railroad Museum in Portola, California, is a treasure house of rolling stock.

The California State Railroad Museum in Sacramento is part of the state's extensive park system. I would like to thank Cara J. Randall, Librarian, and Kathryn Santos, Archivist, at the museum's library. Thanks also go to two people from the State Department of Parks and Recreation: Pati Brown, District Services Manager, Capital District State Museums and Historic Parks; and Phil Sexton, Director of Public Programs, Sacramento History and Railroad Sector. To find out more about this wonderful museum, here is the website: http://www.csrmf.org. Plan a trip to Sacramento, go to Old Town, and climb around on locomotives and rail cars, including a sleeper car that moves and a dining car with tables set with railway china.

At the Colorado Railroad Museum, my thanks go to Kenton Forrest, Archivist, and Kathy McCardwell, Archivist and Librarian, at the Robert W. Richardson Railroad Library, which is located on the museum site. To find out more, go to: http://coloradorailroadmuseum.org. Pay a visit and climb around on the trains.

Thank you to Gail McClure and Loren Ross, two of the "willing people" at the Western Pacific Railroad Museum in Portola, California. This museum dedicated to the WP is the location of several cars in my fictional train consist, including WP locomotive 805-A; the Silver Hostel, the dome lounge car; and the Silver Plate, the dining car. The WPRM is also the site of the Run-A-Locomotive program, and I highly recommend it. Read more about it at http://www.wplives.org.

Thanks also to Eugene Vicknair, *Zephyr* Project Manager of the Feather River Rail Society. Find out more about this organization dedicated to preserving the history of the Western Pacific Railroad, at http://www.wplives.org/frrs.html.

The Internet provides a wealth of resources, including boards and listservs for dedicated railfans. Among these are Train Orders at http://www.trainorders.com. Many thanks to Bruce Yelen, who provided me with first-hand knowledge of the inside of a *California Zephyr* dome observation car, having worked on the restoration of the Silver Crescent at the Gold Coast Railroad Museum in Miami, Florida. For more information on that car, see http://gcrm.org/index.php/exhibits/silver-crescent.

My thanks to several members of the Denver & Rio Grande Western Yahoo group for answering my questions about train operations on the Main Line Through the Rockies. These include Jerry Day, Jimmy Blouch, John Templeton, Duane Cook, Tom Krummell, Bob Huddleston, and Glenn Leasure.

I recommend the *California Zephyr* Virtual Museum at http://calzephyr.railfan.net. Here I found old timetables, menus, and brochures, as well as information on the Zephyrettes.

The Amtrak version of the *California Zephyr* is not the same as the sleek Silver Lady of days gone by. But it's great to ride a train through most of the same route, getting an up-close look at this marvelous country. The journey may take longer, but the scenery is spectacular and the relaxation factor is 110 percent. Besides, unless you hike in, there's no other way to see Gore Canyon.

The *California Zephyr* story, and that of railroading in America, is told in books and films. Some of them are listed below, along with other sources I used in writing *Death Rides the Zephyr*. Many of these books are full of photographs and first-hand accounts of working on and aboard the trains.

PUBLICATIONS:

Portrait of a Silver Lady: The Train They Called the California Zephyr, Bruce A. McGregor and Ted Benson, Pruett Publishing Company, Boulder, CO, 1977. Full of beautiful photographs, lots of history and technical information, and first-hand accounts of what it was like to work on this train.

CZ: The Story of the California Zephyr, Karl R. Zimmerman, Quadrant Press, Inc., 1972. Excellent overview of the train's history, with lots of old photographs.

Zephyr: Tracking a Dream Across America, Henry Kisor, Adams Media Corporation, 1994. An account of Kisor's journey westward on the Amtrak *California Zephyr*.

Waiting on a Train: The Embattled Future of Passenger Rail Service, James McCommons, Chelsea Green Publishing Company, 2009. A thought-provoking account of the author's travels on various Amtrak routes and his interviews with passengers, employees, rail advocates, and people in the railroad business, with discussions about the future of passenger rail in the United States.

A Guidebook to Amtrak's California Zephyr, Eva J. Hoffman, Flashing Yellow Guidebooks, Evergreen, CO, 2003, 2008. There are three volumes: Chicago to Denver, Denver to Salt Lake City, Salt Lake City to San Francisco. I discovered these courtesy of a railfan while riding the Amtrak *CZ*. A detailed milepost-by-milepost guide to what's outside the train window, with history and anecdotes thrown in. A useful resource for finding out how far it is from one place to another and how long it takes to get there.

Rising from the Rails, Pullman Porters and the Making of the Black Middle Class, Larry Tye, Henry Holt & Company, 2004. There is also a PBS video. The book discusses the history of the Pullman Company, African Americans working on the railroad, and their legacy.

The Pullman Porters and West Oakland, Thomas and Wilma Tramble, Arcadia Publishing, 2007. A look at the lives of porters in Oakland, California. Full of wonderful photographs.

Readers familiar with the Rosenberg case will note that Julius and Ethel Rosenberg were actually executed on June 19, 1953. At the time the novel takes place, the execution date had been set for January 11, 1953. The Rosenbergs were granted a stay of execution on January 10. Several more dates were set and postponed before the executions were actually carried out.

The information on David Greenglass, Ethel Rosenberg's brother, his activities at Los Alamos, and his role in the espionage trial come from *The Brother, the Untold Story of Atomic Spy David Greenglass and How He Sent his Sister, Ethel Rosenberg, to the Electric Chair*, by Sam Roberts, Random House, 2001.

For an excellent overview of what it was like at Los Alamos, New Mexico during the Manhattan Project, I recommend *109 East Palace: Robert Oppenheimer and the Secret City of Los Alamos*, Jennet Conant, Simon & Schuster, 2006.

Information on the Korean War comes from *The Coldest Winter: America and the Korean War*, David Halberstam, Hyperion, 2007. The story of how Gunnison, Colorado quarantined itself during the 1918–1919 Spanish Flu epidemic can be found in *The Great Influenza: The Epic Story of the Deadliest Plague in History*, John M. Barry, Viking Penguin, 2004.

FILMS:
The California Zephyr: The Story of America's Most Talked About Train, Copper Media, 1999.

The California Zephyr: Silver Thread Through the West, Travel-VideoStore, 2007.

The California Zephyr: The Ultimate Fan Trip, Emery Gulash, Green Frog Productions, Ltd., 2007.

American Experience: Streamliners: America's Lost Trains, PBS Video, 2006.

Promotional films from the *CZ* and other trains are viewable on YouTube.

The original *California Zephyr* appeared on film in the 1954 movie *Cinerama Holiday*, as well as the 1952 noir *Sudden Fear*, starring Joan Crawford and Jack Palance. During the train portion of that movie, a Zephyrette comes to Joan Crawford's bedroom to tell her it's time for her dinner reservation. That Zephyrette is Rodna Walls, whom I interviewed for this book.

I hope you enjoyed *Death Rides the Zephyr*. Now go ride a train!

ABOUT THE AUTHOR

Janet Dawson has written ten books about Oakland private eye Jeri Howard, including *Kindred Crimes*, winner of the St. Martin's Press/Private Eye Writers of America contest for Best First PI Novel, and a nominee for several Best First awards. Her most recent Jeri Howard book is *Bit Player*, which was nominated for a Golden Nugget award for Best California Mystery.

Dawson has also written two stand-alone mystery novels, plus a number of short stories, including a Shamus nominee and a Macavity winner. A past president of Norcal MWA, she lives in the East Bay region, and works for Lawrence Berkeley National Laboratory. Dawson welcomes visitors at www.janetdawson.com and at her blogs.

More Traditional Mysteries from Perseverance Press
For the New Golden Age

Albert A. Bell, Jr.
PLINY THE YOUNGER SERIES
Death in the Ashes
ISBN 978-1-56474-532-3

The Eyes of Aurora (forthcoming)
ISBN 978-1-56474-549-1

Jon L. Breen
Eye of God
ISBN 978-1-880284-89-6

Taffy Cannon
ROXANNE PRESCOTT SERIES
Guns and Roses
Agatha and Macavity awards nominee, Best Novel
ISBN 978-1-880284-34-6

Blood Matters
ISBN 978-1-880284-86-5

Open Season on Lawyers
ISBN 978-1-880284-51-3

Paradise Lost
ISBN 978-1-880284-80-3

Laura Crum
GAIL MCCARTHY SERIES
Moonblind
ISBN 978-1-880284-90-2

Chasing Cans
ISBN 978-1-880284-94-0

Going, Gone
ISBN 978-1-880284-98-8

Barnstorming
ISBN 978-1-56474-508-8

Jeanne M. Dams
HILDA JOHANSSON SERIES
Crimson Snow
ISBN 978-1-880284-79-7

Indigo Christmas
ISBN 978-1-880284-95-7

Murder in Burnt Orange
ISBN 978-1-56474-503-3

Janet Dawson
JERI HOWARD SERIES
Bit Player
Golden Nugget Award nominee
ISBN 978-1-56474-494-4

Cold Trail (forthcoming)
ISBN 978-1-56474-555-2

What You Wish For
ISBN 978-1-56474-518-7

Death Rides the Zephyr
ISBN 978-1-56474-530-9

Kathy Lynn Emerson
LADY APPLETON SERIES
Face Down Below the Banqueting House
ISBN 978-1-880284-71-1

Face Down Beside St. Anne's Well
ISBN 978-1-880284-82-7

Face Down O'er the Border
ISBN 978-1-880284-91-9

Elaine Flinn
MOLLY DOYLE SERIES
Deadly Vintage
ISBN 978-1-880284-87-2

Sara Hoskinson Frommer
JOAN SPENCER SERIES
Her Brother's Keeper
ISBN 978-1-56474-525-5

Hal Glatzer
KATY GREEN SERIES
Too Dead To Swing
ISBN 978-1-880284-53-7

A Fugue in Hell's Kitchen
ISBN 978-1-880284-70-4

The Last Full Measure
ISBN 978-1-880284-84-1

Margaret Grace
MINIATURE SERIES
Mix-up in Miniature
ISBN 978-1-56474-510-1

Madness in Miniature (forthcoming)
ISBN 978-1-56474-543-9

Wendy Hornsby
MAGGIE MACGOWEN SERIES
In the Guise of Mercy
ISBN 978-1-56474-482-1

The Paramour's Daughter
ISBN 978-1-56474-496-8

The Hanging
ISBN 978-1-56474-526-2

The Color of Light (forthcoming)
ISBN 978-1-56474-542-2

Diana Killian
POETIC DEATH SERIES
Docketful of Poesy
ISBN 978-1-880284-97-1

Janet LaPierre
PORT SILVA SERIES
Baby Mine
ISBN 978-1-880284-32-2

Keepers
Shamus Award nominee, Best Paperback Original
ISBN 978-1-880284-44-5

Death Duties
ISBN 978-1-880284-74-2

Family Business
ISBN 978-1-880284-85-8

Run a Crooked Mile
ISBN 978-1-880284-88-9

Hailey Lind
ART LOVER'S SERIES
Arsenic and Old Paint
ISBN 978-1-56474-490-6

Lev Raphael
NICK HOFFMAN SERIES
Tropic of Murder
ISBN 978-1-880284-68-1

Hot Rocks
ISBN 978-1-880284-83-4

Lora Roberts
BRIDGET MONTROSE SERIES
Another Fine Mess
ISBN 978-1-880284-54-4

SHERLOCK HOLMES SERIES
The Affair of the Incognito Tenant
ISBN 978-1-880284-67-4

Rebecca Rothenberg
BOTANICAL SERIES
The Tumbleweed Murders
(completed by Taffy Cannon)
ISBN 978-1-880284-43-8

Sheila Simonson
LATOUCHE COUNTY SERIES
Buffalo Bill's Defunct
WILLA Award, Best Softcover Fiction
ISBN 978-1-880284-96-4

An Old Chaos
ISBN 978-1-880284-99-5

Beyond Confusion
ISBN 978-1-56474-519-4

Shelley Singer
JAKE SAMSON & ROSIE VICENTE SERIES
Royal Flush
ISBN 978-1-880284-33-9

Lea Wait
SHADOWS ANTIQUES SERIES
Shadows of a Down East Summer
ISBN 978-1-56474-497-5

Shadows on a Cape Cod Wedding
ISBN 1-978-56474-531-6

Shadows on a Maine Christmas
(forthcoming)
ISBN 978-1-56474-531-6

Eric Wright
JOE BARLEY SERIES
The Kidnapping of Rosie Dawn
Barry Award, Best Paperback Original. Edgar,
Ellis, and Anthony awards nominee
ISBN 978-1-880284-40-7

Nancy Means Wright
MARY WOLLSTONECRAFT SERIES
Midnight Fires
ISBN 978-1-56474-488-3

The Nightmare
ISBN 978-1-56474-509-5

REFERENCE/MYSTERY WRITING

Kathy Lynn Emerson
How To Write Killer Historical Mysteries:
The Art and Adventure of Sleuthing
Through the Past
Agatha Award, Best Nonfiction. Anthony and
Macavity awards nominee
ISBN 978-1-880284-92-6

Carolyn Wheat
How To Write Killer Fiction:
The Funhouse of Mystery & the Roller
Coaster of Suspense
ISBN 978-1-880284-62-9

Available from your local bookstore
or from Perseverance Press/John Daniel & Company
(800) 662–8351 or www.danielpublishing.com/perseverance